Whispers in the Wind

Whispers in the Wind

Sarah Clark

To order additional copies of this book, contact:
Xlibris
1-888-795-4274
www.Xlibris.com
Orders@Xlibris.com
793016

To all the victims of domestic violence,
never give up, somebody will always be there to save you.

Chapter 1

The night is chilly, cloudy, and dark. Riley looks out the window of the living room as the car of her older brother Kasey pulls up in the driveway, coming home from working late. She checks the time: it is ten fifteen,

The door clicks as her brother unlocks it and walks in. She looks over to him knowing he's going to be irritated that she had not gone to bed yet.

Kasey stares at his little sister, biting his lip, unsure what to say to her.

"Riley, why are you up?"

Her eyes meet his bright green eyes, and she shrugs her shoulders, wondering what her brother could be up to on a Friday night.

"I don't know. Couldn't sleep in a big house alone."

Kasey sighs feeling bad for Riley. He hangs his keys up on the antler-shaped key holder.

"Well, Dad said he'd be out of town for a couple more weeks, could be longer. Have you eaten?"

Riley nods her head slowly, lying, not really wanting to deal with him being in a bad mood since he of course had a good side and a bad side—sometimes he cared, sometimes he didn't, just like her father.

Kasey turns and locks the door. He feels better thinking that his sister had already eaten something, and so he walks over to her, hugging her.

"Go get some rest, okay? You have bags under your eyes."

She bites her lip and looks up toward the wooden, circular staircase, not wanting to go up to her room alone.

Kasey looks at her, pulling her back out of her gaze.

"What's up, buttercup?" A smile grows on Riley's lips, still biting them, trying not to smile at her brother.

"Nothing, Kasey. I'm just not tired."

Kasey shrugs, letting it go.

"Well, I haven't seen a smile like that on you in a while."

He walks into the kitchen that's connected to the living room with an overhead arch hanging a little lower than the ceiling.

Riley shrugs not wanting to talk and decides about going to bed earlier, just to avoid talking. She stares at her brother, waiting for another comment.

"Hey, are you okay with a couple friends coming over?" Kasey asked.

Riley raises an eyebrow and narrows the other eye.

"I guess. Why does it matter what I think?"

Kasey shrugs while eating a sandwich. Riley stares at his blue scrubs and smirks amused.

"If you have a girlfriend coming over, you might want to change."

Kasey smiles at his little sister. "Riley, I don't have a girlfriend. It's just Erik and Ana. A couple friends from work."

Riley nods getting the hint and has a quick hurt look in her eyes that fades. Kasey catches it.

"What's wrong, Riles? You know you can talk to me about anything. You're my baby sister."

Riley sighs a sad sigh, wishing she didn't feel like they were all lies.

"It's nothing. I'm fine." She turns to run upstairs. Kasey grabs her wrist, catching her before she runs off. Riley does a three-sixty almost meeting her brother face first.

"Riley, just talk to me."

Riley shakes her head, yanking her hand away. He catches a glimpse of a bruise on her wrist.

"What's that from?"

Riley bites her lip nervously. "Nothing. I just hit my wrist against the door. I'm fine." She pulls her rose-pink, long-sleeve shirt down over her bruise and runs up the stairs. Before Kasey can follow her to talk, Erik and Ana arrive. Kasey walks outside to talk to them.

Riley shuts the door to her bedroom and sits on the white carpet in her bedroom. She grabs her aqua-colored laptop and opens it as Ana walks in with a smile on her face. Riley looks up at her and then back at her laptop.

"Can we talk for a second?" Ana asked.

Riley sets her laptop on the floor with an annoyed huff.

"About what?"

Ana sits beside her on the floor.

"You have a hurt look in your eyes, Riley, and I can't ignore that. Are you okay? Did somebody hurt you?"

Riley pulls her sleeves over her hands, thinking maybe she saw the bruises.

"No, I'm okay. I just have a lot going on, you know?" Ana nods wanting to help her in anyway.

"Like what?" Riley bites her lip and gets up, shutting her bedroom door. She lifts her shirt revealing bruises on her side. She then shows Ana the bruises on her wrist. Ana stands up shocked, her heart racing.

"Riley what happened? Does Kasey know? What about your dad?"

Riley holds a finger over her lips in a hush kind of way and rolls her eyes like they would care.

"Nobody knows except Liam. He got mad a couple weeks ago. You know when I came back to live with my dad. I had classes at school, and he didn't want me leaving the house. We fought about it in front of the apartment stairs and one step backward and down I went."

Ana looks at her in disbelief.

"He put his hands on you?"

Riley looks down, feeling guilty and pathetic.

"Riley! Why didn't you tell anybody? You've had these dark bruises for two weeks? You know Kasey is going to be angrier that you didn't say anything to him!"

Riley bites her lip becoming annoyed, feeling heartbroken.

"Yeah, well he isn't going to find out. This secret stays in this room and doesn't go beyond these walls."

Ana takes a breath with a serious look in her eyes. "Riley, I'm sorry, but I can't do what you're asking me to do."

Riley sits back on the floor, picking up her laptop, no longer wanting to talk. Ana sits back down beside her.

"Please talk to Kasey, he's your brother. Yeah, he'll be mad but he's Kasey. He won't be mad at you, and he won't do anything his baby sister asks him not to do. You know that. Kasey is a doctor, sure, but he can help you, Riles."

Riley chews on the inside of her cheek, feeling scared. Ana stands up and holds her hand out.

"I'll be beside you the whole time, I promise."

Riley looks up at her brother's friend, who's more like a sister to her, flashing a scared look in her eyes.

"Are you ready to go talk? Kasey is worried about you, and you know he won't sleep without knowing for sure his sister is okay."

Riley takes her hand standing up and puts on her brave face thinking that he won't care at all. He was wishy-washy like that after all. Ana smiles at her, happy to talk to her. They open the door and walk down the stairs together.

Kasey smiles at his sister, happy to see her socializing. Ana looks at him with a sad look in her eyes. Kasey's smile fades. He walks over to his sister and holds out his hand.

"Let's go talk."

Chapter 2

Riley takes a shaky breath, feeling scared to talk to him; she covers her hands. She then takes his hand remembering things will only get better. She knows her brother will keep her safe. She nods her head okaying it. They go outside to the big, white wrap around porch and sit on a light brown-colored wooden swing.

"So what's up?"

Riley bites her lip, breathing slowly and deeply. She meets her brother's eyes. Tears fill her eyes. Kasey takes his sister's hand, worried about her.

"What's wrong, Riles?" Riley takes a breath, being brave and looks around.

"I have to tell you something serious, Kasey."

Kasey lets go of her hand.

"You're not pregnant, are you?"

Riley laughs amused.

"Lord no! But thanks for the laugh. I needed that. It's about something that happened to me."

Kasey notices Ana in the window pointing at her side and arms. Kasey looks back to his sister taking her hand again, making her let go of her sleeve.

"Can I see?"

Riley chews on the inside of her cheek.

"Buhbah . . . It's what Liam did."

Kasey bites his lip knowing what she is about to say and holds his anger in.

"I just want to see, Riles." He pulls her sleeves up, finding bruises all over her wrist and forearm. Riley stares at her brother scared of his reaction.

Ana lifts her jacket up on one side pointing. Kasey touches Riley's bottom of her shirt and looks up at his sister squeezing her eyes shut.

"Riley, are you hurt?"

Riley bites her lip keeping her eyes squeezed. Kasey grabs her hand.

"Riley, answer me. Are you hurt?"

Riley opens her eyes and looks at her brother, whose face is turning red.

"I fell down the stairs."

Kasey looks into her eyes in all seriousness. "Riley, that's a lie. Don't lie to me. What did he do?"

Riley shakes her head no, scared of her brother being mad, realizing he might care for once.

"Riley, I need to know. Are you hurt? Can I see your side?" Riley turns her head away from him. Kasey moves to the other side of her and squats down meeting her eyes.

"I'm not going to hurt you, Riles, you are my sister. I love you, okay?"

Riley nods, looking at her brother. "I'm okay, Kasey. I promise. I can fight my own fights." She moves to stand up and flinches from being sore.

Kasey texts Ana and Erik to come out to talk too. Riley stays sitting down and hugs her knees to her chest, looking away from her brother.

"Nothing is wrong." Ana hears her as she's walking out and looks at Kasey meeting his eyes and decides to tell Kasey for her.

"Liam got mad at her for having to get to her classes, and she was fighting with him in front of the apartment stairs and said she stepped backward and went down. He put his hands on her, Kasey."

Kasey looks away from Ana, stands up and looks at his sister in disbelief. Riley looks up at her brother with tears in her eyes.

"You need to go get checked out, Riles." He holds his hand out. Riley shoves his hand away, not trusting his caring act and not wanting his help but at the same time wanting him to care.

"No, I don't, Kasey." She stands up and walks inside, slamming the door shut and wiping her face.

Riley goes up to her room and shuts her door. She closes her curtains and turns on music from her laptop and lies on her bed facing away from the door and on the opposite side that is bothering her.

A few minutes pass by and Kasey opens her door. He sits on the side of her bed.

"Hey," says Kasey.

Riley wipes more tears away. "What?"

Kasey gets up and walks to the other side of the bed, and squats down.

"You're my sister. You're too pretty to cry over stupid boys. You know that?"

Riley smiles a small smile at her brother. He wipes the tears off her cheeks.

"Can we talk, please?"

Riley sits up holding her breath.

"Yeah I guess," Riley replies.

Kasey holds out his hand. Riley takes it standing up.

"How bad is it?" Kasey asks.

Riley shrugs, unsure what to say but doesn't want him worrying about her.

"Not really that bad. It happened a couple weeks ago before I moved in with Dad again, and then he took off."

Kasey nods in understanding. "I know he was upset that you wouldn't come out. So he took a surgery case in Georgia."

Riley nods not understanding why he all of a sudden cared just like her brother.

"Yeah."

Kasey grabs the bottom of her shirt.

"Can I see it? I won't touch just want to see it."

Riley sighs agreeing.

"Sure, why not." She lifts her shirt half way as far as she can without being in screaming pain. Kasey's jaw drops at the blue and purple bruise going down her side.

"Riley, this really doesn't look good. If I promise they won't hurt, will you allow me to take you to get checked out?"

Riley looks annoyed with her brother.

"Kasey, I know what a break and a fracture is I also know what bruises are. It's not serious. Concrete stairs do bruise, you know."

Kasey shakes his head and holds out his hand disagreeing.

"And I know what breaks and fractures and internal bleeding look like. Obviously, you would've already been in the hospital if you had internal bleeding, but you need X-rays."

Riley shakes her head disagreeing with her brother. "Kasey, bruised ribs can look horrible too."

Kasey sighs, letting it go.

"Okay, but you have to promise you'll go if it gets any worse. I'm sure people would love to see you at the hospital. Well at your office, I'm sure they miss you."

Riley gets a bigger smile on her face. It fades quickly.

"Yeah, but Liam knows where I worked."

Kasey shakes his head becoming annoyed. "And you think I would let anything happen to you?"

Riley nods walking toward her door. Kasey stands and crosses his arms tilting his head, wondering where she is going.

"You have company. You can't leave them down there alone forever."

Kasey chuckles amused.

"Riles, they already left so we could talk."

Riley smirks at her brother getting an idea.

"Well tell them to come back."

Kasey shakes his head no.

"No, you need to get some rest."

Riley's stomach growls loudly. Kasey crosses his arms. "Did you lie about eating too?"

Riley looks away not answering.

"Hello?"

She starts out of her room to go down to the kitchen. Kasey clears his throat waiting for an answer. Riley stops mid step and turns to her brother.

"Yes."

Kasey sighs, shaking his head.

"We used to be so close you used to tell me everything. What happened?"

Riley shrugs making her way to the kitchen with her brother behind her.

"I grew up, Kase. It happens."

Kasey looks at her with hurt eyes. "Yeah guess so."

He turns around and goes to his room. Riley sits on the couch and texts her brother apologizing.

A few minutes later, Liam texts her saying, "Come outside, we need to talk." Riley takes a breath calming herself and puts a brave face on.

She gets her shoes on and opens the door and closes it. She stands on the porch, and Liam walks up to her.

"I just want to tell you I'm sorry, Riles. Can we try again? Please?" Riley thinks for a second, feeling the fear build up.

"I'm sorry, Liam, I can't."

Liam grabs her wrist he already bruised. "You can. Come with me. Now."

Riley's eyes widen; fear flashes in them. She feels the sharp sting in her wrist as he holds her wrist tighter.

"Just forgive me and get your stuff, let's go."

Riley tries to pull away. "No, Liam."

Liam tightens and looks her in the eye with an angry look—the look that scares her more than anything.

"What did you say to me?"

Riley looks at him with begging eyes.

"Please, Liam, just let me be. Give me a couple weeks, okay?"

Liam shakes his head with an evil grin. "You just had two weeks, Riley. Times up. Let's go."

Riley catches a glimpse of her brother walking by the window. She looks back at Liam wanting him to let go and talks loudly to get Kasey's attention.

"Liam, stop! You are hurting me!"

Liam yanks her arm, dislocating her shoulder. "I do what I want. Get your stuff and let's go." He yanks her arm again before letting go.

Riley screams in pain. Liam hits her right in the eye.

"Shut up, you're going to attract people."

Riley tries to suck it up.

"Liam, just STOP." About that time Kasey opens the door, walking out. "Riley, get in the house now."

Riley doesn't budge. Liam grabs the opposite arm yanking it away from her face.

"She's fine."

Riley looks away from her brother. Kasey puts himself between Liam and his sister forcing Liam to let her go.

"Liam, if you are not off my property in five seconds, I will have you arrested. Goodbye."

Liam takes off as Erik pulls up to help get him away from Riley. Riley is sitting behind the swing with her knees to her chest crying.

Kasey walks over to his sister and kneels beside her. He touches her chin gently and makes her turn her head toward him.

He sees a swollen eye bruising around it. Kasey stands up and holds out his hand.

"Come, let's get you inside." Erik runs up to the porch wondering if Riley is okay.

"She okay?" Kasey shakes his head no.

Riley looks up at her brother not able to open her eye.

"Come on, Riles. Let's go in."

She looks at her brother blankly and over to her arm. Kasey notices her shoulder looks a bit different. His heart shatters, he backs up holding his breath pacing in anger.

Erik talks to Kasey quietly, then walks over to Riley and squats down.

"Hey, love, let's get you fixed up, alright?"

Riley shakes her head no. Erik nods yes to her.

"You know I won't hurt you and you know your brother for sure won't." He holds her hand out to her.

Riley looks at him scared and in pain.

"Come on love let's go," says Erik.

Riley shakes her head no again.

Kasey is already hanging up the phone with his dad. "Dad is getting on a plane home now, Riles."

He walks over to Riley squatting down on her other side.

She reaches one arm to him. Kasey picks up his sister. She leans her weight against him. Kasey carries her inside and sets her down on the kitchen island.

Erik follows behind. He looks at his sister apologetically. "First things first, we need to get your shirt off and reset your shoulder. I'm not going to lie . . . it's going to hurt."

Erik looks up at Kasey. "Ana is here."

Ana runs into the kitchen with her boyfriend Justis following her. Ana throws off her jacket and hops up on the island with Riley.

Riley stares at her shocked.

"I'm sorry you're really going to hate me," says Ana. She pulls a pair of scissors out of her pocket and cuts down the back of Riley's shirt and pulls it off and then holds Riley still.

"On three." She looks at Kasey and Erik, who are both staring at her shocked.

"And we thought we did everything thanks to nurses."

Ana whispers in Riley's ear. "Take deep breaths, think happy thoughts, and look the opposite way."

Riley squeezes her eyes shut. Ana resets Riley's shoulder without the help of Erik and Kasey, who both continue to stare at Ana and wait for Riley to start screaming.

"Hey, you're done." She covers Riley with her jacket.

Riley opens her eye and looks at Ana, waiting for the pain to hit. "That's it?" Ana nods smiling jumping down. "Might want a new shirt."

Riley hops down and walks toward the stairs while the four others stand in there talking.

They hear a thud and Riley mumbling. Kasey stands at the bottom of the stairs.

"You okay, Riles?"

Riley decides to be a smart mouth.

"Yup, fantastic!" She finally gets a shirt after walking into her closet door and gets on a dark-blue half-sleeve shirt and walks slowly back down into the living room, her face pounding, her arm feeling like it might fall off, and her wrist hurting.

She walks into the bathroom by her brother's room and shuts the door staring into the mirror at her swollen, bruised eye, feeling ugly.

She sits on the floor just wanting to feel loved and wanted. The tears fall. After about fifteen minutes, Erik knocks on the door.

"Riles?" She wipes her face and nose and stands up.

"Yeah?" Her voice sounds shaky.

"Well, I guess that answers my question." He opens the door, peeking in at her, and then walks in as she slides back down on the floor. He sits beside her. Riley looks down on the floor.

Erik puts his hand under her chin and lifts her head up. "You are beautiful . . . stop moping, as your brother puts it. You are too pretty to cry. You wear that bruise proud because you won this battle. Got it?"

Riley meets his eyes, not used to Erik being comforting; he is usually a jerk to her.

"You have your whole life ahead of you and who knows your hero is probably sitting right in front of you."

A smile forms on her lips. Erik smiles back at her. "See, you have a smile that could kill. Who couldn't resist that?"

Riley's face blushes pink.

"Ready to get up and go to bed? You could use some sleep. Your dad would like to talk to you."

Her face lights up. "My dad is home already?" Erik smiles nodding, her smile fades, remembering he probably wasn't really there for her. Most likely, it was just to get away.

"It's only five in the morning." He stands up and holds out his hand. Riley takes his hand with her bruised wrist.

Erik bites his lip in anger, seeing her covered. Riley meets his gaze and looks up at him. He puts his hand on her cheek and meets her eyes.

"Hey, you are better than that. Don't you ever take that again, love."

Riley nods, touching his hand and feeling the caring touch from him. Erik lets go and they go into the living room.

Jase looks up from his phone on the couch at his daughter. He looks exhausted, aggravated, and sad. His blond hair is slicked back, and he's still in scrubs. Riley looks away from her dad, afraid and afraid of letting him in.

Jase stands up and walks over to her. He hugs her, as she flinches scared. He sits on the coffee table and is at her level.

"I love you, sweetheart. I'm sorry I wasn't here to protect you. I have a surgery in a couple days, but I needed to know you were okay."

Riley nods, looking away from him, feeling her heart shatter knowing this is a fake kind of caring from him.

"Hey, go get in my bed. Get some rest, honey. You need it."

Kasey laughs amused. "Yeah, right. Riley, sleep? I don't think she's slept since she came home."

Erik pulls Kasey into the kitchen talking to him. Riley stares at Erik and his tattoos down his arms. His tanned-colored skin and high and tight hairstyle, and the tattoo on the back of his neck.

Jase catches his daughter's attention. "RILEY!" Riley jumps and looks back at him.

"Yes?"

Jase smirks at his daughter. "I can tell them to replace me for this surgery. Kasey said you wanted me."

Riley shakes her head disagreeing. "No, Daddy, you need this."

Jase smiles and pulls her into another hug.

Kasey walks into the living room and mouths "come here for a second" to his dad. Jase nods and lets go of his daughter.

"Why don't you go get a warm shower and get some sleep, and I'll see you when you get up, okay?" Riley shakes her head no.

Ana steps in. "I can stay with you in your room tonight, Riles, if you're okay with it and if your dad is okay with it."

Jase smiles wondering where his kids found the right kind of friends.

"That's fine with me, she needs a friend," Jase says.

Riley nods looking at Ana. Ana smiles warmly.

"Good," says Ana.

Riley goes up to get a shower while Jase talks to Erik and Kasey. Ana sends her boyfriend Justis home with her car. Riley comes down in pink-plaid pajama shorts and a tight-fitting, black T-shirt. She looks at Ana feeling like the side of her face is swollen.

"I feel like I got hit by a train." She giggles jokingly.

Ana raises her eyebrows. "I'm sure you do! Your eye looks a little more swollen."

Riley shrugs and walks into the kitchen to get some Tylenol. Jase, Erik, and Kasey are all staring at her, smiling.

Riley looks at them a little worried and stares at them the whole way to the counter and walks into it knocking the breath out of herself.

The guys laugh at her. Erik walks over to her and holds out his hand.

"I need to talk to you."

Riley looks at him for a second, unsure, and then climbs onto the counter and opens the medicine cabinet above the sink. Jase bites his lip nervously watching her.

"Riley, you don't need to be doing that."

Riley hops down and takes a couple of pain meds. "Yeah, well you get hit by a train, and see how you feel."

Kasey chuckles, liking his sister for being more cheerful.

"Erik really needs to talk to you though."

Riley sets the bottle on the counter and walks outside to the porch with Erik. They sit on the swing.

"So after I talked to Kasey and your dad and have their permission, I have a question for you."

Riley looks at him curious. "What's that?"

Erik smiles hopeful. "Well, I'd like to ask you to be my girlfriend."

Riley looks at him shocked, jaw dropped, speechless. Riley smiles meeting his eyes again.

"Yes. Yes, I will."

Erik smiles cheerful. "I promise I will treat you right."

Riley giggles and hears everybody yelling in the house. She looks up at the window, seeing the curtain move as everybody hides.

"I already told Ana she could stay with me tonight," says Riley.

Erik smiles cheerfully. "Well you do need some girl time as well. But for now, go get some rest."

Riley smiles standing up and walks inside with Erik behind her. Kasey looks at Erik in a serious way.

"I hope you're not planning on sleeping with her."

Erik chuckles, taking Riley's hand. "No, she's going to bed."

Riley looks at him with an eyebrow raised. "Am I?"

Erik nods very sure. "Yes, ma'am, you are."

Riley smiles excitedly and hugs her brother and father goodnight finally.

"I love you, guys." Kasey and Jase hug her back and talk together. "Goodnight, Riles."

She walks over to Erik and hugs him as well.

"Goodnight." Erik hugs her back being easy.

"Goodnight, love." Riley goes up to her room, gets in her bed, and falls asleep by six in the morning, with Ana sleeping on a bed she made.

Chapter 3

At around eleven in the morning, Riley wakes up thinking everything was a dream until she trips over Ana and hits the door, hitting her head on the doorknob.

"Well, that felt lovely." Ana giggles and looks over to her.

"You okay?"

Riley nods getting up. "Yup, just peachy." She opens her door finding Erik, Kasey, and Jase standing at the door.

"What?"

Erik tilts his head curious. "Well, we all heard a loud thud."

Riley laughs amused. "Yeah, I tripped over Ana."

Ana gets up a little annoyed. "It isn't my fault. You didn't open your eyes and pay attention."

Riley smirks amused. "Sorry!" She walks out of her room and down into the kitchen, followed by everybody. She makes herself a cup of coffee and turns to everybody staring at her.

"What?"

Kasey shrugs and walks over to his sister and makes a cup as well.

Riley's phone starts dinging constantly. She picks it up from beside the sink where she left it and sees the ten texts from Liam, one saying he "will be back for her, this isn't the end."

Riley throws her phone back on the counter and goes back to her room locking herself in alone. She lies on her bed and faces the wall, hugging a pillow. Kasey knocks on her door.

"Riles?"

Riley ignores him; she is not in the mood to talk. She gets up when he walks away and grabs a bag from her closet and throws clothes into it. She specifically grabs her scrubs and work uniforms and then her phone charger. She zips up the black bag and gets changed into a tight pink T-shirt and leggings that look like dark-colored jeans.

She grabs her pink tennis shoes and slips them on and then grabs her car keys. She walks downstairs and looks at her brother, Jase, and Erik.

"I have to go. I have to get away from here. He's just going to keep coming back."

She walks to the door and walks out, letting the tears fall down her cheeks. She gets into her blue-colored SUV and throws her bag into the back seat.

As she reaches for her door, she spots Liam walking up. She tries to yank the door shut fast, but he beats her to it.

"Where do you think you are going, Riley Carter?"

Riley takes a breath to calm down.

"Just leave me alone!"

Liam smiles an evil smile, refusing to let go of the door. She shoves him back, and he grabs her arm pulling her out of the car.

They both hit the ground together. Riley gets up quickly, out of breath as the hit on the ground knocked the breath out of her.

She looks at Liam who is already up. She bites her lip deciding what to do and grabs a big rock throwing it hitting the window on the house and catching everybody's attention.

She takes off to the wood line and finds herself in the middle of the woods. She looks around hoping Liam isn't too close and takes a second to catch her breath.

All of a sudden, something sharp hits her in the back of her calf.

She looks down and sees a piece of glass poking out with blood. She looks up and thinks to herself.

"I can't catch a break!"

Liam steps up behind her. "No, you can't because you are coming home with me." Riley takes a breath and runs finding a road. She finds the street sign and reads Cantrell Way.

She figures out where she is and runs toward the fire department that's just a mile down the road.

Finally, she reaches it and bangs on the door trying to find the breath to scream for help.

A thin-tanned skin guy with bright blue eyes and blond hair opens the door to her.

"Hey, do you need something?" asks Chase.

Riley stands there, catching her breath.

"Yes. I'm running from an abusive ex, and I need to call my dad." The guy shuffles her in quickly and slams the door shut as he sees a man run out from the wood line, looking around confused.

A short, skinny girl with short red hair walks around the corner with a smile and looks up, meeting Chase's gaze.

Her smile fades when she sees Riley standing there in panic mode. Alyssa runs over to them.

"Who is this, Chase? She looks half dead."

Riley is finally able to breathe normally and bites her lip. "Look my brother works at the hospital with me. I just need to call him or my dad. I'm sure they are worried about me."

Alyssa looks at her confused and pulls out her phone.

"Who is your brother?"

Riley chews on the inside of her cheek, knowing they are just trying to help her.

"Kasey, he works in the emergency department." Alyssa scrolls through her phone and pulls up Kasey's number.

"I hope it's the same Kasey." She calls him and explains to him what's going on and then hands Riley the phone.

Riley takes it, hurting from the glass still stuck in her leg and feeling like she might die.

"Hey, Liam was outside he got me, Kase. I'm hurt. I'm at the fire department please come get me."

Within minutes, Kasey shows up to get her and gets in quickly from the guys. Riley is sitting in the lounge room trying to figure out how to get the glass out.

"I don't know where the glass came from. I just know it was there from the second I hit the ground and somehow ended up in the middle of the woods. I just kept running until I got to a road and figured out where I was and ran here."

Kasey looks at his sister with his arms crossed disappointed.

"Just fight back, Riley, quit running! Erik is so worried about you as well as our father."

Riley stands up understanding where her and her brother now stand. "I can't rescue you forever, Riley. You're twenty-two and staying home would have been smarter than running. Let's go."

Riley rolls her eyes and gets in the car with her brother still rambling on about how stupid she was. When they get home, Riley hops out and slams the door, still ignoring Kasey. When they get inside Kasey rambles on to his dad about what happened.

Riley turns to her brother annoyed.

"Just shut up, Kasey! You are the one that said you were always there. You are the one that said you wouldn't let him get me again so maybe for once if you paid attention to me when I walked outside none of this would have happened, and I could have just left like I wanted to. You don't want to be there anymore, fine! I don't want you to be there either."

Kasey and Jase stare at Riley, shocked that she stood up for herself to them.

She takes an irritated breath and goes into the bathroom, slamming the door. Kasey knocks on the door within seconds.

"I'm sorry, Riles, and you have to get out here to get that glass out we can help you." Riley holds her breath and yanks it out then cleans it and makes sure nothing is torn. She then grabs a super glue and super glues the skin together.

She walks out of the bathroom and looks at both her dad and her brother.

"I don't need help from either one of you. You may both be doctors but, you know, I'm a nurse. I had to learn not only emergency medicine but also OB medicine. So just shut up and leave me alone."

Riley goes up to her room, slamming the door. Erik walks up and sits beside her on the bed.

"Can we talk for a second?"

Riley faces him. "What?"

Erik shrugs and holds up his hands. "You need to grow up before you settle with somebody like me. So I wish you the best of luck, and know that I am always here for you. Maybe it's just that you need time and then we can talk, but you need to think about what you want to do."

Riley stares at him as he walks out. She gets up and shuts her door. She messages a co-worker asking if she is okay to come back to work. They message back instantly.

"Of course! We miss you and OMG you must meet the new OB here. He is single! And cute!"

Riley takes a breath and grabs scrubs changing. She once again grabs her keys and black work shoes and walks out of her room. As she's walking out, she grabs her pink stethoscope.

She stuffs it in her pocket and walks out to the living room and stares at her brother, Erik, and her dad. Kasey tilts his head, confused.

"Where are you going?"

Riley shrugs not really wanting to make peace with them. "To my office." She walks out the door and to her car.

As soon as she reaches her car, Erik grabs her car door before she shuts it. She looks up at him with hurt eyes.

"Mind if I catch a ride with you? I got called in."

Riley shrugs again and nods. "Sure, why not." Erik hops in the passenger seat, and she drives off to work. Erik turns her music down and looks at her curiously.

"So you said you studied OB nursing?" Riley nods, still not really wanting to talk.

"What office do you work in, if you don't mind me asking?"

It hits her as they pull into the parking garage that Erik is that new OB. She stares at him once they park. Erik meets her eyes.

"What?"

Riley bites her lip. "You're the new doctor, aren't you?" Erik looks a little confused.

"Well I came from a different—" He pauses, and it dawns on him that she is the nurse that had been on leave for a couple weeks.

"You're her?"

Riley nods, piecing it all together. "Sure am."

Erik smiles a cheerful smile. "Well, why don't we make it a new thing when we go in. Why don't we remain a couple?"

Riley smiles, liking the idea. "I'd like that."

Erik smiles back, gets out of the car, and opens the door for her. He takes her hand, and they walk into the practice together.

Jordan, her co-worker, stares at Riley shocked. They go in the side door together and Riley gets the info she needs for taking over for a sick nurse. Jordan pulls her aside.

"Girl! That's the single doctor! How did you guys meet?"

Riley giggles cheerfully. "He's my brother's friend. Not so single anymore."

Jordan touches Riley's cheek where the bruising remains.

"Oh, honey, what happened?"

Riley takes a breath not ready to talk but knew going to work that people would ask.

"Liam happened. I'm covered in bruises. Erik helped me."

Jordan shakes her head and stares at Erik.

"Well, you got a better guy now."

Riley nods agreeing. "Sure do."

The receptionist hands Riley a file.

"There's only two for Dr. Taylor left but thank you for coming in."

Riley nods taking the file and gets everything ready for the patient. She walks around the corner to get the patient and walks into Erik. Papers fly everywhere.

All the nurses stare at her in the corner, waiting for him to yell. Erik grabs her arms keeping her from falling.

"Are you okay, love?"

Riley nods and meets his eyes. "I'm sorry."

Erik smiles and helps her pick up all the papers. "It's okay."

Riley gets all the papers, gathered them together, and put them in the right spot. Erik stops her before she walks off.

"Are you sure you're ready to be back?" Riley nods trying to be in her work mode.

"Yes, I'm fine." Erik nods and lets her go. Riley calls a patient in and takes them to a side room.

She gets their weight and blood pressure. After writing it all down and getting it into the computer, she realizes Dr. Taylor isn't in and is in a delivery. The computer prompts her to take her to the next doctor, which would be Erik.

She pauses and makes herself understand that Erik only cares for her. She walks the patient to the room and goes to Erik's office, knocking on the door.

"Hey, patient in Room 2."

She sticks the file in his box outside the door and walks back to get the second patient waiting. She grabs the second patient's file and gets them.

She gets their weight as well as their blood pressure and takes them to a room, realizing this patient is thirty-six weeks pregnant. She hands the patient a sheet to cover with.

"Undress from the waist down and he'll be in in a second."

The young girl looks at her, irritated. "Um, excuse me? Dr. Taylor is supposed to be my doctor today." Riley nods, understanding her patients concerns.

"I understand but Dr. Taylor is in a delivery right now, so they have you set up with another."

The patient shakes her head no. "Then you can reschedule me because I won't see another."

Riley shakes her head and walks away from the patient's room. The patient walks out and grabs Riley's hair, pulling her back.

"Excuse me, I was talking." Jordan catches a glimpse of the girl; she gets a couple other nurses and run to Riley's rescue. Erik walks out of his office seeing nurses run down the hall.

They get the patient off Riley and shut the door, leaving the patient alone. Jordan stands by the door with Riley as Erik comes to find what the fuss is about.

"You okay?"

Riley nods wondering what everybody's problem is today.

"Peachy."

Erik looks at her confused. "What's going on?"

Riley looks away. "Somebody's being a jerk, that's all. Have fun!" She shoves the file into Erik's hand and walks off.

After a long day of the same repeated things, she gets in her car with Erik. He looks at her shocked.

"I have to give it to you. I didn't think you would make it today. How are you feeling?"

Riley smiles thinking he is joking, not being used to the caring kind of treatment. "I'm okay other than fighting a pregnant jerk."

Chapter 4

After a couple months of getting back into the grind of work there is no sign or word from Liam, and Riley is getting used to being with Erik and out of a bad relationship. Riley is starting to feel less and less afraid of Liam.

Riley gets up out of bed early, waking up Erik, hoping her brother isn't up yet. Erik lies in bed, smiling at her. Riley pulls on her pajama shorts and a long-sleeve shirt.

She turns to Erik, not expecting him to be awake, and she jumps when she sees him move. She puts her hand on her chest.

"Lord, you scared me!"

Erik chuckles and holds his hand out. "Get back in bed, love. You're off today . . . rest up."

Riley giggles amused. "My brother can't know you slept in here—he'll flip."

Erik shrugs and agrees. "Yeah. I don't think I want to deal with a cranky Kasey." He gets out of bed and pulls on his gray sweatpants and a red T-shirt.

Riley opens the door and looks on both sides of the hallway and rushes Erik out. Riley meets him at the door on the porch and kisses him.

"Let me know when you get home?"

Erik nods agreeing. "You know you could come with me, love."

Kasey walks outside and looks at his sister who looks frozen and to Erik.

"Here so early?"

Erik smirks amused. "Yeah, she was up anyways."

Kasey shrugs, opening the door. "Why don't you both come inside where it's warmer."

Riley laughs keeping her secret. "Actually, I was about to go with Erik."

Kasey looks his sister up and down.

"Not in pajamas I hope."

Erik nods agreeing with him. "He is right, love."

Riley pulls Erik inside with her and goes up to her bedroom and changes into a camo-looking dress with a hood and half sleeves, black leggings, and black boots.

She goes into the bathroom and washes, dries, and straightens her hair. She gets pulls out her makeup bag as Erik walks in to check on her. He puts his hand over it.

"You don't need that gunk on your face. You're too pretty."

Riley smiles and looks at him. "But I do."

Erik shakes his head, disagreeing. "No, you really don't."

Riley grabs her bag and sticks it back under the sink. Erik grabs her and walks down with her. They walk to the door. Kasey turns to them in the kitchen.

"Riles?"

Riley looks at her brother. "Yeah?"

Kasey pulls out his phone.

"I have this girl that constantly keeps coming to the ER, and I think she is being abused." Riley looks at him confused.

"And?" Kasey shrugs thinking.

"I don't know . . . there is just something about her. She seems so broken. Is that how you were?"

Riley bites her lip not wanting to remember. "I—"

Erik cuts her off. "She may not want to remember it, Kasey."

Kasey shrugs, sighing. "I want to get a house. Will you guys live with me?"

Riley looks at Erik shocked. Erik smiles cheerfully.

"Of course, we will. Let's go." Kasey smiles excited.

"Great, because I already bought it and moved. Your turn, sis!" He tosses her a set of keys.

Riley looks shocked at her brother. "Is that a 'you better spend your day packing' kind of hint?"

Kasey nods, smiling. "Dad is moving to Georgia, he met a girl. Might sell the house. You can't live with Dad forever."

Riley giggles, agreeing. "I wasn't going to, but it was my safe place." She turns to go upstairs to get some stuff thrown into bags.

Kasey clears his throat.

"Hey, Riles?"

Riley turns to her brother afraid what he's about to ask. "Yeah?"

Kasey smirks happy. "You look pretty, sis."

Riley smiles perky. "Thanks."

She goes up to her room and finds boxes by her door but not expecting them to be there. She grabs the box and tape and goes into her room and begins packing up everything that isn't last minute.

When she gets her room packed besides a couple uniforms and a couple regular outfits and a set of pajamas, she gets her bathroom stuff packed.

After getting everything else packed, she shoves boxes into her car and hugs Erik goodbye.

"I'll see you soon?"

Erik nods, kisses her, and leaves. Riley goes with Kasey to his house and finds a bedroom downstairs and two upstairs with a living room.

She drags her boxes upstairs and goes out to her car. Kasey goes with her to get furniture and the rest of their stuff.

She goes back with Kasey to his house and gets everything unloaded and into a bedroom. She places everything but her bed in place and gets everything unpacked quickly.

Erik comes over with his stuff which isn't but a couple boxes full. They get stuff placed and their bathroom set up the way they want.

Erik puts a TV on a TV stand in the living room for them, and they get the house decorated the way they want upstairs. Riley comes down and finds her brother had a bunch of furniture delivered and already put together in the house.

Riley hugs Erik excitedly. "I can't believe we're living together."

Erik nods agreeing.

Kasey gets paged into work for the same girl.

"This girl is back again!"

Riley looks at her brother confused. "Are you sure she isn't on drugs?"

Kasey nods very sure. "Yes, she is the fire fighter that saved you, that called me."

Riley's jaw drops shocked. Kasey nods, feeling bad.

"Look, I know I asked you guys to move in with me but maybe you could stay at Dad's house? I mean he's probably going to give the house to you, anyways."

Riley throws her crap back in the boxes and into her car.

"Sure, why not. We'll be gone by the time you get home." She and Erik get all their stuff except their dresser and TV and couch. They drive back over to Jase's house and unpack everything again.

By the time they finish, the day is already gone. Erik sits on the black circle couch, bored.

Riley walks over to him and lays her head on his lap. He puts a hand on her. She flinches and almost jumps up. Erik rubs her back.

"It's okay. It's just me." He calms her down. Kasey calls Erik and talks to him about bringing Alyssa to his house.

Erik talks to him about it being a good idea to keep her safe. Riley gets up and walks into the kitchen to grab her phone.

She texts her dad asking if she could have the house. Jase replies with a picture of a lady named Melanie saying sure! With a thumbs up.

Riley walks back into the living room with Erik grabbing his car keys.

"Hey, I'm going to help your brother calm down Alyssa, okay?"

Riley bites her lip afraid he might not come back. "Okay."

Erik walks out of the house leaving. Riley texts him a few minutes later saying she loves him.

When eleven that night hits, and he still hadn't come back home, Riley texts him again asking where he is.

After waiting thirty minutes for a reply, she gives up and goes up to her room and gets into pajama shorts and a black T-shirt.

She then goes into her brother's empty room and lies on the floor, wishing he would come back too. She hears the door open and close and then footsteps.

Unsure if it is Erik, she hides in her brother's closet and realizes it's Liam again. She turns her volume down in hopes that he doesn't find her.

She gets a text from Kasey asking if she is alright being there alone right now. Riley sees the light come on in the bedroom and holds her breath, not texting him back.

"Riley, I know you are here your car is sitting outside. Come out, come out, wherever you are." Tears flow down her eyes. The fear consumes her.

After about twenty minutes she hears the footsteps leave and the door open and close.

Riley sits in the closet hearing a car speed off. Kasey calls her phone. Riley hits ignore just in case it's a trick. After an hour of her not answering him or Erik, Erik comes back and walks in.

"Riles are you okay, love?"

Riley texts him saying "Closet, Kasey's room." Erik walks in and opens the closet door. He finds a frozen Riley with a fearful look in her eyes. He sits on the floor beside her.

"What's up?" Riley bites her lip scared to even move.

"He came in here."

Erik looks at her confused. "Who?"

Riley stares blankly into the air. "Liam. He came in here. I've been in this closet for two hours."

Erik stands up and holds out his hand.

"Well I'm here now you're safe, love." Riley doesn't move. Erik walks out of the room and calls Kasey. Within minutes, Kasey is at the house and walking into the room.

"Riles?"

Riley doesn't respond to him or move from the closet. "Riles what's wrong?" Kasey squats down meeting her eyes. "Hello?"

She looks at him for a second flashing her fear in her eyes and then away. Kasey sits in the closet with his sister. She leans against him letting the tears fall again.

"I can't be here, Kasey. I can't do this anymore!"

Kasey holds his sister tight. "It's alright, Riles. Buy yourself a house or live with Erik at his."

Riley shakes her head. "I don't think Erik can handle me, Kasey." Kasey bites his lip, knowing Erik is tired of dealing with her and Liam.

"Riles, I think you and Erik need to talk."

Riley gets up, puts her brave face back on, and goes into the kitchen where Erik is standing with Alyssa. Alyssa turns to Riley.

"How do you do it?"

Riley looks at her confused. "Do what?"

Riley sees all the bruises on her. "Oh. I don't."

Erik huffs annoyed. "She runs and hides."

Riley rolls her eyes. "Can I talk to you, please?"

Erik walks with her onto the porch. Riley shuts the door, already feeling her heart break.

"Tell me the truth. Do you want to be with somebody not like me? Not broken?" Riley looks away from Erik while she talks, fighting the tears back.

Erik lifts her chin toward him and kisses her.

"If I didn't love you, Riley, I wouldn't have come back. Stop this. You are broken, you need somebody there for you. Just as Alyssa needs people there for her. She just had her husband beat her at work. She needs a friend. Your brother is doing what he does best."

Riley nods gathering that hers is old news and doesn't need to be helped anymore.

"Basically, you're saying I'm old news and this just happened, right? That's crap, Erik, and you know it." Riley turns to go inside. Erik grabs her arm, stopping her. Riley turns toward him not wanting this again.

"Please let me go." Erik pulls her into a hug.

"I love you, Riley. She just needs your help." Riley shrugs not caring.

"And I needed my brother and my boyfriend for two hours. Did anybody care then? Of course not." She pushes Erik away and goes inside leaving him on the porch. Kasey looks at his sister confused.

"Hey! Chill out, Riles." Riley turns toward her brother, irritated.

"You are one to talk. Leaving me here alone when I needed you the most. Screw you, Kasey. You are too busy chasing druggies and whores to help your sister."

Riley walks up to her room, locks her door, and gets in her bed. She rolls over wanting Erik beside her more than anything but isn't ready to talk to him either.

She hears tires drive away. Figuring everybody has left her alone, she rolls over and goes to sleep. In the morning, she gets up and dressed in fuzzy black pajama pants and a long-sleeve gray shirt.

She slides on socks and walks down the stairs she trips on the last stair and slides down. Erik sits up on the couch and looks at her confused.

Riley jumps when she sees Erik when she stands up.

"Stop doing that!"

Erik chuckles and pats the couch. "Come here."

Riley walks over to him and sits beside him. "What?"

Erik hugs her sideways. "I'm sorry."

Riley smiles, feeling his warm, comforting touch again. "I was scared he was going to kill me last night."

Erik holds her tightly. "I didn't think anything of it, Riles. I thought he has given up by now."

Riley sighs wishing. "I can dream."

Erik chuckles in a sarcastic way. "I'm sorry I should have come back earlier. Your brother and Alyssa seem like a good fit. I think you will like her if you give her a chance."

Riley shrugs ignoring the comment. "I don't like much of anybody."

Erik stares at her shocked. "You're a nurse why?"

Riley giggles amused. "Because I wanted to be a labor and delivery nurse but ended up in an office."

Erik shakes his head thinking okay then. "I couldn't picture you being nice enough to be a nurse."

Riley smirks and sits up feeling comfortable. "I could. Hey, guess what!" She thinks about her bruises changing the subject.

"What?" Erik looks over to her, wondering what kind of adventure she might take him on this time.

Riley pulls up her shirt showing her bruises almost gone. Erik smiles cheerfully.

"Look your scars on the outside are almost gone. Time to work on the inside. I'm serious, Riles, Lyssa could use a friend who could help her through some of this. Just text her."

Riley takes a breath not ready to talk about her and Liam.

"Erik, there are things that I went through with Liam, things I'm not ready to talk about."

Erik nods in understanding and pats the seat beside him.

"Well, you know I will be here to help you through it all. Maybe try talking to a counselor?"

Riley shakes her head no. "I'd be paying to sit in a room and stare at walls." Erik nods in understanding.

"Well, you know when you're ready to talk about it all, I'm here." Riley nods thinking she'll never be ready. She gets off the couch and goes into the kitchen and makes herself a cup of French vanilla coffee.

She dumps sugar into her cup and French vanilla creamer and then walks into the living room.

Erik shakes his head while sitting on the couch. "I think you're going to give yourself a caffeine over dose one day."

Riley's jaw drops. "I didn't think that was possible."

Erik nods feeling smart. "Yeah. I've seen this girl come into the ER she overdosed on caffeine and looked like she was on drugs."

Riley shrugs, not worried about it. "Well, if it happens it happens, right?" Erik shakes his head taking her cup.

"You've had several cups. Slow down." Riley gets off the couch and goes up to her room to change. She hears the door open and close. She texts Erik asking where he's going.

He texts back and says, "Nowhere, your brother and Alyssa are here."

She grabs a tight pair of jeans and gets changed. She goes downstairs and sees her brother and Alyssa.

Riley walks right past her brother, ignoring his existence, and grabs Alyssa's arm, pulling her outside to the porch. Riley sits on the swing and looks up at her.

"You wanted to know how I did it? How I learned to be human again?" Alyssa shrugs and sits beside Riley.

"How do you live every day in fear?"

Riley shrugs not thinking before answering. "Some days are better than others. I think the worst is knowing that he shows up when I'm alone. He feeds on my fear. One day it'll be easier. Can I ask who hurt you?"

Alyssa looks away. "Chase. The guy who helped you. I have broken ribs, and your brother is so caring. I don't trust the other guy in your house. He looks mean."

Riley giggles amused. "Erik? Think of him like this. He helped me like Kasey is helping you. Maybe we could have a party tonight? It'd be fun. Let loose. I promise if Kasey would let you have a night of fun with me, you will be okay. I need it too."

Alyssa smiles, feeling like she needs a friend. "Yeah, that would be great! But I don't think your brother will let you have a party."

Riley giggles even more amused. "My brother has no authority over me or my house. Erik is a different story."

Alyssa nods still afraid. "He won't hurt me?"

Riley stands up holding her hand out. "No, Erik wouldn't hurt a fly."

Alyssa nods but not ready to let herself go.

Riley sighs crossing her arms.

"Well, you have to get ready if you want to have a party tonight! You need a friend and I need a friend. It works both ways. Believe me, Erik scared me too. Until one day he walked into the bathroom and sat on the floor with me and talked to me. That's all it took. Try it. Show my brother you aren't helpless."

Alyssa nods and gets up, not taking Riley's hand. She walks into the house with Riley. Erik and Kasey stare at the two girls waiting for one of them to talk.

Alyssa goes into the bathroom. Kasey looks at his sister irritated.

"What did you say to her, Riley? She needs a friend not somebody who is going to break her even more."

Riley shrugs not caring. "She wanted help I can't help the way she takes what I say. And if you must know, I told her to man up and not act like a coward around you. She isn't helpless, Kasey. If she has to pee, let her go in peace. Good grief!"

Erik steps in between the two siblings and faces Riley and points toward the couch.

"Walk away, Riley. It's not a fight you want." Riley sighs and walks toward her father's room. Alyssa opens the door at that point, walking out and looks directly at Kasey.

"I'm not feeling too well. Can we go home?" Riley pulls Alyssa into her dad's room with her.

Before Kasey can get to them, she shuts the door and locks it. She looks at Alyssa, disagreeing.

"Just go get ready. There is a bathroom there. I got this."

Alyssa stares at Riley fearful. "Look I just puked my guts up. I really don't feel too great okay?" Riley shrugs and moves out of Alyssa's way of the door.

"Nobody is stopping you from leaving. You are the one that needed a friend. If you can't take jokes then move on."

Alyssa looks at Riley annoyed and then smirks. "You're pregnant."

Riley looks at Alyssa amused.

"That's—" She thinks for a second and bites her lip. "Okay, this is a secret between us, so do not say a word to Kasey or Erik."

Riley goes into the bathroom pulling out a test from under the sink, praying she isn't. She takes a test and gets a positive.

Riley looks up at Alyssa with an "oh crap" look. "Girl, that isn't even funny!" Alyssa shrugs and crosses her arms.

"You're moody, eat weird combinations. Erik hasn't figured that out yet?"

Riley texts Erik saying, "I'm going to beat you this better be some screwed up joke." Erik texts back, "Well if you unlocked the door I could figure out what you're talking about." Riley sends him a picture with an angry face under it saying, "This isn't funny."

Alyssa opens the bedroom door and walks out with a smirk, feeling amused. Riley goes out behind her. Erik stands behind Riley and clears his throat.

"Make sure it wasn't an expired one?"

Riley jumps not expecting him there. "Or I can go have a blood test done which is exactly what I'm going to do. Thank you."

Erik shakes his head. "I'm joking, love. You can't get a false positive."

Riley bites her lip. "There are cases you could." She goes down the line of cases, and Erik holds up his hand stopping her.

"I know all these cases, Riles. There is nothing wrong with this."

Riley looks at him aggravated.

"Yes, there is! There are things wrong with this because I have an IUD so yes, yes there are many things wrong with this."

Erik shrugs not worried. "Well, setting up an appointment and ultrasound will be the easiest way."

Riley shakes her head, grabbing her keys.

"No no no. I am going now." She walks out with Alyssa following her. Riley smiles, happy that Alyssa is going with her. They get in Riley's car and drive to the health clinic.

After going in as a walk-in and getting everything done, the blood test shows negative. They take Riley in for an ultrasound and find a sac with nothing there.

Riley is told the words that nobody wants to hear. "You are having a miscarriage. We'll check next week to see if anything changes and set up a d and c with your OB."

Riley gets her appointment set up for the next week and drives home, not talking to Alyssa.

"Honey, things like this happen all the time. You're okay."

Riley texts Jordan while driving to tell her to get her an appointment set up with Taylor. She pulls into her driveway not expecting Erik to be out on the porch.

Riley gets out and walks over to him. Erik looks up at her wondering what happened.

"I told you something was very wrong with that." Erik meets her eyes with a sad look.

"Did you get an abortion?"

Riley looks at him like he lost his mind. "No! Of course not! It's just that there is no baby—just a sac."

Erik looks away from her.

"You miscarried?"

Riley shrugs disagreeing.

"They say that. I believe I would be in the hospital if I did, don't you? I mean I'm not even bleeding, Erik, think about that."

Erik stands up taking her hand.

"So you are saying you are too early to see?"

Riley nods, not wanting him to worry.

"Erik, I'm an OB nurse. If I were really worried it would be because you were. We both know the same things."

Erik meets her eyes and holds her close to him. "You want to know what I think?"

Riley looks up at him. "What's that?"

Erik takes a breath not wanting to hurt her.

"That you are wrong. That you should be in the hospital and that we should find out what is really going on."

Riley takes a step back. "Erik, I know what you are thinking, and you know it's okay."

Chapter 5

Riley did miscarry, after fighting the depression and not talking to anybody about it. She has the IUD birth control removed without telling Erik about it. Riley is sitting at the island planning her party for the night when Erik walks in from work. Riley turns toward him and kisses him.

"Good day?"

Erik smiles and sits beside her. "I found something out about you." Riley's eyes get wide wondering what it could be.

"Yeah? What was it?" Erik hands her her medical file. She looks up at him shocked.

"So you found out I got the IUD removed?"

Erik smiles nodding. "Sure did."

Riley shrugs and holds up pills. "But what you didn't see was that I got pills instead." She giggles feeling amused. Erik laughs at her.

"Sure, I did. Doctors talk to each other, you know. Quinn just didn't know you were my girlfriend, that's all. Asked me to take over you as a patient."

Riley laughs not paying attention to him. "We got Lyss, Kasey, Alyssa's dad, and Jordan coming over tonight by the way." Erik opens the fridge, finding two cases of beer and cheer wines in the fridge.

"Why?" He turns to Riley unamused. Riley shrugs looking away from her laptop.

"Sorry, I forgot to tell you."

Erik shakes his head no. "I mean, why so much alcohol?"

Riley pauses trying to find a good answer. "It's a party. I needed it."

She gets up, puts her laptop in the cabinet in the island, and grabs a strawberry cheer wine; she opens it and turns to face Erik while leaning on the counter.

"And tonight, is going to be a good night."

Erik walks over to her smiling. She wraps her arms around his shoulders. "You think so?"

Riley bites her lip smiling. "I know so."

Kasey walks in with Alyssa and Derek. Alyssa giggles seemingly amused, and Kasey clears his throat apparently annoyed.

"Get a room!"

Riley peeks at her brother and smiles amusedly. "Oh, I'm sorry you came into my house, Kase." Kasey rolls his eyes unamused.

"And we have company, Riles."

Derek looks at the two confused. "Erik?"

Erik turns toward Derek and smiles. "Derek."

Riley smiles cheerfully.

"Riley! Sorry, I felt left out," Riley says.

Kasey grabs his sister's arm, feeling irritated and takes her drink from her.

"You don't need to be drinking. You are still in recovery."

Riley yanks her drink back from her brother. "My house my rules, thank you."

Kasey rolls his eyes irritated with her. "Technically, it's Dad's house."

Riley crosses her arms now annoyed with her brother. "Yeah, well he lives halfway across the country with his girlfriend and her kids and signed the house to me. So it's my house not Dad's. He's not coming back, Kasey. Just get over it already."

Derek cuts into the conversation. "Your father may not be coming back, Riley, but he has asked help from brother to keep an eye on you."

Riley bites her lip not answering Derek. Alyssa smirks amused.

"Good luck. My dad is fun to deal with." Derek shoots Alyssa a hush-up look.

Riley walks over to Erik and hops up on the island. "And I am an adult, Kasey. I can take care of myself."

Erik chuckles amused at her. "You can?"

Riley looks irritated at Erik who has his arms crossed and is leaning on the island beside her.

"Yes, Erik. I can. I'm not like clumsy bones over there almost killing herself every step she takes."

Alyssa looks as her jaw dropped. "At least I didn't bust my butt getting out of my car."

Riley finishes her drink. "Yeah, well in my defense. I was half asleep and was asked to cover a shift in labor and delivery thank you."

Erik stares at Riley waiting for the story. "So you fell out of your car?" Riley giggles a cute innocent giggle.

"It wasn't a fall it was a slip, there is a difference. We all know I don't pay attention without my coffee."

Erik takes the coffee pot and throws it in the trash. "And you can continue to live without the caffeine. It won't kill you."

Riley shrugs and hops off the island. She pulls out a coffee maker that makes one cup at a time.

"I have them stashed don't you know that. I live on a nursing income and only have a few bills. Although I would like to get a new car soon."

Erik nods agreeing. "Yeah, yours is starting to fall apart."

Derek stares at everybody, watching. Alyssa looks at everybody.

"Okay, well I have an announcement," says Kasey, while smiling in a loving way. "We have an announcement." Riley looks at both waiting. Alyssa smiles a big grin.

"We're pregnant!"

Riley busts out laughing. "Really? I'm sorry I just can't picture my brother being a father. Poor kid."

Kasey elbows his sister. "Can't you be nice? For just once."

Riley shrugs not feeling bad.

"Yeah, I could. You know about six months ago. When you lived with me."

Kasey yanks his sister outside with him. "I've had enough of your smart-mouth comments. We have guests and you are acting like a brat."

Riley crosses her arms. "Don't ever grab me like that, Kasey."

Kasey stares at his sister angrily. "Can't you just be nice to my fiancé? Just one time? You know I'm sure Erik is getting tired of your crap too."

Riley bites her lip, choosing not to answer her brother. "Well, at least I didn't leave you behind, at least I didn't leave you in a closet. You want to throw Erik up in my face? I'll throw everything up in yours."

Kasey and Riley get in each other's faces.

"At least I didn't leave you at the fire department hurt, Riley. Remember that? Remember when I came to your rescue?"

Riley huffs at her brother. "I remember that being the night you became a jerk, Kasey!" at that point Liam walks up on the porch, smiling with a rose.

"It's my peace offering, Riley." Riley turns to Liam and gets in his face. "If you do not stop showing up here and not stop harassing me, I will have you thrown in prison! So go away, Liam!"

Kasey stands back, watching his sister in case he should intervene. Liam towers over her.

"You want to play that game? Let's go, little girl. You couldn't take me if you tried."

Riley shoves him off her stairs.

"For all those times you beat me, all those times you put me down." Liam walks backward and runs off.

Riley walks back onto the porch and looks at her brother.

"Thanks for helping, jerk."

Kasey shrugs. "I thought you could handle it. If I didn't, I wouldn't have just stared at you."

Riley goes inside, slamming the door on Kasey's face. Kasey follows his sister up the stairs yelling.

"Who slams the door in their brother's face when they are still talking? Do you know how disrespectful that is?"

Riley turns at her door to face her brother. "Oh, you didn't like that? I thought it was quite amusing. Here let me do it again for you." Kasey catches the door as she tries to close it. Erik sits on the couch on his phone. Alyssa sits beside him listening to them fight.

"You're okay with that?"

Erik shrugs listening to them argue. "I'm used to it. It's a normal thing."

Kasey yells at Riley. "I hope Erik finds somebody better then you!" Riley's jaw drops. Erik sets his phone down and hops up.

"And that is my cue to cut in."

Riley stares at her brother hurt. "You don't mean that!" Kasey crosses his arms.

"You have issues, Riley, and I do mean it."

Erik pops up at the door. "Okay, guys, just stop."

Kasey turns to Erik. "I bet he would be at my house all the time if it weren't for you, Riley!"

Riley crosses her arms still flashing a hurt look.

"Oh really? I bet he wouldn't even talk to you."

Erik steps in between the two of them. He grabs Riley's shoulders meeting her eyes. "You need to chill out."

Kasey stares at the two annoyed. "We're talking, Erik!"

Erik turns to face Kasey, holding Riley behind him. "Kasey, I think you need to leave or go downstairs with Alyssa."

Kasey huffs and walks out. Erik shuts the door behind Kasey and sits on the bed with Riley. She lays her head on his lap, feeling hurt. Erik plays with her hair.

"You know your brother is just in a bad mood. It'll be okay."

Riley nods feeling down. "Are you ready to go down and socialize?"

Riley shakes her head no. "No, he can leave." She rolls over closing her eyes.

"Love, what's wrong?" asks Erik.

Riley sighs tired. "I just fought Liam off outside, and Kasey just stood there. He isn't my brother anymore."

Erik nods trying to be a good boyfriend to her.

"Talk to him calmly."

Riley sits up. "Okay."

Erik takes her hand and they walk down into the living room together. Riley seems more cheerful to everybody. Kasey looks at Erik oddly.

"What'd you do?"

Riley looks at her brother, biting her tongue thinking to herself like it's none of your business what we do.

"Can we talk please?"

Kasey laughs amused at her.

"Sure."

He leads the way to the porch. Riley sits on the side closest to the window.

"I'm sorry."

Kasey looks at his sister confused and shocked.

"What?"

Riley bites her lip.

"I'm sorry for being emotional, for being a jerk. There is a lot going on, you know."

Kasey nods accepting her apology.

"Well I'm sorry for leaving you on your own. But you could share Erik, you know he was my friend first."

Riley giggles amused. "Yeah and you could share Alyssa. I could like her if we got to hang out, you know."

Kasey laughs at her comment. "Yeah good luck with that one. Lyss doesn't share well."

Riley gets up and sighs. "Yeah I didn't think so."

Kasey stands up smiling at his sister and hugs her. "I'm sorry for all the hurtful things I said to you."

Riley shrugs and looks toward the stairs, worried Liam will show up again.

Kasey puts his hands in his pockets. "Hey, we're all here. He won't come back. We got it this time, okay?" Riley nods and feels like her brother actually cares for once.

"Yeah, maybe not." The memories of Liam shoving her down the stairs, and him busting in to her house in Kasey's room flash in her mind. Her smile fades.

"How are you doing?"

Riley shrugs letting it go. "The memories will always be there, the nightmares are still around. I think I should move away."

Kasey shakes his head, apparently disagreeing.

"No, I think you have this. Don't run, Riles. I bet Derek could help. He's a good person to talk to, you won't know until you try."

Riley sighs, not really wanting to try or even talk to somebody she doesn't really know. Then again, her father wasn't exactly there for her either.

"Please, Riles? I promise you'll love him!"

Riley takes a breath, afraid to let somebody else in and be able to read her like a book.

"I don't know Kasey I'm not ready to talk."

Kasey nods and opens the door, motioning for Derek to come out. He looks at his sister hopeful.

"Just let him talk for now."

Derek walks out on the porch, kind of confused.

"I told her you would be a good person to talk to. You know, she went through a lot of abuse like Lyss."

Riley looks up at Derek, sitting on the porch seemingly unsure. Derek sits beside her with a friendly smile.

"You'll get used to me. Your dad just needed comfort, I guess—with his kids here and him in the south. You know I have two daughters. Both pregnant at the same time. It's nice to be around somebody who isn't."

Riley smirks at his comment.

"Well, maybe one day, we can get to know each other."

Derek smiles, liking the idea. "Sweetheart, I'm a close friend of Erik's Kasey's, and your father's. I'm here no matter what."

Riley nods accepting the friendship. "Thanks."

Derek meets her eyes. "Now let's talk for a second. What exactly did this guy do?"

Riley looks toward the Woodline, not ready but knowing talking might help.

"Well, it all started when I had to go to work one time. He got mad and hit me . . . busted my lip. I waited for it to go away before I came home to see Kasey and my dad. The next couple days were rougher. He held me at gunpoint, told me if I left or told anybody I wouldn't live to tell another soul. The next day, he started yanking me around and then the apologies started."

Derek cuts her off. "Does anybody else know your story?"

Riley bites her lip not making eye contact.

"Kasey doesn't know it all. Just that I was shoved down the stairs after an argument, and he was there when Liam hit me when I was fighting back. He was there when a friend came to reset my shoulder. He was there when I was hiding in his closet when Liam busted in looking for me, and he was there when Liam showed up recently."

Derek nods listening. "So when you say Kasey wasn't there, he was. Honey, your brother has been through most of it with you. Does Erik know it all?"

Riley nods looking down. "He does . . . most of it. You know Alyssa saved me once?"

Derek smiles, proud of his daughter. "Did she?"

Riley nods, meeting his eyes with tears in them.

"One day, Liam showed up and yanked me out of the car. I ran. I ran until I got to the fire department once I realized I was hurt. Kasey came and got me."

Derek smiles happy to hear that siblings can get along just not his daughters apparently. "See, Kasey saved you too."

Erik walks out with a blanket for Riley. "You look a little cold, love."

Riley smiles looking up at him. "Thanks."

He holds his hand out helping her up. "Why don't you guys come in and talk. It's getting cold."

Riley bites her lip and goes in with Erik in front of her and Derek behind her. She sits on the black leather couch and shivers. Erik hands her the blanket.

She covers up and picks up her phone. She sees a missed call from Jordan and two texts from Dr. Taylor. Riley reads the texts asking her to come in to cover in labor and delivery for the night.

Riley jumps up. "Erik!"

Erik jumps when she yells. "I'm right here you don't have to yell."

Riley smirks apologetically. "Sorry, but why didn't you tell me I was being called in? I have to go!"

Erik shrugs looking at her not sure. "Well, it's your phone, your privacy. I trust you."

Riley smiles feeling loved. "Awh! Well I have nothing to hide. You can always go through my phone if you wanted to."

She replies to Dr. Taylor saying, "I'm on my way." She runs up to their room and changes into a light lilac-colored scrubs, then she runs back down.

She kisses Erik quickly and grabs her car keys, rushing out the door. She hops in her car and drives to Hopkins Hospital.

She parks and rushes into the hospital to the labor and delivery floor. Jordan smiles when she sees her friend.

"Thank goodness you're here! Dr. Taylor is thinking of asking you to take day shift over here."

Riley smiles, putting her keys in a lock box, and goes with Jordan to meet the doctor. A young male doctor walks into her.

"Sorry." He keeps walking.

She meets Jordan's gaze. "Not Erik at all!" They both giggle remembering when she bumped into him at work.

They go into a room and Dr. Taylor looks up smiling. The patient who looks to be in a lot of pain stares at both of them.

"What are you guys waiting on?"

Riley hooks the patient up to the monitors and gets vitals. Dr. Taylor waits outside the room for Riley and Jordan.

"Okay, honey, what's your pain level?" Riley types as the patient talks. She watches contractions while talking to the patient.

"Are you getting an epidural?" The patient nods.

"Has anybody called anesthesiology?"

Jordan breaks into the conversation.

"No and Dr. Taylor needs to talk to you as soon as you are done in here." Riley holds a thumbs up. She then turns to Jordan.

"Dilation?" Jordan nods.

"She's a five." Riley types it in with the time and then looks at the patient.

"Alright, Mrs. Cutney, I'll go page for the epidural and we'll be right back."

She walks out of the room meeting Dr. Taylor.

"Hey, Quinn called out, Erik is on call, and Derek is on call for us tonight. Can you replace my overnight's charge nurse? She quit last night." Riley looks at her shocked.

"Yes, absolutely!" Dr. Taylor smiles warmly.

"Thank you! So don't come into the office. Just come in tomorrow seven to seven, and we'll get it fixed tomorrow. I'm calling in one of the guys on call. We have six in active labor."

Riley's eyes widen, and she moves to the computer taking over the charge nurse's laptop. She finds the files she needs and monitors the other five patients without needing help. The nurses light comes on for Room 4 where she was an hour go.

"Yes, can I help you?" Mrs. Cutney is basically on the other end, begging for an epidural.

"Yes, ma'am, we will get your nurse for you." Riley looks at Jordan with an *oops* look.

"Hey, you have Cutney right?"

Jordan nods looking up from a laptop. "Yeah why?"

Riley pages for an epidural for the patient. "We have to go in in a second."

Riley catches hard contractions out of the corner of her eye for another patient. She hops up while Jordan takes care of Room 4. She goes into Room 2 to check on the patient. She figured Jordan had been in there.

"Hey, I'm Riley. I'm your nurse for the night. How are you feeling?" She walks over to the monitor. Ms. Tris looks comfortable and happy.

"Great now that I got an epidural."

Riley smiles, checking the time she got it. About an hour ago. She gets everything she needs to check dilation.

Tris pulls her legs up and Riley checks her. "About a seven maybe eight." Riley puts it in the computer and walks out.

Erik and Derek walk in about the time Riley walks out of the room.

"Oh, she called you both in?" Riley looks at Derek a little confused. You're over here now?"

Derek smirks amused. "Sure am!"

Riley nods adjusting to this new thing. Jordan rushes up to Riley out of breath. "Okay three is a nine you need to get Taylor, six isn't dilating anymore, and five was sent home."

Riley walks behind the desk and texts Dr. Taylor for Room 3. She looks at the monitors then to Jordan.

"When was the last time you went into one and four?"

Jordan pulls up her logs. "One, I haven't, and four was about an hour ago."

Riley prints out discharge papers for one and pulls up Room 4.

"Go check four, I'll get one. Dr. Taylor is on her way."

Another nurse walks in late.

"Sorry I'm late guys. I have a sick kid at home. Had to wait on the father to get there. Who's the charge tonight?"

Jordan points at Riley. "It's all on her." She runs off. Riley sighs gathering up things.

"Okay. Six needs on call so pick one and Taylor has three then I want you to check three." The nurses scatter, and Krista looks at Derek and Erik deciding.

"Well, one of you just go" Riley discharges Room 1 and moves on to 2 again. "Hey, Tris. How are you doing?"

Tris looks exhausted and hurting.

"What's your level?" Tris holds up eight fingers.

"Alright so the epidural needs a boost. Let me page them for you and let me check again." Riley checks her to see how far again. She is at a nine.

"Alright let me go get a doctor."

She walks out of Room 2, bumping into Derek.

"Sorry!"

Derek smiles cheerful. "It's okay! How's Tris doing?"

Riley opens the door. "She's a nine."

Derek goes in. Riley goes to three to check on them, meeting Dr. Taylor at the door.

"Riley, I need you in four, please."

Riley nods and moves on to four. Jordan is getting everything together and paging NICU for help. Riley walks in and helps Jordan, and then the two girls deliver Mrs. Cutney's baby.

Erik walks in after the baby is born and does what he's supposed to do. Riley moves back to the desk, with all the help she can sit down for a second.

Once everybody has delivered, Riley checks the time and realizes its already five in the morning. She does her rounds for each room for medicine and gets everything put into the computer.

Jordan helps with getting vital checks, and they get everything ready for the next shift. Riley walks in with Mary, the day shift nurse to two different rooms, and gets ready to go. Erik walks over to her.

"You make a good charge nurse you know," he says to her.

Riley smiles cheerfully. "I took a night-shift position as a charge nurse."

Erik smiles happy for her. "And I have a question for you."

Riley looks at him half asleep.

"What's that?"

He holds her hand and places a ring on her ring finger.

"Will you marry me?"

Riley smiles cheerfully. "Of course, I would!"

Chapter 6

Riley gets up at around two that afternoon with Erik. Erik hands her a cup of her favorite coffee in bed.

"Aw, that's so sweet!"

He smiles cheerfully. "I figured you could use it. Do you work tonight?"

Riley nods sipping her warm cup. "Thank you for turning on the heat. I forgot about it."

Erik smiles happily. "I turned it on before you left."

Riley gets up and grabs some sparkly gray pajama pants and one of Erik's black T-shirts.

She goes to the bathroom and takes a shower. When she gets out, she dries her hair and puts on her pajama pants and his shirt.

She walks out and walks downstairs to meet Kasey, Derek, and Alyssa in the living room.

"Erik said you got a new job, just wanted to congratulate you!" says Kasey.

Riley hugs her brother. "Thanks, Kase. You know it's always been what I wanted to do."

He nods in agreement.

"Sure is! Welcome to the real world of Hopkins Hospital! How does it feel to be a charge nurse?"

Riley smiles happy. "It can be slow or it can be busy, I guess."

She sits on the couch with her knees up to her chest. She stares into space. Erik catches her attention.

"How are you feeling?"

Riley looks up at him. "I'm just groggy. I'll be okay."

He laughs at his fiancé. "So have you told anybody yet?"

Kasey, Derek and Alyssa all look at her, confused. She looks at her ring on her hand smiling.

"I thought I dreamed it. Hey, guys, we're engaged." She looks up at everybody. Kasey lets out a breath of relief.

"You don't even know what I thought you were about to say."

Riley giggles amused.

"No, Kasey. I am definitely not pregnant. I'm on the pills, I promise you that one."

Alyssa coughs a fake cough and talks at the same time. "You can still get pregnant aha."

Riley laughs, amused at Alyssa. "At least you're the one that got pregnant not me!"

Alyssa rolls her eyes. "Yeah, yeah, make jokes."

Riley smiles and looks at Erik. "I'm sure, one day, I'll be there . . . not just now."

Erik smiles a bright smile. "You could always stop taking your pills, you know."

Riley nods biting her lip. "I'll think about it."

Erik smirks jokingly. "Hey, that's all on you, not me."

Riley bites her lip not really interested in children at the moment. Yeah. I'd wait on that one it might be awhile."

She hops up and walks into the kitchen getting another cup of coffee, feeling tired. Kasey smirks at his sister amused.

"What's the matter? Can't handle the heat of the night?"

Riley shoots her brother an ugly look. "I mean I was up for twenty-four hours, Kasey. Not my normal. I'm not exactly in my party days anymore."

She checks the time on her phone and realizes it's five in the evening.

"Crap!" She throws her still-full cup in the sink and runs upstairs to get ready for work. She throws her hair up and make up on, then gets dressed in purple scrubs and rushes down the stairs with one shoe off and one on.

Erik looks at her like she is crazy. "What are you rushing for?"

Riley holds up her phone. "It's five forty-five. I have to get food!" She rushes into the kitchen still with one shoe on and stuffs bread in her mouth, eating fast.

She puts a clip in her hair to help hold it up and goes into the living room shoving her shoe on. She hops up and grabs her blue light zip-up jacket and throws it on quickly then grabs her keys.

"Okay, I for real have to go." She kisses Erik and rushes out to her car to start it, before realizing there is snow on the ground and ice everywhere, and she is freezing.

She tries starting the car, but it won't even choke. She notices she left her headlights on and runs in sliding across the floor, then faces Erik.

"Okay, my car won't start because I'm stupid and left the headlights on. Take me to work? Please?"

She gives Erik a sweet look. He stands there with a smirk on his face at her begging him.

"Riles, I'm the one on call tonight and have to be there anyways for a code white. Of course, I'll take you." He changes and gets ready quickly.

Riley stands there impatiently. Finally, he walks down with a hoodie on and green scrubs.

Riley grabs his keys and runs out ready. She slides all the way to his car and gets in, starting it with the heat on full blast. Erik meets her out there and turns the heat down.

"Chill out, love. You won't be late." He drives out carefully and to Hopkins Hospital. They get to the hospital rather quickly.

Riley hops out and runs in quickly clocking in and putting her stuff up. She is at the desk by seven ten. She notices there are only three patients, and she is working with a girl she hadn't met yet.

The blonde nurse walks over to her. "Hi, I'm Sarah I'm kind of new." Riley nods understanding that and checks the monitors.

"Well, I'm Riley. I'm your charge nurse, and you have Rooms 1 and 3 tonight!" She walks around pulling up Room 2 with high contractions.

"Alright, when was the last time they were checked?"

Sarah shrugs not sure.

"I was with Krista and she went to page on call for somebody."

Riley sighs irritated. "Alright, you'll be with me. Let's go." She walks in to Room 2 and smiles cheerfully.

"Hey, I'm Riley. This is Sarah, she is new and learning. How are you feeling, Mrs. Roberts?"

Mrs. Roberts, a rather small lady that looked all baby, is pale. Riley checks vitals and hands Sarah stuff to check dilation.

"What is her dilation?" Riley looks at her while typing vitals. "I'd say an eight maybe nine." Riley checks for herself to be sure.

"Nine and fully effaced get on call."

She looks at the patient rubbing hand sanitizer on her hands. "We'll be right back." She walks out and goes to Room 1, checking on them.

"Hey, I'm Ril—" She stops and looks dead at her brother and Alyssa. "Didn't I just see you, guys?"

Kasey nods amused. "Yeah. Alyssa started hurting so we're here to be checked out."

Riley looks to see if Sarah got her on the monitor yet.

"Sarah hasn't come in?"

Kasey looks confused. "No, you would be the first."

Riley shakes her head annoyed. "Okay."

She hooks Alyssa up to the monitors and gets her vitals as well. "Okay, drugs, drink, smoke?" Alyssa looks at her crazy like.

"Yeah, right."

Riley moves through the normal questions. "Okay, and pain rated zero to ten?"

Alyssa thinks for a second and looks at Kasey. "I guess at six."

Riley nods standing by the computer looking up at the monitor seeing a few strong contractions. She walks out of the room grabbing the first doctor she sees.

"Room 1 is premature labor. I think they need a doctor quickly."

Derek looks at Riley seriously.

"Okay, I'm kind of busy."

Riley bites her lip not realizing it was him. "It's Alyssa." He rushes into the room. Riley moves on to Room 3.

"Hey, I'm Riley. Has Sarah been in here?" Sarah pops her head out of the bathroom.

"Yeah, I'm right here." Riley walks out and waits on Sarah. Sarah walks out a couple minutes later.

"Have you checked on 2?" Sarah shakes her head no. Riley looks irritated and texts Erik to ask if he was paged. She goes in to Room 2 to check on Mrs. Roberts.

She checks dilation, and she is full and complete. She looks up at her biting her lip. "Don't push!" She rushes around getting things together quickly.

Erik calls her trying to figure out where he was needed. She opens the door finding Erik in the hallway.

"Hey, in here." He doesn't hear her, and she goes back into the room and helps get ready to deliver the baby on her own.

She pages NICU quickly and by the time Erik walks in, she has already delivered the baby and looks at Erik in relief.

"Thank God, she needs you." She shuts off one of the monitors and walks out of the room and slides down to the floor behind the nurses' desk and hears the monitors beeping for Room 1 —Alyssa's room. She jumps up and runs into the room and doesn't see anybody but Alyssa in there asleep.

She checks monitors and then wakes up Alyssa. "Hey, I'm going to check you, okay?"

Riley checks her dilation and gets a three. She moves the monitor around for the baby's heart rate and finds it.

"Okay, how are you feeling?" Alyssa shrugs not really talking. She looks over at the monitors.

Riley takes her vitals getting a low blood pressure and high baby heart rate. She texts Erik saying Alyssa is in Room 1 and needs you. Riley walks out and walks over to her desk, watching Alyssa's room closely.

Strong contractions begin when Erik walks up with Sarah and Kasey. "Hey, what's up?"

She pulls Erik over and shows him the monitor. "What is she?"

He is clueless since he hasn't been in there or read his texts.

"She's a three, baby has a high heart rate." Sarah looks over his shoulder and turns to Kasey.

"Room 1."

Kasey drops his coffee and rushes into the room. Riley turns and faces Sarah irritated.

"That's his wife!" Sarah has an *oops* face. Erik looks at Riley shocked.

"Meet me in OR one for a C-section, get her ready."

Erik runs off. Riley sighs annoyed and goes into the room pulling her off monitors. Kasey looks at her worried, holding Alyssa's hand.

"What?" Kasey asks.

Riley bites her lip, not answering him. She starts prepping Alyssa for a C-section, then looks up at Kasey.

"Sarah is bringing you stuff. She's going for a C-section."

Riley waits and waits for Sarah and walks out, finding her on her phone. She shoves past her and grabs the things he needs and walks into the room handing it to him.

Kasey changes and goes down the hall with Riley. She goes into the OR with them and sees Erik has nurses ready for her along with NICU.

Riley turns and walks out to go back to the labor and delivery floor. She walks past Derek who was looking upset. She ignores him talking and goes straight to Sarah.

"Go home."

Sarah looks at her confused. "Why?"

Riley looks at her with no light in her eyes.

"You haven't helped me with anything or even listened to me. You just did your own thing. Go home, I don't need you here." She goes to Room 4 for a new patient and gets the patient set up on a monitor.

The new shift starts coming in, and Riley is exhausted and still on a code white hold. A code for snow. She walks into Room 2 for Mrs. Roberts.

"Nicole, she is your nurse for the day!"

Mrs. Roberts smiles cheerfully holding her baby.

"This nurse is a legend. I'll always remember her!"

Riley smiles cheerfully and walks with Nicole to Room 3. She introduces the day-shift nurse to the patient and then to Room 4 and does the same.

Riley walks into the showers and takes a shower and changes into dark-blue scrubs. She goes into a room with beds and goes to sleep. Somebody bangs on the door.

Riley jumps up and opens it, checking her phone. She has three missed calls from Dr. Vickery. She runs past Erik and to the labor and delivery floor bumping into Dr. Vickery.

"Hey, we need you. We got six in active labor all between sevens and eights."

Riley goes over to the desk meeting the day-shift charge nurse.

"Hey, I'm overnight charge nurse where do you want me to start."

Mickey, a tall skinny girl with glasses smiles cheerfully. "I'm Mickey! I'm so happy to meet you! Uh help me with what you can. Just pick rooms and go. One was your C-section, right?"

Riley nods, biting her lip. "She is back in there, everything went well. She is having a blood transfusion for losing too much blood and had low iron. I guess just start there then two and three are being discharged."

Riley takes a breath and starts. She goes into Alyssa's room to check on her and take her vitals. She sees she is asleep with Kasey holding her hand.

"Breathe, Kasey. She's okay, I promise."

Kasey looks up at his sister unhappy. "Don't ever promise patients. It just makes it worse." He looks away.

Riley checks Alyssa's vitals, seeing her blood pressure coming up along with everything else.

"She's doing good." She walks out and goes into Room 2 while rubbing hand sanitizer on her hands.

"Hey, Mrs. Roberts. How are you doing today?"

The patient smiles cheerfully at her. "I thought you worked nights, honey! Get some rest!"

Riley giggles cheerfully and gets her last set of vitals.

"Alright, let me go get your discharge papers! I'm here until the code white is lifted. For snow."

She walks out getting the discharge papers and brings them to Mrs. Roberts for her to sign then walks her and her baby out to her car.

Riley moves on to Room 3 with discharge papers and does the same. She moves to Room 4 and checks for dilation.

"Oh, girl, you're full and complete. Let me get the doctor." She goes out of the room and gets Dr. Vickery and walks back in. She pages NICU and gets everything ready. She helps with delivery and gets vitals after.

She then goes into the next room and helps with delivery there with Mickey. Unfortunately, the baby's heart beat is lost, and they are rushed to a C-section where the baby lived, and the mother did not.

Riley takes a hard hit to her heart for it. She slides down outside the OR room, crying. Mickey sits beside her.

"They're still trying to revive Mom."

Riley looks up at her. "Really?" Mickey nods sad.

Riley jumps up and runs in to assist. They get her back and into ICU. Riley looks exhausted by the time her shift is supposed to start. Erik finds her tired.

"Have you slept?"

Riley smirks half asleep. "Like three hours, yeah." Erik hands her a to-go box.

"What about food?"

Riley shakes her head. "No, have you heard the crazy on the floor today?"

Erik looks at her confused. "I haven't because I went to the ER for sleep."

Riley huffs annoyed. "Erik, we almost lost a mother." Erik looks at her apologetically.

"They're talking about lifting the code, which means we can go home." Riley rolls her eyes shoving the box back him.

"I'm not hungry." She turns to see Dr. Taylor, who smiles cheerfully at Riley. "Hey, honey, go on home. Get some rest. You've pulled a twenty-four. I've got you covered tonight. You're off tonight tomorrow and the night after."

Riley nods tired and leaves with Erik to go home.

Chapter 7

Riley goes straight to bed without changing her clothes. Erik covers her up as she falls asleep and holds her closely to him. Kasey blows up Riley's phone asking where she is because Alyssa wants to see her. Riley wakes up to his texts. Erik picks up her phone.

"I got it. Go back to sleep, love."

Riley nods, barely awake, and goes back to sleep.

Shortly after that, Derek knocks on the door. Erik gets up then wakes up Riley. She hears them downstairs talking. Riley walks down the stairs still rubbing her eyes.

"Hey, sleepy! I heard you delivered a baby by yourself," says Derek.

Riley nods still barely awake. "Yeah, I did."

Derek smiles cheerfully. "Sorry for coming by so early. Lyss wanted to see you."

Riley looks confused and looks at the clock. Six in the morning.

"Okay?" She crosses her arms and realizes she's still in scrubs. They video call Alyssa. Alyssa answers her phone half asleep.

"Yes, Dad?"

Derek hands the phone to Riley.

"Hey, how are you feeling?"

Alyssa's eyes widen. "Hey, I wanted to tell you thank you for saving me and my baby."

Riley shrugs and smiles cheerful. "It's my job, glad you guys are okay. And it was Kasey and Erik."

Alyssa nods starting to fall asleep.

"Okay, well I'll let you go Alyssa. I'm going to bed myself."

She hands Derek his phone and turns to Erik.

"Okay, I'm seriously going to take a shower."

Erik laughs and lets her go. She goes into the bathroom and gets a shower then walks out in a towel. Erik chuckles and hands her clothes.

"I knew you forgot, so I got you some."

Riley smiles happy. "That's sweet. Thank you." She goes into the bathroom and gets dressed into fuzzy pink pajama pants and then puts on his black T-shirt.

She walks out feeling like a groggy zombie and lies on the couch with Erik. Erik frowns not wanting to upset her.

"I have to go to work though, so I'll see you tonight. Ana is coming over to hang out with you, so you aren't alone."

Riley kisses him and locks the door behind him. She falls asleep waiting on Ana and jumps up to the banging on the door, thinking she was still at the hospital.

She realizes she is home and without looking, she picks up a baseball bat and opens the door swinging. Ana hops back.

"Lord, girl, you're trying to kill me!"

Riley giggles apologetically. "Sorry. I thought you were someone else."

Ana nods understanding. "Erik wanted me to stay with you just in case you had issues."

Riley sits up trying to stay awake on the couch.

"I'm sorry I'm just tired."

Ana stares at Riley studying her.

"What?"

Ana bites her lip seeing a glow. "Have you been taking your pills?"

Riley's eyes pop open, and she runs into the kitchen grabbing her pack of birth control and then looks at Ana.

"Nope! Of course not. Not even after the first week."

Ana smirks looking at her. "Sickly?"

Riley shakes her head no.

"No and no I'm not pregnant. I took a test like two months ago and have been too busy at work."

Ana giggles and texts Erik about it.

Riley goes into the kitchen and makes herself peanut butter toast. She eats it not really having an appetite.

"Okay maybe that wasn't the best idea." She walks into the bathroom throwing it all back up.

Ana texts Erik that Riley is sick too. Riley sits on the couch with Ana, watching horror movies all day and eating apples. Ana looks at her, thinking she's a weirdo.

"You've had like four apples!"

Riley giggles amused. "Yeah, I like apples. It's crazy I used to hate them and now it's like I want them on everything."

Erik walks in from work as Riley is stuffing her face with apples. Ana stands up smirking.

"Dude, she has eaten like a million apples today!"

Erik looks between the two and walks into the kitchen. Ana looks over to Riley perky.

"And that is my cue to go have a great night!" Ana leaves.

Erik walks into the living room with his arms crossed. "Didn't know you weren't taking them anymore."

Riley looks up at him with her smile fading.

"I didn't either. I just forgot them. I'm Riley. I forget medications all the time for myself. You know this."

Erik holds out a test for her. Riley rolls her eyes and gets up taking it. She goes into the bathroom and takes the test, feeling annoyed.

She walks out before it's even ready. "Well?" Erik stares at her waiting for answer.

"I don't know. I didn't want to hang around to see."

Erik goes into the bathroom and pulls her along. He hands it to her with a smile. Riley sees a negative sign. She looks up at him smirking.

"I told her I wasn't. She just didn't want to listen."

Erik nods agreeing. "She just made it out like you were."

Riley giggles and hugs him cheerfully.

"I knew I wasn't. I just took it not to argue with you."

Erik laughs, walking out with her to the living room.

"So what do you think about us taking the downstairs bedroom?" Riley thinks about it knowing her dad left a king-sized bed in there.

"Sure!" She pulls him up to their room grabbing clothes and throwing them into an empty box.

Erik carries the clothes downstairs to the bedroom and gets everything hung up while Riley carries down the phone chargers into the bedroom and plugs them in.

She walks past Kasey's room that she hasn't been in since that night. She thinks about opening the door but decides not to.

She sits on the floor of their new bedroom and looks over to her dad's bed, who she hasn't heard from in a couple months. She texts him asking how he is and tells him about the new job she's been in for a few weeks. Without a reply, she sets her phone down and walks out to Erik.

"So can I talk to you about something serious for a second?"

Erik nods, sitting on the couch and looks up to her. "I wouldn't mind having a child after we've been married for a year or two."

Erik nods agreeing with her. "I'm for that. But we also need to start planning our wedding."

Riley nods agreeing with him. "That we do." She looks over to Erik wearing a big grin.

"What?"

He looks confused. "I think you would be a complicated pregnant wife."

Riley shrugs somewhat agreeing with him. She picks up her laptop and opens it up to look at her work schedule online.

"Yeah let me do what I want, and you'll be just fine."

Erik shakes his head disagreeing. "We'll get to it when it happens."

Riley chews on the inside of her cheek nodding. She looks at her schedule seeing she works one night off the night on the week coming up.

"We will." She shuts her laptop and puts clean sheets on the bed then pulls a big purple silk like comforter out and puts it on the bed. She then goes into the hallway and checks the temperature on the thermostat for the heat.

Set on seventy. Sounds good to her! She goes back to her room where Erik sits on the bed watching her. She crawls into bed and pats the space beside her.

Erik chuckles at her amusingly. "Bedtime at eight?" Riley nods tiredly.

"Yeah! I'm tired you know!" Erik lies beside her, they both drift to sleep.

Chapter 8

Riley gets up in the morning, realizing it's another night off and her last night off. She feels well rested and is very cheerful. She goes into the bathroom connected to their now room and gets a long hot shower. She gets dressed in a long sleeve navy-blue shirt and black leggings.

She scrunches her long brown hair and pulls her bangs back making a poofy on top. She puts on socks and her black ankle boots and then does her makeup just to look pretty for a day and to surprise Erik.

She walks into the kitchen to get a cup of coffee and sees her coffee pot sitting unplugged. She turns to Erik, who is sitting at the kitchen island on his laptop.

Riley gets a mug down and makes a cup of hot chocolate with lots of mini marshmallows. She sits at the island beside Erik. He looks up at her and then down at his laptop and back up at her taking a double take.

"Well somebody is perky today!"

Riley smiles cheerfully. "Well, it maybe coffee-free but I have sacrifices to make too. So less caffeine the better, right?"

Erik stares at her blankly studying this new Riley; he is trying to decide what's wrong with her.

"Are you sick or something?"

Riley giggles and shakes her head no. "Of course not! I'm just in a good mood. Do you want to go out and do something? Get away from the house for a while?"

Erik thinks for a minute while staring her down.

"Or just an idea, we could hang out here today since you have every other night off after tonight," suggests Erik.

Riley shrugs thinking she knows where he is going with this. She gets up, finishes her hot chocolate, and rinses the cup out in the sink, then sticks it in the dishwasher.

She goes into the living room and finds her favorite Christmas movie on *Maxine the Glowing Reindeer.* She smiles remembering her and Kasey watching it every Christmas when they were kids.

Then her smile fades as she thinks of how much she wishes her mother would have been around. People disappear all the time, but this one was different.

This was her mother. If only she had one memory, even a small one, of her mother; and her father was always gone at work at Hopkins to make sure she and her brother had everything they needed. Meanwhile, her brother practically raised her.

Riley texts Kasey saying, "Hey, Maxine the glowing reindeer is on." When the movie is over, Erik stands in the doorway of the kitchen and living room with his arms crossed and a big smile on his face. She looks up at him while wiping a tear away.

"Shut up. I'm not emotional!" She turns the TV off and goes toward their room. Erik blocks her and holds her in a hug.

"I just thought it was adorable! You are crying over a kids' movie!"

Riley looks up at him, embarrassed that he caught her crying.

"I was not crying it's allergy season!"

Erik laughs at her defense.

She sits back on the couch and picks up her phone to see if Kasey replied but he only read her text. She figures he was just busy with Alyssa and a newborn of course. Erik plops down beside her.

"Where would you like to go?" Riley shrugs and thinks for a minute.

"Maybe the park? Somewhere fun? I don't know. Just wanted to get out and about but we don't have to."

She looks at the clock. Twelve in the afternoon. What a shock. The days always go by superfast for her nowadays.

Erik stands and takes her hand. "What about a walk?" Riley takes his hand standing up smiles happy.

"Sure, sounds good!" They both walk to the door. Erik grabs a gray hoodie and her light-blue jacket. They walk out together and down the porch. Riley walks in front of him, worried that Liam might pop back out of nowhere.

"So I was thinking, what about a wedding in the yard? You know, get an arch and decorate it the way you want and rent some tables and chairs."

Riley thinks about his idea and starts to like the idea.

"Yeah! Hey, you know my birthday is a couple months away we could totally do it on my birthday!"

Erik takes her hand, interlocking her fingers with his and stops her, pulling her to face him. "I think whatever you want to do is up to you. I think that no matter what, I will always love you and will take care of you. If you let me, that is."

Riley's eyes fill with tears. She stares into his feeling as if her heart were full. So many emotions rush through. The fact that somebody could care for her so much meant a lot to her, especially with her past.

Erik was the first to ever love her, to take care of her, and it was time she really let him in. "I promise I will."

"Are you sure you're okay, love?" Erik wipes her tears away and kisses her gently before she can answer him. Snow starts to fall again. He pulls her back toward the house with him.

"Yes, I'm okay. You just mean the world to me." She smiles sucking up her tears and wonders why she is crying about everything!

The snow starts to fall harder. The wonders of Washington, right? She picks up snow off the grass and makes a tiny snow ball and throws it at Erik.

He laughs and chases her back to the house and catches her in the driveway, from behind. Riley giggles playfully putting her arms around his.

Her feet hit the ground when Erik lets go. They walk toward the porch. She hops over a hole that she didn't know was there and beats him to the porch, rushing inside. She looks at the clock again and then to him shocked.

"That was a long walk!" Erik nods agreeing. She pulls off her jacket and grabs his as well, then she goes into their bedroom and grabs all the dirty clothes up and throws them in the washer.

She starts the washer; she then goes back to the living room. She plops down on the couch and grabs a green and pink crocheted lap blanket, covering up with it to warm up. Riley gets a text from Ana asking if she could come over. She replies with a yes and looks up to Erik.

"Ana is on her way over to hang out. Is that okay?" Erik shoots her a why ask look and nods, not worried about her having friends over.

Within minutes Ana is opening the door and coming in.

Erik starts making lasagna for dinner. Riley hops up and hugs Ana excited. "I miss you! By the way are you sure you aren't the one pregnant?" Ana bites on her lip anxious to tell her but not Erik.

"Girl, I am! I actually just found out like two hours ago." Riley smiles excited for her and hugs her tighter.

When supper is done, Riley gets the plates together and for the first time, they sit at the island eating together. When everybody is done, she puts away leftovers so Ana can talk to Erik. Riley does the dishes, starts the dishwasher, and cleans up the kitchen.

Ana waves to Riley after being there for a couple hours, as she is still cleaning up. Erik walks up behind Riley and hugs her from behind, placing his chin on her shoulder.

"Are you ready for an Erik and Riles movie night?" Riley turns to him shocked that he actually wanted to do something other than sleep with her.

"Sure!" She runs off into their room and puts on black fuzzy shorts and a white tank top. She turns on their TV and lies in bed with Erik. He finds a movie for them. Riley falls asleep in the middle of it.

Chapter 9

In the morning, Erik kisses Riley's forehead before leaving for work.

Riley shakes her head no. "Uh uh!" Erik chuckles at her while walking toward the door. "Get up so you can get some rest for tonight."

Riley pulls the blanket over her head. He walks out, and Riley gets up sad that her warmth is gone. She pulls on a pair of sweatpants and a long-sleeve shirt. She walks into the kitchen and makes a cup of coffee, dying for one. She sits down at the island and sips it, barely holding her eyes open.

After her cup she makes herself resist another and puts the cup in the sink. Riley drags over to the couch and covers up turning on the TV. She gets a text from Erik that says, "hey crazy hair don't forget to get a shower and only one cup of coffee today love you." She smiles at his silly text and texts him back saying, "I'm up don't worry I only had one." She lies on the couch feeling as if she is dying of exhaustion.

She falls asleep. After most of the day is gone, Riley wakes up at four and hops up feeling wide awake.

"CRAP!"

She texts Erik letting him know she fell asleep and runs into the laundry room forgetting to switch on the laundry. She sighs a sigh of relief when she notices he got the laundry switched for her.

She grabs her light-purple scrubs and a clean towel out of the dryer and rushes into the bathroom and takes a shower. She gets dressed, then dries, straightens, and pulls her hair up into a pony. She puts on makeup to surprise Erik again; she grabs a thick white jacket.

She sits down feeling like she is starving and eats a big plate of lasagna. She then puts it in the dishwasher and brushes her teeth.

Riley pulls on her shoes and grabs her keys, then walks out locking up the house. She gets in the car and drives to work.

When she gets there, she runs into Erik in the parking garage. "Riles, are you sure you aren't getting sick?"

Riley nods still groggy. "Yeah I'm sure." Riley hugs him tightly and walks into the hospital holding his hand. He walks her to the doors.

"Taylor is on call tonight, so it should be a smooth night." Riley smiles feeling like he cares so much more for her since she decided to change some things about herself starting with her coffee.

"Thank you. I love you and let me know when you get home, so I know you made it safe."

Erik nods and kisses her, letting her hand go. Riley stands at the door and watches him walk away. She turns and walks to the labor and delivery floor.

She puts her keys and jacket up in a locker and takes charge. Nicole walks up to her cheerful. "Hey, Riles! I switched to nights to help. Sarah was moved to days to train better."

Riley smiles cheerful to see her. "Well thank you! I definitely could use some help. Is Jordan here tonight?"

Nicole shakes her head no. Riley walks over to check monitors and finds only two patients are there tonight. She smiles happy to have an easy night and goes to start her rounds. She walks into Room 3 for the first patient.

Mrs. Debloo is sound asleep. Riley checks her contractions, which are continuous and high. She checks the epidural pump to make sure it is working, and she wakes up the patient.

"Hey, I'm Riley. I'm your nurse tonight. I need to get your vitals and check dilation, okay?"

The patient consents and Riley gets her vitals. Everything looks good. She checks dilation. She is only a four. Riley walks out of the room and logs everything. Dr. Taylor walks over to her.

"Have you checked Room 3?" asks the doctor.

Riley nods and starts to feel nauseous. She pushes it aside since she is at work.

"Yes, I have. She's a four." Dr. Taylor nods accepting that and stares at Riley as the nausea sets in. Riley holds up her index finger, signaling him to hold on a second. She runs into the bathroom and vomits. Everywhere.

Doctor Taylor watches Riley as she walks back toward her, looking red faced.

"Riley, are you sure you're okay to work tonight?" Dr. Taylor asks.

Riley nods, hoping the nauseating feeling will go away.

"Yes, ma'am. It was just for a second. I actually feel better. I don't know why I would get sick when I ate the same thing yesterday." Dr. Taylor gives a sly smile on her face and starts to walk away.

"I know what you are thinking it's not that!" Riley calls after her.

"Sure, it isn't honey." Dr. Taylor walks away.

Nicole stares at Riley, shocked, thinking the same thing as Dr. Taylor. Riley shakes her head no.

"No no, I am not! Don't even say it!"

Riley sits down feeling sluggish and then hops up and goes to the snack machine. She picks a peanut candy bar and eats it, hoping it could just be her sugar or something.

She sends Erik a text telling him what's going on. Erik replies with "probably a bug just come home."

Riley walks over to Dr. Taylor feeling sick again.

"Okay, I'm really not feeling well." Dr. Taylor nods calling in a charge nurse to cover. Riley drives home feeling exhausted and wonders what in the world could be going on with her. Then it hits her. She stops at the nearby store and takes a test in the bathroom.

When it comes back positive, her eyes widen. She takes a picture and sends it to Erik. She drives home slowly and carefully, since there is ice and snow everywhere. When she gets home, she walks in thinking Erik is going to be like her brother.

She sees him sound asleep in their bedroom. She walks in and lies down beside him. "Hey, sleepy, I need you to wake up for a second."

Erik jumps not expecting her to be home already and sits up. "What is it, love?"

He barely has his eyes open. Riley bites her lip nervous to say anything but must tell him. She holds up her phone with the picture.

"Yeah. I know what that is . . . what of it?" Erik rubs his eyes looking at it.

Riley looks at her phone and then sets it down.

"Well, Riles, what is it? What is so important that you need to wake me up in the middle of the night?"

Riley looks up at him, meeting his tired eyes. "Erik, that's mine."

Erik grabs her phone and pulls up the picture, now more awake.

"You're pregnant?" Erik asks.

Riley nods, now sitting on her knees on the bed, staring at him. She waits for a reaction.

Erik hops up putting her phone down, still not believing her. "No, you aren't! You're joking!"

Riley shrugs wishing she was then she stands up feeling a little light-headed.

"No, I'm really not. I took it on the way home, well not in the car, but you know what I mean."

Erik hugs her tightly excited for this new adventure.

"Well, you need to rest. We'll talk about it in the morning, okay?" He kisses her gently. Riley gets in bed with him and they both go to sleep.

Chapter 10

Riley wakes up first and gets up thinking she was dreaming. She looks at her phone and finds the picture. Nope, definitely it wasn't a dream. She gets up and puts on a pair of sweatpants that cling to her skin and an olive colored T-shirt.

Erik rolls over, staring at her with a smile. "Good morning, love."

Riley smiles and sits beside him on the bed.

"Good morning!" She climbs under the blanket again, snuggling up to him, wanting his warmth. Erik puts his arm around her and stares into her eyes.

"You are so beautiful, you know that?"

Riley smiles thinking, *Suck up.* She gets up and pulls him up out of bed. She goes to the kitchen and makes a cup of hot chocolate since this would be her life for a while because she is cutting out caffeine during this time.

Erik meets her in the kitchen a few minutes later. He shoots her a look. "That better not be what I think it is." Riley shakes her head no as if reassuring him.

"No, it's hot chocolate."

He stares at her doubting it and walks over to see for himself.

"Good." He smirks sitting beside her. "Called to make an appointment yet?"

Riley shakes her head no. She looks up from the island finding him staring at her. She gives him a *what?* look.

"Nothing. You just look exhausted, love." Riley bites her lip, hiding a smile knowing she is, but it's nothing. It'll pass eventually. She looks away and hears her phone ringing. She hops up and rushes into their room, grabbing it. She reads Kasey across the screen and answers quickly.

"Hey, what's up?" Kasey had already hung up by the time she answers. She shrugs assuming he'll send a text to her and goes back into the kitchen leaving her phone behind.

Erik looks up at her from his phone.

"They are asking for you to go in for day-shift coverage."

Riley thinks for a second about what she really wants to do. She sits on the stool at the island and looks at him meeting his gaze.

"Love, it's really up to you however you feel about going," says Erik.

Riley bites her lip still thinking and decides not to go.

"I really don't feel like it today, to be honest."

Erik nods while texting Kasey to inform him.

Riley moves into the living room with a headache and lies on the couch. She grabs her blanket from the back and snuggles up to it.

Erik walks in to check on her. "Hey, love, not feeling good?" Riley shakes her head no. She falls asleep on the couch and sleeps on through the night.

Chapter 11

Erik wakes Riley up in the morning. He sits beside her on the couch, not wanting to leave her alone. Riley rubs her tired eyes; her nose is clogged up along with a congested cough.

"Riles, you need to go to the doctor."

Riley covers her face with her blanket, not wanting to move. "No, I'm okay. I'll just take something until it's gone."

Erik stares at her in shock, thinking she might do that just to make the cough go away faster.

"Here, let me help you move to our bed. You'll be more comfortable there. And I'll get you some breakfast and medicine. Sound good?"

Riley nods and gets up, wrapping herself in a blanket and walks slowly into their room. She lies on their bed and snuggles up to the pillow, closing her eyes.

Erik wakes her up a short time later with potato soup. Riley shakes her head no.

"I don't even want to think about food," says Riley.

Erik sits beside her, putting the bowl down on the nightstand, and lets her snuggle up close to him. She looks up at him, meeting his eyes.

"Maybe some crackers?"

Erik gets up walking out. Riley hears somebody at the door and Erik talking to another man. She gets up and walks into the living room. She catches a glimpse of Derek at the door with Kasey.

Riley wonders what might be going on and makes her way over. "Is Alyssa okay?"

Erik turns to her shocked that she is up. "Riles, what are you doing up?"

Kasey shoots his sister an irritated look. "Why didn't you come in yesterday when I needed you!"

Riley crosses her arms. "I'm sick! That's why!" She rolls her eyes aggravated that all he wanted was to come see why she didn't go in. She turns around and walks away to their room, shutting the door.

The guys continue in a conversation, until Riley hears her name being called. She gets up out of bed again and opens the door.

"What!"

Erik peeks around the corner at her with a smile. "Come in here for a second please."

Riley sighs and goes into the living room to figure out what he wants. She sees Derek and Kasey sitting on the couch and Erik standing by the TV with a grin. She looks at Kasey and Derek, then back to Erik.

"Well, why aren't you sitting down? That's worrisome," she says.

Erik smirks at his soon-to-be wife and pulls here over to him. "We haven't really told anybody. I thought maybe you might want to tell your brother."

Riley thinks for a second then realizes what he's talking about and looks to her brother sarcastically.

"I'm pregnant, there you go . . . that's our big secret. Okay, I'm going back to bed, if you guys don't mind." She walks back to their room and gets back in bed for what feels like the one hundredth time and closes her eyes.

She feels as if she is being stared at and sits up opening her eyes. She whacks her head against Erik's and holds her head laughing.

"I'm sorry!"

Erik laughs along with her doing the same thing. "It's okay, love!"

Riley giggles at him and hugs him tightly trying to make him feel better. She makes the discovery that she doesn't really feel as bad and gets up perky.

She runs out of the room, and Erik catches her from behind laughing with her. He holds her close while resting his head on her shoulder.

"I sure love you. Our little bear as well." Riley smiles cheerfully, turning to face him. She kisses his cheek not wanting to get him sick.

"I love you too. I have to call and get an appointment set up. I'm picking Natalie Youngblood to be my doctor."

Erik nods, taking her hands, and happy that she feels and looks a little better.

"I think you just really needed some rest, love. You don't look pale, but you still look as if you don't feel good. Maybe take another day to rest? I have to go to work tomorrow though, you know."

Riley nods understanding. "I figured you do have a day job."

Erik smiles at her, loving that he found somebody who understands his job. His phone starts ringing, so he walks away to answer it. Riley goes to the fridge and pulls out her bowl of soup and heats it up in the microwave. She sits at the island and eats it.

The warmth of the soup makes her throat feel better. After eating, she puts her bowl in the empty dishwasher, then goes back to bed, noticing it's already eight o'clock in the evening.

Chapter 12

Riley has a rough night. She wakes up constantly coughing, now wheezing, and her throat hurts much worse. She notices Erik isn't there and figures he was called in. She texts him telling him she wants to go to the doctor, then eventually she falls asleep.

Erik wakes her up after coming in. She gets up feeling sick and rushes into the bathroom, throwing up. Erik holds her hair up for her and then helps her back into bed.

She snuggles up to him and falls asleep. She wakes up late morning and sees that he's already left for work. Riley gets up and gets dressed then grabs her car keys and drives to the health clinic down the road to get checked out.

She gets out and walks inside, signing in. They call her back and take her vitals. One hundred point seven.

"What are your symptoms?" she looks up at the nurse.

"Sore throat, coughing, wheezing, also I'm pregnant." The nurse looks at her seemingly shocked and takes her into a room. The doctor walks in within minutes and checks her throat and listens to her lungs.

The doctor then checks her ears.

"Symptoms?"

Riley sighs not really wanting to talk. "I have a sore throat, wheezing coughing, and I am pregnant."

The doctor nods and sends a nurse in to take her blood samples.

The young nurse smiles cheerfully and takes her blood then looks up at her. "You look so familiar."

Riley smiles trying to be perky. "I work at Hopkins in labor and delivery." The nurse's eyes widen.

"I'm Ella! Roberts!" Riley smiles looking at the patient she had and remembering her.

"I remember you. I haven't been back to work in like a week. I left sick at my stomach. A couple days later, found out I was pregnant, and now I'm sick."

Ella nods after taking her blood. "Well, it was nice to see you again! I hope you feel better! They'll have results in a few minutes." She walks out.

Riley gets a text from Erik asking how she is feeling. She texts him back telling him she is at the doctor's now getting checked out. He sends a thumbs up. The doctor walks back in and frowns.

"Well, Ms. Carter, you have the flu. I understand you are a labor and delivery nurse, so we need to get you feeling better fast. You'll get an antibiotic shot as well as medications."

Riley nods, understanding it all. The doctor walks out, and Ella comes back in to give her the shots.

After the shots Riley gets her prescriptions filled and then she leaves to go home. She texts Erik, letting him know she's home; she takes her medication then goes to bed.

She wakes up that afternoon and decides to get a shower. She puts on a pair of black yoga pants that cling to her skin and a green short sleeve V-neck. She makes herself a bowl of cereal and sits on the couch to eat while watching a movie. She loses time, and Erik walks in after work. Riley looks up at him from the couch and looks at the time.

"Well, that was a fast day."

Erik smiles and hands her a baggy from the store. Riley takes it, thinking he went and got another test. She opens it to find a box of chewy candy. She looks up at him with a smile.

"Thank you," Riley says.

She walks into the kitchen and puts it on the counter, not really wanting sweets at that moment. Erik hugs her from behind.

"You look much better than this morning."

Riley smiles; she is indeed feeling a little better than she did this morning. "That's good because I really feel better."

Erik hops up on the island counter and stares at her, admiring her. Riley makes an egg sandwich with ketchup and cheese. Erik looks at her food, disgusted.

"That doesn't look *that* great," Erik comments.

Riley sits at the island eating as if she is starving. Then again, she just went a couple days not really eating much.

"It's actually really good, want to try it?"

Erik shakes his head, hops down, and makes himself a turkey sandwich. Riley puts her plate in the dishwasher and sits beside him at the island.

Erik stares at her in admiration. "You are so beautiful, you know that?"

Riley smiles a perky smile. She takes his plate and puts it beside hers. She takes his hand and locks the front door, closing the curtains. Erik gets a sly grin.

Riley shakes her head and crosses her arms.

"No, I do not feel that great, you've lost your mind."

Erik smirks and picks her up off her feet. Riley clings to him while not expecting it. They go into their room, and he sets her down gently on the bed.

Riley sits with her legs crossed. "So how was your day?"

Erik changes into sweatpants and walks out of the bathroom, shrugging. "Could have been better. Taylor asked how you were doing. I told her you have the flu, so you are covered on that one until you are one hundred and ten percent."

Riley shrugs thinking it works for her. She hops up grabbing her laptop and sits back on the bed. Erik looks at her like she lost it.

He takes the laptop and sets it on the TV stand. "You really need to get some rest. Maybe if you feel any better in the morning you can go to work."

Riley sighs, feeling a little bit irritated and walks around the bed picking up her laptop.

"I was working on making a list for the baby for gender-neutral colored stuff, thank you!" she mutters.

Erik sighs, ignoring her, and lies on the bed, facing the opposite direction, with his back on her.

Riley feels defeated and sets down the laptop. She sits down on the side he's facing. When she doesn't get his attention, she lies down with her face right by his and stares at him. He opens his eyes and looks at her.

"Yes?"

Riley giggles amusingly. "I'm sorry I just really want to be super prepared and my emotions are just . . ." she pauses, thinking of the word.

Erik puts his arm around her. "I know, love. It's just hormones."

She hides her face in his chest and feels his warm caring touch.

"Taken your medicine yet?"

Riley's eyes pop open. "Yes. I think."

Erik chuckles and gets up to go check. He comes back in the room nodding. "You did."

She nods and scoots over to her side. She lies her head on his chest and falls asleep.

Chapter 13

Riley wakes up to Erik's alarm going off on his phone. She gets up, shutting it off, and wakes him up. "Hey, your alarm went off."

Erik waves his arm around before opening his eyes. "Already?"

Riley giggles feeling a lot better than she did the past couple days. "Absolutely."

She puts on black leggings and a white sweater dress. She scrunches her hair and puts on makeup. Erik walks into the bathroom behind her in green scrubs and looks at her surprised.

"What are you getting fancy for?"

Riley smiles and looks into his eyes. "You!"

She walks in the living room with Erik following her curiously. "What about me?"

Riley shrugs, now making him a cup of coffee. "I just wanted to surprise you. I thought maybe it would make you happy."

Erik smiles and kisses her forehead.

"Riles you don't feel as warm as you have been. Guess they gave you a strong dose of antibiotics."

Riley smiles perky. "I also feel a lot better. I was thinking of going into work tomorrow if you're okay with that?"

Erik nods grabbing his laptop bag. "Of course, I would be. I'll let Taylor know."

Riley nods accepting that answer.

She picks up her phone and looks up at him. "You know it's time that you leave, right?"

Erik looks at her oddly. "What's the rush?"

Riley holds up her phone showing him the time. He hops up realizing she isn't rushing him off and kisses her quickly then leaves. Kasey texts her telling her Derek and his wife are coming by to see her.

She makes sure the house is straightened and pulls on black ankle boots. She goes over to the door as Kasey, Derek, and a lady she had not met before approach the door. She opens it with a perky smile while letting everybody in.

"What are you perky about? I thought you were sick?" Kasey looks at her strangely.

Riley shrugs cheerful. "On another note, I've only been on medication for a day and feel a million times better."

Everybody makes their way into the living room. "Well Derek wanted to stop by to see how you were."

Riley turns to everybody. "I'm fantastic. Why aren't you guys at work?"

"Because we heard you had the flu. Figured you wouldn't feel this good yet." Derek feels as if he were talking to Alyssa.

Mabel, Alyssa's mother, steps forward. "I'm also a new doctor working on your floor at night. I'm Mabel. I wanted to meet my charge nurse."

Riley smiles warmly. "Well it's nice to meet you too." She sits on the couch. Derek points at her belly.

"She's your pregnant charge nurse."

Mabel looks at Riley shocked.

"No way! Have you picked your doctor yet?"

Riley nods her head yes.

"Yes, it's Youngblood. She's amazing! She's really sweet I adore her!"

Mabel smiles warmly. "That's fantastic! When do you go?"

Riley bites her lip looking away.

"I haven't exactly had a chance to set up my appointment yet." She shoots Kasey a look. "Don't worry. Erik reminds me almost every day. It's only been a couple weeks since I found out."

Kasey hands his sister her phone. "Well you have a chance now."

Riley rolls her eyes and walks into her bedroom, calling and making her appointment.

She texts Erik letting him know her appointment is the day after tomorrow. She walks into the living room, sticking her phone in her boot. "It's set up."

Mabel smiles cheerfully standing. "Well, it was nice to meet you, but I'm on call for today to get to know people. So I'll see you tomorrow?"

Riley nods, watching them leave. She shuts the door and locks it. She sits on the couch and decides to be lazy. Erik texts her saying there is a new doctor covering labor and delivery and maybe she could get in today.

Riley calls him, getting curious. "Who are you talking about? I hope it's not Mabel, Derek's wife. She is friendly and all, but I really like Youngblood."

Erik backs down letting her do what she wants. They get off the phone.

She gets laundry done and then pulls out her laptop and starts putting together a list for colors for the baby. She gets up in the middle of it and makes herself two egg sandwiches.

She eats both then takes her medicine. She turns on the music and cleans the house spotless. Erik walks in to her dancing around cleaning and laughs, recording her in a video.

Riley spots him and stops with a smile. "You totally recorded that, didn't you?"

Erik nods smiling and holds his phone up. "Only a kiss makes it disappear."

Riley giggles in a flirty way and kisses him.

"I love you." She pokes his nose and takes his phone, catching him off guard. She deletes the video and giggles.

"You know you love me!"

Erik nods and smirks. "So your appointment is the day after tomorrow?"

Riley nods and realizes she'll be exhausted because she works tomorrow night. She looks at Erik hopeful.

"Are you going to come with me?"

Erik takes her hands, with a grin. "Of course, my love."

She smiles excited and then pulls out chicken from the freezer, thaws it in the microwave, and stuffs it in the oven. After about thirty minutes she gets supper thrown together and makes Erik a plate while he's in the shower.

Erik walks into the kitchen in comfortable sweats and a navy shirt. Riley hands him his plate and sits at the island counter with him to eat.

After dinner, she gets dishes put away and goes into their room with him. She lies in bed excited for tomorrow, to go back to work, and to get back to normal.

She falls asleep happy, laying her head on his chest.

Chapter 14

Riley wakes up in the morning with Erik already gone for work. She gets up and pulls on red snowflake leggings and a bright-green long-sleeve shirt. She gets on her black ankle boots and a white crocheted scarf.

She goes into the kitchen and makes an egg then puts ketchup on it and makes some buttered toast.

She eats her breakfast and texts Alyssa asking if she wanted to hang out today. Alyssa replies with, "Sure, I'll come by and pick you up." Riley gets excited to have a friend.

Riley takes her medicine and makes a cup of hot chocolate while waiting. She decides to call Erik to let him know where she will be and who she is with. Erik replies to her saying, "that's fine have fun."

Alyssa pulls up honking the horn. Riley hops off the stool and puts her half-empty cup in the sink. She grabs her keys to lock the door and walks out to the car, getting in.

Riley smiles excited when she gets in the car. She looks in the back not seeing the baby.

"Where's the kiddo?"

Alyssa bites her lip not wanting to hurt Riley's feelings. "She's with your parents."

Riley looks kind of confused.

"My parents? Is my dad in town or something?"

Alyssa keeps her mouth shut, biting her lips.

"They kind of just bought a house and just moved in a couple days ago. She's got two kids, a boy and a girl both almost grown, and your dad proposed. If you want to see them, I could take you by."

Riley thinks and feels a little sad but takes the opportunity.

"Sure, sounds good. Just not long, please. My dad doesn't care that much for me."

Alyssa nods, not saying anything and drives to Jase's house. She parks and gets out with Melody and Jase walking out confused.

Riley gets out putting on a fake smile. Jase looks at his daughter shocked and walks over to her.

"My Riles, how you have grown! I hardly recognized you." Riley hugs her dad thinking he hasn't seen her in like seven or eight months. Of course, she has grown.

Melody walks over and smiles a warm smile. "Hi. I'm Melody, you are?" Riley frowns realizing her dad hasn't said a word about her to his, whatever she is.

"I'm Riley, his daughter." Jase's smile fades.

Melody shoots Jase a surprising look. "Well, it's nice to meet you. I have a son that lives around here. He actually dated somebody with the same name as you."

Melody's teenage daughter pulls up behind Alyssa in a small fancy sports car. She hops out. Riley turns seeing a teen wearing a short dress and has long brown curly hair and makeup pounded on her face.

She looks almost as snobby as Melody. She walks past and goes inside.

Melody points toward her door. "You are welcome to come inside."

Riley follows behind Alyssa, Melody, and her father. They all sit on the couch. Alyssa picks up Gracie her daughter and hands her to Riley to hold. Jase looks at his daughter, not liking the image of her holding a baby.

Alyssa turns to Melody and Jase. "You know she saved mine and Gracie's life. Erik delivered."

Jase looks at his daughter interested. "She did what? Not my Riley. She's just a nurse in a doctor's office."

Riley looks at her dad hurt. "Actually, I work on the labor and delivery floor as a charge nurse now." She looks down at Gracie, admiring her. Alyssa smiles.

"What are you guys hoping for?" asks Alyssa.

Jase looks at the two women, confused. "Hoping for? What do you mean?" His face starts to turn red and angry.

Riley looks up at her father and to Melody, who now has her arms crossed. "Well, I think Erik wants a girl and I want a boy." She ignores her father as if he cared for her now.

Jase stands up crossing his arms. "You better not be saying what I think you are."

Riley smiles, feeling as if the tables had turned. "Yes, actually I am, Dad. I'm pregnant."

Jase pulls out his phone walking out. Riley lets out a sigh getting that out of the way. Alyssa takes Gracie and lays her in her bed. Melody stares at Riley, as Liam walks in the door.

All the color rushes out of Riley's face. She hadn't had to deal with him in months. The fear hits her, she freezes terrified. Liam meets her eyes and smiles.

"Long time no see, Riles. Come back for me?" Alyssa walks in to the room and stares. She sits in front of Riley.

"Riley, breathe!"

Riley hops up. "I need to go. I have to go. Now." Alyssa, though not understanding the problem, grabs her keys and walks to the car with Riley. She gets in and has an anxiety attack.

Alyssa goes into paramedic mode. "Hey, you have to breathe normal, Riley."

Riley stares out the window, still freaking out. She looks as if she saw a ghost. Her skin becomes pale.

"RILEY! If you don't breathe normal and calm down, you are going to pass out!"

Riley pulls out her phone and points to Erik's number. She becomes very shaky and then nothing. Everything goes black.

Chapter 15

Riley opens her eyes; bright lights are everywhere. She looks around seeing an IV hooked up to her and a sonogram machine sitting beside her bed. She sees Erik watching the monitors beside her bed. She sits up, a little freaked out.

Erik holds out his hand to keep her from getting up too fast. "You passed out. Are you okay? Did you eat anything this morning?"

Riley takes a second to adjust to everything. "I . . . Liam . . ." Erik's eyes widen. He hugs her tightly.

"It's okay. I'm here, you are safe." A slight grin forms on his lips. "Guess what I saw? Well, mostly because I'm on call today."

Riley looks at the machine beside her and then to him. "You did not!"

Erik's grin grows. "I sure did. Love, you're eight weeks. But our baby is okay and growing exactly as it should be."

Riley looks at him jealous. "So not fair!"

Erik chuckles and the blood pressure cuff takes her blood pressure. It comes back as 90 over 40. Erik makes an *oo* face. He looks at his fiancé.

"Alright, you get some rest. I need your pressure back up, okay?"

Riley looks annoyed and crosses her arms. "Okay."

Erik frowns feeling bad that she's a little irritated.

"Sorry love. It's kind of my call. Give it an hour or so and we'll see then, okay?"

Riley gets irritated, hating being in the hospital, and nods.

Erik walks out. She grabs her phone and texts him saying she dislikes him at this exact moment. Nicole comes in perky about thirty minutes later to check her vitals.

Riley looks at her still annoyed. "My fiancé is a jerk, you know."

Nicole looks at her confused and laughs. "Why is that?" The cuff takes her blood pressure again.

"Because my fiancé is Erik, that's why."

Nicole laughs amused and types in the info. "Let me go ask him what he wants to do, your blood pressure is a little better. It's 100 over 70."

Nicole walks out. Riley thinks to herself, *Is this how much of a jerk I sound to my patients?* Another thirty minutes go by. Nicole walks in again and checks her vitals again.

"I know this is irritating, let me check again. Just want to make sure it's not dropping again." The cuff tightens. The results come back as 110 over 80. Nicole smiles putting it into the system.

"Perfect! Erik will be by when he can." Nicole walks out. Riley texts him saying he better get his butt in here to release her. In about forty-five minutes, Mabel walks in with a perky smile.

"Hey, sweetheart, how are you feeling?"

Riley smiles a fake smile at her. "Fantastic, can I go?"

Mabel giggles amused, she checks the monitors and logs. "Pressure is back up, you have color. Let's get one more look at the baby and we'll let you go. How does that sound?"

Riley nods agreeing to that. Mabel does the ultrasound printing pictures for her. She hands them to Riley.

"Looks great. Let me get started on the papers."

Another hour goes by, and finally Riley is released. Riley walks over to the nurses' desk to talk to Dr. Taylor as she is coming in.

"I hear you are coming back tomorrow. Are you excited?"

"Of course!" Riley smiles happy.

Erik walks up to her looking exhausted. Riley turns to him, giving him the I'm-not-happy-with-you look. She turns back to Taylor. "I'll see you tomorrow!" She walks out with Erik following her. They get to his car and Riley gets in the passenger seat and buckles.

Erik looks over to her, feeling the tension. "Riles, you aren't seriously mad, are you?" Riley shakes her head no.

"No, I know you did what you had to. I'm okay, I promise." Erik nods driving home.

When they get home, Riley goes into the kitchen and makes a big bowl of crispy crunch. She eats it as if she is starving. After a while, she puts her bowl away. After eating she gets a shower and gets in bed, snuggling up to Erik.

"I love you."

Erik holds her close. "I love you too."

Chapter 16

When morning came, Erik wakes up Riley. She gets up and takes a shower then puts on jeans and a hot pink short-sleeve V-neck that clings to her skin. She puts on rose-pink tennis shoes.

Riley scrunches her hair and puts on some makeup, even dark burgundy lipstick, and walks out excited to try something new.

Erik stares at her up and down. "You are so beautiful."

Riley smiles perky. "Thank you."

She eats a slice of cheese and onion omelet Erik made her for breakfast, then she takes her medicine. Almost done with breakfast, she grabs her keys and hands them to Erik.

He grabs them and drives to the doctor with her. She walks in holding his hand and signs in. They sit down, being the only ones there.

Riley is called back quickly for an ultrasound. The baby measures eight weeks and six days. They get vitals, weight, and then she is taken into a room.

Doctor Youngblood walks in. "Hey, Riley! How are you doing?"

Riley smiles friendly. "Great!"

Doctor Youngblood looks at her file she is holding.

"Alright, baby looks great, vitals are great. I understand you were under Doctor Dawkins and Doctor Sheeran yesterday?"

Riley smiles a big smile looking at Erik who is sitting behind her on his phone. He puts his phone down and looks up.

"She was. She passed out. She's fine now though."

Doctor Youngblood smiles and looks to him. "Well, if passing out is going to be a concern, you need to take it easy on your night shifts. Let the staff work for you. Next time you come, we will get some blood work. Any questions?"

Riley shakes her head no. "No and to be honest, I just freaked out about somebody and that's what happened. So passing out will not be a concern."

Doctor Youngblood looks at Erik with uncertainty. "Alright, well you still need to take it easy for a couple days. And you are good to go!"

Riley hops up after she walks out. Erik follows her out. She sets up her next appointment and goes to the car with him.

"Take me home before you go to work?"

Erik nods then takes her hand. "See, that's why I don't like her very much. You should see Mabel instead."

Riley looks lost, not understanding. "I adore her! I used to work with her, you know." Erik shrugs getting in the car and driving home with her. Riley kisses him before he leaves.

She goes inside and goes to bed before she has to go to work. Her alarm goes off around five. She gets up and gets ready—fixing her hair and makeup then she dons a navy-colored scrubs with a white long sleeve on it and black tennis shoes.

Riley eats a ham and cheese sandwich and grabs her keys. She drives to Hopkins Hospital and parks. She walks to the labor and delivery floor and gets her keys put up.

Krista smiles cheerfully upon seeing her. "Long time no see!"

Riley giggles.

"Yeah. Sick then pregnant and who knows what else. Feels good to be back."

Riley gets her patients and checks monitors before making rounds. She walks in to Room 2.

"Hey, Mrs. Cherry. I'm Riley. I'm your nurse for the night. How are you feeling?"

Mrs. Cherry looks at Riley as if hurting. Riley sees the pain in her face. She gets her vitals and then begins asking her normal questions while watching the monitor.

"What's your pain level?"

Mrs. Cherry clinches the rail of the bed. "About an eight, and I'd really like to get an epidural."

Riley nods, typing it in and paging the anesthesiologist through the computer. She gets the stuff to check dilation. She looks up at Mrs. Cherry shocked, feeling a nine and a half and complete.

Riley walks out to the desk and looks to see who is on call. Derek. She pages Derek for Room 2 and goes in setting up things for delivery.

Mrs. Cherry looks at Riley confused.

"Is something wrong?"

Riley shakes her head no. "No, ma'am. You just don't have time for an epidural."

Derek walks into the room with NICU nurses. Elissa, a new nurse overnight that Riley hadn't met yet, walks in.

Riley looks up at her. They deliver the baby within fifteen minutes. After the first delivery, Riley goes on to Room 3 where the patient is Mrs. Mayes.

"Hey, Mrs. Mayes. I'm Riley. I'm your nurse tonight. How are you feeling?"

Mrs. Mayes looks almost exactly like her last patient—in pain. She takes her vitals and checks dilation. Only a seven. Riley puts it into the system.

"Are you getting an epidural?"

Mrs. Mayes shakes her head no. Riley nods and moves on to Room 5 since Elissa is in the next room with the next patient.

"Hey, I'm Riley. I'll be your nurse for the night. How are you feeling?"

Ms. Morris smiles brightly. "I feel fantastic!" Riley double takes and sees the epidural pump. She takes her vitals, checks the pump, and then checks dilation.

"About an eight." She hears the monitor beeping and looks at vitals for both baby and mom. Mom's blood pressure is high, and the baby is in distress.

"Okay, Ms. Morris. I need you to calm down."

She lays her back and flat. She pages for Derek. When Derek did not respond, she goes to the next on call. Mabel.

Mabel rushes in and grabs Riley. "You are going into this C-section with me. Elissa is covering pretty good, let's move."

They get the patient into the OR with NICU, making sure she is completely numb. They start the C-section. Riley holds the patient's hand, keeping her calm and talking. When it's over, Riley shows Mrs. Morris the baby—a ten-pounder!

They get the patient closed up, and Riley continues talking to her.

"My baby is okay, right?"

Riley smiles warmly. "Yes, ma'am. Your sweet little girl is just fine!"

After the C-section, Mabel walks out with Riley to the desk and smiles happily.

"How are you feeling after your spell yesterday?"

Riley, never having her mom around that she can remember starts to take to Mabel. "I feel pretty good today actually."

Mabel smiles cheerfully. "That's fantastic! But I do think you need to take it easy tonight, okay?"

Riley nods, listening to her. Mabel hugs her as if she were her own daughter.

"I care for you honey, you and that sweet little baby!"

Riley starts thinking about changing to Mabel as her doctor.

"Hey, can I ask you a question?"

Derek walks up as Riley is talking to Mabel.

"Of course, honey!"

Riley smiles happy. "I just wanted to ask if you work in the same office as Dr. Youngblood?"

Mabel thinks she already knows where it's going. "I sure do. Youngblood isn't as warm-hearted as I've heard."

Riley nods, agreeing. "Yeah, I saw her today. She wasn't but that's all I wanted to know."

Derek tilts his head curious. "Why?"

Riley jumps not even noticing him. "You just scared the crap out of me. Because I wanted to switch doctors."

Mabel smiles warmly. "I'd love to, sweetie. Do you already have your next appointment set up?"

Riley nods.

"Yes, I go back in a month. Of course."

Mabel makes an odd face. "Oh no no, that is not going to work. Make another for me in two weeks."

Riley hears monitors beeping and takes off. She goes into Room 4, a room she has not visited. She finds Elissa having a complete melt down as a mother just passed out on her.

Riley gives her a chance. "What happened?"

She pulls her stethoscope to listen to heartbeats and breathing: quick heart rate and quick breaths.

"Derek and Mabel are both at the desk, get them. Tell them I'll meet them in the OR."

Elissa takes off. Riley hooks up the portable heart monitor and moves quickly to the OR, meeting them inside.

Derek and Mabel work quickly together. They do a C-section. Meanwhile the mother has stopped breathing, and Riley is doing CPR in the process.

They get the mother back while NICU nurses are working on the baby.

After a long eventful shift, Riley is paged by Elissa to Room 6 for a new patient. Elissa stares at her as she walks in frozen. "The head is out."

Riley looks a little irritated and directs Elissa to get things together. She pages Mabel to the room and gets ready to deliver the baby on her own. When Mabel gets in, the father is already cutting the cord, and Riley is handing off the baby to the NICU nurses.

Mabel checks for tears and other things. Riley stands at the desk exhausted and drinking a bottle of flavored water. Erik walks in to start his shift as Riley is taking Krista to her rooms.

She meets Erik in the hallway. "Long night I heard?"

Riley nods exhausted. "Oh, most definitely. Two C-sections, and I just delivered a baby."

Mabel walks up to the two. "And she needs rest today even if I have to sit at her house and make her rest."

Erik smiles a sly grin. "She could spend the day with you. I'm sure she'd love spending time with another female!"

Riley shoots him an oh-no look.

Mabel smiles cheerfully. "Me too."

Riley follows Mabel to her house since Erik volunteered her for a girl's day.

Chapter 17

Mabel sits on the couch with Riley, as she refuses to sleep even though she is exhausted.

Mabel watches her and meets her tired eyes. "Honey, why don't you go into our extra room and get some rest? You look so tired."

Derek nods, agreeing with his wife. "You're pregnant, sweetheart. You need the rest."

Riley feels as if they were really her parents. She had never felt that kind of caring before except from her brother and father occasionally.

"I'm okay."

Natalie walks downstairs meeting her parents; she gives them a crazy look.

"Take in somebody?"

Mabel shoots her daughter a hush look. "Excuse me? That was very rude, young lady. You best be apologizing!"

Natalie rolls her eyes with an attitude and carries on to the kitchen.

Mabel looks at Riley apologetically. "I'm sorry, that would be my daughter Natalie."

Riley, half asleep, nods. "It's okay."

Mabel stands up and points to the stairs. "It's the bedroom in the hallway closest to the door at the end. Go get in bed, missy."

Riley shakes her head no. "No, no, I'm fine."

Mabel crosses her arms. "Riley, don't make me go mother bear on you. Get in bed and get some rest."

Derek catches the conversation after dealing with Natalie in the kitchen and gives Riley a look.

"Is there a problem?"

Natalie peeks in to the living room. "You really don't want him getting involved."

Riley shakes her head remaining on the couch. "Guys, I'm fine really."

Derek, now crossing his arms, the same as Mabel looks a little irritated. Mabel steps away. "Nat's right. Derek adores you like you were his own. I don't think I'd be testing the water."

Riley sighs not wanting to fight with him, or go to bed, but at the same time, she is so exhausted.

Derek walks over to her, holding out his hand. "Let's go. Move it. Don't think I won't treat you like I do my girls."

Riley, a little afraid, gets up and goes to the room with Mabel going behind her. She hands Riley a white comforter. "Make yourself at home, sweetheart."

Riley gets in bed and falls asleep quickly.

Around one that afternoon she wakes up and feels odd. Kind of like something was wrong. She gets an oh-crap look and hops up feeling a tight stabbing pain in her back and sides.

She opens the door and feels weak. "Mabel?" She has tunnel vision. She sits on the floor beside the bed, figuring she just needs to eat something, and texts Mabel asking her to come in there for a second.

Mabel comes to the door. "Everything okay, honey?" She sees Riley sitting on the floor pale. She rushes over to her.

"What is it?"

Riley tries to focus on her. "Do you have any crackers or toast or anything?"

Mabel texts Derek telling him what's going on. "I do. How are you feeling?"

Riley takes deep breaths. "I think my blood sugar dropped that's all."

Mabel watches her. "It's alright, we'll get you something to eat and see how you're doing after that, alright?"

Riley bites her lip feeling embarrassed. "Okay."

Derek walks in with peanut butter crackers. "She okay?"

Mabel opens her mouth to say something but Riley cuts in.

"I'm peachy."

He hands her the crackers obviously feeling concerned for her. Riley eats them and feels a little better, but now she is having a pounding headache.

Mabel watches her, feeling bad for her. "Maybe we should do weekly appointments."

Riley shakes her head disagreeing. "No, no, I'm fine. I assure you I'm fine."

Riley stands up, feeling much better than before. "I'm sorry I just got ahead of myself, I guess. Normally, I don't eat when I get home."

Mabel disapproves of this. "Well, you need to. I'll let Erik know to watch you for blood pressure and blood sugar."

Riley nods understanding. They all go down to the living room and sit on the couch.

Derek looks at Riley with a smile. "Maybe you should teach Alyssa how to be this open! I would give anything for her to be as simple as that!"

Riley laughs, thinking he's joking, then realizes he is serious. "Wait she for real doesn't say anything when something is wrong?"

Derek shakes his head no. "Absolutely. She will not tell anybody until she's already on the floor."

Riley makes a what face. "You're kidding!"

Mabel shakes her head. "We're not."

Riley shrugs. "Well, if you teach my dad to actually care about his daughter instead of his step-daughter then I'll teach Alyssa to speak up."

Derek gives her a sympathetic look, meeting her eyes. "Sweetheart, I'm not trying to sound like a jerk, but your father is a jerk. The only person I've seen him care for is Kasey. I would gladly take you in as my own."

Mabel cuts in. "Even though you are grown. Every girl needs her mother, and every girl needs her father, and you've definitely got us even if we are not biological."

Derek nods agreeing with her. "And you are a very hurt and broken young lady. Even though you have Erik, you do need somebody to care for you like parents as well. We are here for you, honey."

Riley smiles feeling loved. "Thanks."

She gets a call from Erik asking how she is feeling. "I'm good. I promise."

Erik asks her to stay with Mabel and Derek until he gets off. She agrees and tells him she loves him. He gets off the phone a bit rudely.

"Erik asked me to stay here until he gets off, if that's alright?"

Mabel smiles warmly. "Of course, honey! You are welcome here anytime!"

Riley smiles perky. Mabel goes into the kitchen leaving Riley alone with Derek. Riley feels a little awkward alone with him. Derek tilts his head.

"What's on your mind?"

Riley snaps back to reality. "Nothing. Sorry, I was thinking . . ."

Derek nods. "About?"

Riley chews on the inside of her cheek. "Just now I'm realizing how crappy my father is."

Derek nods, agreeing. "Yes, but anybody can make a baby. It takes a real man to take care of that child and a village to raise it."

Riley smiles, agreeing. "It does."

Time flies, and Erik is pulling up to their house. He walks in smiling and hugs Riley tight.

"I'm glad you spent the day with Mabel. You know she adores you."

Riley kisses him and holds him in a hug. "Me too."

Erik takes her hand and sits on the couch, visiting with Derek and Mabel for a while.

Mabel gets an idea and talks to Derek in the kitchen. The two walk into the living room with a smile.

"You guys know there is a spare bedroom you are welcome to stay the night. Maybe have a game night or something?"

Riley looks at Erik for an answer. Erik smiles enjoying being around friends.

"Sure! If Riley is up to it," says Erik.

Riley nods. "Of course! It's been awhile since we've been around other couples."

Erik nods agreeing. "Far too long. Ana and Justis are busy with a baby and just don't get out much anymore."

Mabel smiles perky. "Perfect!"

She pulls out a game that you have to go around the board knocking people out of their place and they have to restart but the goal is to get to the finish before anybody else.

They stay up until one in the morning, playing the game, and Mabel wins.

Riley starts getting tired and rubs her eyes. Erik runs to their house and gets an overnight bag real fast. Riley sits on the couch hugging her knees to her chest while talking with Derek and Mabel.

Mabel hands her a warm cup of hot chocolate. "I would give you coffee, but you don't need it right now." Riley nods agreeing.

"Actually, I cut coffee out of my life when I found out."

Mabel smiles happy to hear.

Derek looks at her shocked. "A daughter that actually takes care of herself! This is crazy!"

Riley giggles amused. "Alyssa doesn't?"

Derek shakes his head. "She's too busy trying to get all the attention she can."

Riley nods, feeling kind of bad for her brother. "Well, good. Kasey is a good fit her for then."

Erik gets back and gives her black fuzzy pajama shorts and a gray T-shirt. Riley changes and notices a small bump forming. She smiles cheerfully.

When she walks out, Mabel touches her belly. "So cute! You are just so tiny it already shows! Derek, look!"

Derek smiles amused while talking to Erik. Riley starts having thoughts of C-section because of a big baby.

She meets Mabel's eyes with a frown. "Just promise you won't do a C-section unless absolutely necessary," says Riley.

Mabel frowns agreeing. "Honey, if this baby is too big for you I absolutely will not give you the chance to even try. I won't risk it."

Riley nods, accepting that answer. "Good enough for me." She laughs.

"Okay, but I'm seriously tired, so I'm ready for bed." She looks at Erik catching his attention.

Mabel hugs her goodnight, and then Derek hugs her. "You need to rest, Riles."

Riley nods, agreeing, and goes up to the spare bedroom with Erik, and they both fall asleep quickly.

Chapter 18

Riley wakes up in the morning, feeling refreshed with Erik and excited that he is off today. She lays her head on his chest waking him up. "Good morning, love."

Riley smiles. "Good morning. You know, why couldn't they be my parents?"

Erik laughs amused. "I don't think Derek would be too happy if you were pregnant and his actual daughter. I dare you to say that to him."

Riley giggles curious. "Just watch."

They go down to the living room, meeting Derek and Mabel in there.

Erik smiles slyly. "You guys want to know what Riley said this morning?"

Mabel smiles wondering, and Derek looks to her curious.

Riley freezes being put on the spot. Erik takes over. "She said 'why couldn't they be my actual parents?' and I said, 'I don't think Derek would be too happy if she was pregnant and your actual daughter'."

Riley's face turns red with embarrassment. Derek laughs agreeing. "You know me too well, Erik."

Mabel chimes in. "She would probably be more embarrassed if we were!"

The three of them laugh in unison joking. Riley chews on the inside of her cheek.

Derek decides to add in a few things. "But I would still love her. She's grown, and acts grownup unlike my two."

Riley looks at them, trying to figure out how to respond and elbows Erik. "Well, you're the one that said it, Riles."

"I did." She giggles, and the realization hits her that she has to work tonight. She looks at Erik hopping up. "Erik!"

Erik jumps looking at her wondering what made her jump. "What?"

She looks at the time on her phone noticing it's about eleven that morning. "I have to work tonight!"

Erik shoots her a really look. "Lord, Riles, don't scare me like that!"

Riley smirks. "Well, I just thought you should know."

Mabel looks at Riley with her head tilted. "Are you in a hurry?"

Riley shakes her head no. Her phone starts ringing, and she sighs seeing Taylor's name across her screen.

She walks outside answering. Taylor tells her she needs her to come in and take the night off because they are short—and a day-charge nurse just quit on her.

Riley agrees and walks in, looking at Erik. "I have to go to work. She said to take the night off. They might be moving me to days."

Erik nods and hands her the keys. "I'll get Derek to give me a ride. Go on."

Riley looks at Erik like she has a question to ask but is afraid to. "What is it, love?"

Riley shrugs. "I just need a shower, I'm gross." Erik laughs and grabs a towel for her from the hallway closet.

"I've spent lots of time with Derek. Go get a shower, they won't care."

Riley goes up finding the bathroom and gets a shower then runs into the spare room getting dressed. She throws her hair up in a hair pony with a bump on top and smiles seeing Erik grabbed her makeup.

She puts on gray eye shadow and looks like a snobby kind of nurse almost. She walks out shoving her shoe on her foot and walks into Mabel.

"Sorry!" Mabel laughs and hugs her.

"It's alright. Did you get called in?"

Riley nods answering her. "Sure did."

Mabel smiles excited. "Well at least I know who my charge is today. Let's go."

Riley kisses Erik and hands him his keys. "I'll just ride with Mabel just don't forget to come get me!"

He chuckles kisses her forehead. "Love you."

She gets in Mabel's car and off to the hospital they go. They get there rather quickly, and both rush to the floor.

Riley jumps in, taking over the monitors from another nurse. She looks up meeting Sarah's eyes and makes a huff.

She assigns Sarah to two different rooms as well as Krista. She watches monitors as a new patient walks in.

"I think somethings wrong."

Riley looks a little confused and looks over the desk seeing a puddle.

"Oh okay! Just take deep breaths. Let's get you in a room."

She gets the patient a wheelchair and into a room. She gets the patient's name and personal info.

"Alright and how far along are you?"

Ms. Wallace looks a little frightened. "I'm thirty-four weeks."

Riley looks a little concerned already knowing labor cannot be stopped.

"Okay and you said you are seventeen, right?" The young girl nods scared.

"Please don't let anybody know I'm here." Riley nods hooking up monitors to her getting vitals and baby's vitals. Riley puts in a request for on call ASAP. She checks for dilation and feels a cord.

She tries to hide her finding and keeps calm. "Okay, I know you're scared, and I'm not trying to scare you anymore, but please whatever you do, do not push!"

Riley rushes running straight into Dr. Taylor knocking them both over. Taylor helps her up and looks at Riley a little irritated. "Is there a problem, Riley?"

Riley catches her breath. "I need you to do a C-section now!"

Taylor looks a little concerned. "Honey, I'm off. Your patients are under yours and Sarah's care until on call gets out of another C-section. The next on call is Erik."

Riley texts Erik with urgent 911 get here now! She paces around waiting and goes back into the room, checking her patient and keeping her calm. Ms. Wallace looks very uncomfortable.

"I really feel like I need to push." Riley sits beside her, keeping her calm and shakes her head.

"I'm sorry but you really can't. My on call is in a C-section and the next one is on the way just a couple more minutes, sweetie. I know it's uncomfortable."

Mabel walks in from the C-section, ready to go for the next one.

"What's going on? Erik is stuck in traffic."

Riley walks out with Mabel. "I felt the cord. She is fully dilated and complete."

Mabel rushes with Riley down the hallway with the patient passing Erik. Erik stares.

"Need help?"

Riley turns to him. "We got it! Take my other patients!"

They get the girl into the next OR, and Riley sets up moving quick. Mabel is paged to the floor as Erik is walking in. Mabel rushes.

Not paying attention, Riley does her job, not realizing Erik and Mabel switched. After the C-section is over with Riley keeping the patient calm until she gets her back in her room.

Erik meets his fiancé at the desk after things calmed down. "I didn't think you had that in you, Riles."

Riley giggles watching the monitors. "Yeah, and—"

She jumps up running into a room. Erik follows behind her just in case. She has already taken the vitals and is watching contractions while the patient is getting an epidural.

Erik looks confused. "What?"

Riley, eyes glued to the monitor, talks trying not to scare the patient. "She has high blood pressure both heart rates are up."

Erik steps out with Riley. "So watch her."

Riley looks annoyed. "I was. I'm waiting at the moment."

She goes back in and sits in front of the monitor with Sarah watching the blood pressure drop. Heart rates drop but stay as they should be.

Riley hands Sarah stuff to check dilation after the epidural. "Six" Riley nods keying it in and walks out.

The shift ends and Riley gets the new charge nurse to each patient.

Chapter 19

Mabel grabs Riley's arm and pulls her aside in the hallway. "Would you like to come over for a little while, while Erik is on call?"

Riley nods. "Sure! Sounds good!"

She texts Erik letting him know. She gets in the car with Mabel and goes over to her house.

She walks in with Mabel and sits on the couch, feeling wired.

"You know I think being a trauma nurse would be awesome!"

Derek looks away from watching the news at her. "Really?"

Riley nods and then shrugs. "But I absolutely love my job!"

Suddenly, Riley starts feeling bad and cramping. She thought, *Maybe I'm just tired.*

"Hey, would you be okay if I went up into your spare room and took a short nap?"

Mabel nods getting up. "Of course, honey! Make yourself at home."

Riley goes up into the bedroom and lies down. She falls asleep.

After a couple hours of resting, she wakes up hurting really bad and feels like something isn't right at all. She uncovers and sees blood all over her.

Reality sits in. She had lost her baby. She hops up and rushes down to the living room. Derek looks up at her, since Mabel had gone to bed, and the first thing he sees is her pale skin.

"Are you alright, Riley?"

Riley, shaky shakes her head no.

"No, I'm miscarrying. I need to go to the hospital like now."

Derek jumps up and grabs his keys. He grabs up Riley carrying her to the car.

Riley, thankful for Derek, gets to the hospital quickly.

She gets into the emergency department, and Taylor is called down for her. They get to her right as she loses consciousness.

When Riley wakes back up, she looks around in the hospital room and sees the blood transfusion, and fluids being pumped into her. Erik is sitting beside her with sad eyes.

"Are you okay, love?"

Riley nods feeling her heart shatter. "So I was right? I lost the baby?"

Erik nods sadly. "It's not your fault, Riles. You got help and thank the good Lord for Derek."

Riley smiles through the tears. "Maybe something just wasn't forming right? We may never know but everything happens for a reason."

Erik nods agreeing.

Chapter 20

Riley is released from the hospital the next day, and heart shattered she holds herself together and believes that maybe something was wrong, that it wasn't her fault and that she may never meet that sweet little baby, but she will always hold the love she had in her heart for it.

Erik wakes her up, taking the day off to spend it with her to make sure she really will be okay. Riley rubs her eyes and looks at him. The hurt in her eyes is still very noticeable.

"Everything will be alright, love." He hugs her tightly. Riley lays her head against his chest, not saying a word. She feels her heart breaking more, but there were no tears left to cry.

"Think about those that you have saved though, Riles. You are a miracle worker and you have this. You are a strong woman and you are strong enough to overcome this."

Riley nods listening to the words roll off his tongue. "I love you."

Erik smiles kissing her forehead. "I love you too."

Riley lies in bed with Erik until she falls asleep again. Mabel stops by to see her. She wakes up to Mabel sitting beside her. "Hey, how are you holding up?"

Riley sits up and feels like a mess. "I'm sorry. I probably look crazy. I'll be okay. Things happen for a reason, and maybe the reason was that the baby was forming right."

Mabel nods agreeing, knowing already that it was. "Riles, can I tell you something?"

Riley nods listening. Mabel looks down taking a breath. "The baby wasn't forming right. It was deformed. You will pull through this even if it takes days, weeks, months, and years."

Riley nods. "Yeah." She gets up and walks into the living room with Mabel. Erik is talking to Derek. Riley looks up and sees him and hugs him.

"Thank you. I'm sorry for scaring everybody."

Derek hugs her back. "Don't apologize for something out of your control."

Riley nods and makes herself a cup of coffee. They all sit around in the living room talking.

Eventually, Riley goes to take a shower. When she gets out, she is paged to the labor and delivery floor.

Not realizing she was an on-call nurse, she gets dressed and grabs her keys. She kisses Erik and walks out, not saying a word.

She gets to Hopkins and goes in putting her emotions in the back of her head.

She clocks in and sets her keys down in a lock box. Nicole, today's charge nurse, pulls her to room three for help to calm down a patient.

"She needs a C-section and is hysterical."

Riley sits by the patient and takes her hand. "Hey, you know your baby is going to be one hundred percent fine!"

The more Riley talks, the calmer the patient gets. She goes to the OR with the patient and keeps her talking and calm. A nurse hands Riley the baby, and Riley shows the patient. The patient becomes excited.

After the baby is born they get the patient closed up and back to her room. Riley moves on to the next room.

"Hey, Mrs. Bane. I'm Riley, and I understand you just got moved in?"

Mrs. Bane nods. "Yes, ma'am!"

Riley goes through a series of questions with the patient. She then gets vitals and checks her dilation. "You are a five would you like to get an epidural?"

"Yes!" Riley pages for it and waits. She helps the patient as she is getting it. Afterward, Riley walks to the next room and goes back and forth until she gets to room one.

She walks in and checks dilation. The baby's head is out, and she throws everything together and pages on call.

She delivers the baby as Taylor walks in. She moves over letting Taylor do her job. She hands the baby to the NICU nurses.

After the delivery, the shift ends, and Riley goes home.

Riley hugs Erik for a long time and then gets a shower and gets ready for bed. She lays her head on Erik's chest and meets his eyes.

"I love you. You know that."

Erik smiles. "I love you too."

Riley, her heart feeling full, falls asleep.

Chapter 21

Riley gets up early, hoping not to be called in. She goes downstairs to get breakfast made as a surprise for Erik. She makes waffles and stacks them on a plate in the middle of the island.

Erik walks down, still looking tired, in his green scrubs and smiles at his wife. She hands him a cup of coffee she made for him.

"You seem a little more perky this morning."

Riley smiles a small smile. "What do you think of me going to day shifts? I love my nights just because it's quiet for me, but I think I want to try days."

Erik shrugs, sitting down with his waffles. "Go for it, love. If that's what you want to do."

Riley texts Mabel asking about it. She sits beside Erik and eats a waffle just to keep him from being worried. She cleans up and hands him his keys.

When he leaves, he kisses her gently and puts his hand behind her ear. "I love you, Riles. Everything will be okay."

She hugs him and then watches him leave. She gets ready for her appointment and gets dressed in a black T-shirt and dark-colored jean leggings with her black boots.

She walks in and sits there, feeling alone. She couldn't be mad because she never told Erik that she was going and had this appointment although she assumed he knew.

A nurse calls her back, and she gets her vitals and then takes her to a room. Dr. Madison walks in and smiles warmly. She asks Riley a bunch of random questions.

"I am prescribing you depression medication. Things will be better."

After the doctor's office, she stops by Erik's to go on a lunch date, maybe. She discovers a female nurse sitting at his desk and thinks maybe it's just his nurse.

She walks in with a smile. "Hey, where is Erik?"

The woman looks up at her with an annoyed expression.

"Who are you? Shouldn't you be in a room or waiting room?"

Riley shakes her head no and sits in a chair in front of the desk. "I'm Erik's fiancé."

The nurse smirks. "Yeah, okay."

Riley looks a little confused, and Erik walks in and sees both women; he walks right back out.

Riley hops up and runs up to him. "I wanted to tell you something."

Erik's face a little red, turns to her. "Yes?"

Riley's eyes narrow, feeling a little hurt, she decides not to tell him that she is on depression medication. "Never mind. I'll just see you when you get home."

Riley walks away and gets in her car. She looks down at her ring thinking that maybe she and Erik really needed to just get to know each other. She sure jumped when he was ready to be her hero, but did he really know her?

Riley drives by the fire department wanting to see Alyssa for a second. She gets out and walks in excited to see her sister-in-law. Lindsey walks over to Riley.

"Hey, can I help you with something?"

Riley smiles, trying to get her spirits up. "I just need to see my sister-in-law. Alyssa?"

Lindsey nods and takes Riley to the lounge room. When she walks in, Alyssa looks up at her and jumps up. Unfortunately, the girl she thought was a nurse is sitting there with Alyssa.

"Didn't I just see you?" says Riley.

The girl nods with a smile. "Sure did. I'm just getting my best friend's opinion on my wedding dress for my fiancé."

Riley nods and grabs Alyssa's arm, pulling her aside. Alyssa looks at her, not understanding seeing the ring still on Riley's finger.

"Erik said you guys broke up?"

Riley shakes her head. "No, not that I was aware of, but thanks for the confirmation."

She pulls the ring off her finger and throws it at the girl. "Tell him to get his crap out."

She walks away with tears in her eyes and goes to her car. She drives home, feeling broken, and goes inside not ready to be alone in this house. She goes into their room and sits on the bed, hugging her knees and then decides to call Kasey.

Shockingly he answers. "What's up, Riles?"

Riley takes a breath and holds back the tears. "I know we aren't close I know you don't want me as a sister, but I really need you."

Kasey takes a minute to answer her. "Riles, whatever it is, you'll get through it. I have to go, I'm at work." Click. She texts Mabel saying she needs a friend.

She hears the front door open and close lightly. Riley walks into the living room and sees Erik. She crosses her arms.

"We have to talk."

Erik nods, agreeing holding her ring. "You're right if you think I would really cheat on you."

Riley feels her heart break even more. "I don't think Alyssa told me Erik. I wanted to tell you I was on depression medication. I wanted to talk to you. I walked in with her being in your office! I wanted to go out with you and have lunch together like normal couples."

Erik nods understanding, not having anything to say.

"What? You have nothing to say? I'm giving you a chance to talk."

Erik looks at her with hurt in his eyes and puts her ring in his pocket. "I did it Riley, okay? I cheated on you with a nurse."

Riley nods, holding herself together. "You don't have to stay here if you don't want to, but you are not staying in the same room as me if you do."

Erik goes into the room and moves all his stuff into Kasey's old room. He blows up an air mattress in there and walks into the room where Riley is.

"I'm sorry I hurt you."

Riley shrugs and looks at him with hurt eyes. "I'm used to it."

Chapter 22

Riley stays up late texting Mabel. She decides to text her old friend Sloan, a firefighter she was super close to before Liam. She then falls asleep.

When she gets up, she pulls on tan leggings and a black sweater dress. She does her makeup and straightens her hair. She walks out at the same time as Erik and walks past him not making eye contact or talking.

She goes into the kitchen and grabs a hard plastic to-go coffee cup and then grabs her keys at the same time as Erik.

Riley moves back looking at him. When he stares at her, she grabs her keys and turns for the door. He grabs her hand.

"We have to talk eventually, Riley."

Riley pulls her hand away.

"Where are you going, Riley? You have to work tonight."

Riley meets his eyes. "To meet an old friend."

She walks out the door and goes to the park. Sloan, a tall, dark-headed, tan-skinned, muscular man walks over to her with a smile and hugs her tightly.

"How are you doing, Riles? You look great!"

Riley smiles hiding her heartbreak. "I'm okay. I finally got my labor and delivery job!"

They walk around the walking track at the park together, talking and catching up. Sloan walks her over to her car.

"Well it was great seeing you, Riles. I'm sorry with everything you are going through. Maybe we could hang out. I'll come by the hospital tonight!"

Riley smiles, enjoying her time spent with him. "Sounds great!"

She hugs him goodbye and drives home.

She takes a shower and goes to sleep for the shift tonight. She gets up a couple hours later and gets ready for work.

She puts on purple scrubs and styles her hair half up and half down and goes to work putting on a fake smile.

Mabel walks up to Riley when she gets to the desk and hugs her. "Erik is on call tonight with me. It'll be okay."

Riley smiles hugging her back. "I know. My friend is stopping by later."

Mabel smiles. "No drama."

Riley nods agreeing. She goes behind the desk and sees there are only two patients. Shouldn't be a rough night. She goes into Room 2 and smiles cheerfully.

"Hey, Mrs. Rogers, I'm Riley. I'll be your nurse tonight." She walks over to the computer by the bed and gets vitals and then checks dilation. "Okay, only a six. Are you wanting the epidural?"

The patient shakes her head no. "No, I want a natural birth."

Riley types it in for the patient to maybe get what she wants.

"And your pain level?"

Mrs. Rodgers thinks about it for a second. "A seven or eight."

Riley types it in. "Are you sure you don't want anything for pain?"

Mrs. Rodgers shakes her head no.

"Okay, well if you need anything, let me know."

Riley walks into the fourth room for the second patient and repeats. Except dilation is an eight.

"Alright, I'll page on call it might take him a minute to get here."

She walks out and over to the desk, letting Sloan know now would be a good time to come by if he wanted.

Erik walks in with this new girl by his side and stands to the side of the desk, talking to her. Sloan walks in and smiles with a purple rose. Erik looks directly at him.

"Well, you have some lucky lady, don't you?" Riley walks over to Sloan with a smile.

Before Sloan can answer he hugs her. "I remembered you love the color purple." He hands her the rose.

Riley giggles in a flirty way. "Thank you. It is pretty." She takes it. Erik moves over to Riley and Sloan.

"So you're lucky one is her?"

Riley's smile fades. "I'll walk with you."

She walks down the hallway explaining to Sloan the whole Erik thing.

Mabel walks over to Erik with Krista. "Looks like you have competition." They both laugh.

Tara, the nurse Erik cheated on Riley with, walks over to him. "It's okay. I look better than her."

Riley walks back alone with her flower and puts it in her locker with her keys. She has a smile on her face.

Mabel talks loudly to her. "That was sweet."

Riley looks up at Mabel with all eyes on her, with a smile. "Yeah, he's a pretty good friend. We lost contact because of Liam and we talked last night."

Mabel smiles and hugs Riley. "I'm glad! He's pretty too."

Riley giggles. "That he is."

Erik clears his throat. "Don't you have patients?"

Riley rolls her eyes and checks monitors then back to him. "Yeah, the two in Room 2 and 4? I can balance my life between personal and work, can you?"

She walks into Room 4, checking again. She walks out and motions for Mabel. Mabel hops up and walks into Room 4. Riley gets NICU nurses, and Krista and goes back in.

She sets up for delivery and they assist Mabel. After delivery, Krista walks out with Riley passing by Erik. "You have to set me up with one of his friends!"

Riley shrugs. "He's really just a friend. He knows what happened between me and Erik. He's actually coming over tomorrow night to hang out."

Krista giggles and the two walk to the second room. Riley checks dilation and vitals. "We are a nine. I'll go get everybody."

Krista walks out and tries to get Mabel, but she is busy admitting another patient, so they settle for Erik and NICU.

Krista walks in apologetically. Riley gets everything set up and assists Erik with Krista. When the baby is born, she hands the baby to the NICU nurses and walks out going to the next room.

She gets vitals, asks some questions, and gets it all put in. "Alright and your pain level?"

Mrs. Jeffers looks half asleep. "A four."

Riley nods, typing it in, and checks dilation. "A five." She types it in. "Has your water broken?"

Mrs. Jeffers nods. "Yes."

Riley nods, logging it as well and hooks her up to monitors. "And do you want an epidural?"

"No."

Riley puts it in as well and turns to the patient. "Okay, well if you need anything, just let me know!"

She walks out to the nurses desk and gets everything together for the next shift. She takes Nicole to her patients and then walks over to get her stuff out of her locker.

Erik grabs her hand. "Are you really already seeing somebody else?"

Riley looks up at him, wanting more than anything to just fall into him. Wanting his touch. "No, Erik, he's really just a friend."

Erik, not believing her, let's go. Riley grabs her keys and walks out to her car. She finds her tire slashed and texts Erik, wondering if he would even care.

Riley waits and waits but never gets a response, so she calls Sloan.

Sloan comes in about thirty minutes, Riley looks barely awake. He changes her tire for her. "You know you look too tired to drive. I can just give you a ride home."

Riley gets in his car and they go to her house.

"Thank you."

Sloan looks at her confused. "So he lives with you?"

Riley nods. "Yeah, I told him he didn't have to leave."

Sloan nods and walks her in. She goes into her room changing into fuzzy short pajamas and a long sleeve navy shirt and mix-matched socks.

She walks into the kitchen where Sloan is. "Do you want anything? You know I do share food."

Erik walks into the kitchen after being woken up to another male's voice in the house.

He looks at Riley tired. Sloan shakes his head. "No, I actually have to get going. I'll see you tonight, Riles."

He walks out of the house.

Riley turns and almost walks into Erik. She looks up at him meeting his eyes, his arms crossed. "What? My tire was cut. I had to get home somehow. Wouldn't want to upset your new girlfriend."

She moves to walk past him to go to bed, but he blocks her. He does it to her twice. Riley becomes irritated, and Erik pulls her into a hug.

"I would have gotten you. I was just sleeping. I'm sorry."

Riley hugs him back, missing this. Missing him after one day. She lets go.

"Okay, I'm going to bed." She walks into her room, shuts the door, and gets in bed.

She texts Sloan telling him to let her know when he is at the station. She builds a pillow fort beside her so she can sleep. She hears her door click open and sits up.

Erik walks in and lies down beside her. "I thought maybe you needed a friend."

Riley looks at him like he lost his mind still sitting up. "You can't sleep, can you?"

Erik nods. "Oh, I can. I didn't think you could."

Riley points to her door. "That's sweet and all, but I don't think your girlfriend would like the idea of you sleeping in bed with your ex-fiancée."

Erik gets up and walks back to his room. Riley lies down falling asleep.

Chapter 23

Riley, eyes still closed feels very warm. She feels next to her, feeling a body. She jumps up out of her bed letting out a scream. Erik sits up and looks at her. "What?"

Riley holds her chest and laughs. "I didn't know you were in here."

Erik laughs. "You looked like you weren't sleeping well, so I came in here with you and fell asleep."

Riley rubs her eyes. "Lord, don't do that! Scared the crap out of me!" Erik laughs again and hugs her.

"I'm sorry, love."

Riley hugs him back catching a glimpse of Tara about to open the door. She decides to be a jerk and leans her head against his chest. Tara walks up behind Erik.

"Why is she here?"

Riley and Erik look at her. They let go of each other.

Erik turns to his girlfriend. "We both live here."

Tara shakes her head. "Uh uh, you can live with me."

Erik looks at Riley and then to Tara. "Or you can get over it. We can be ex's and be roommates right, Riles?"

Riley nods. "Yeah, totally."

Riley shuts her door and gets back in bed. She falls asleep and sleeps a couple more hours. She wakes up and gets a shower.

She gets out and realizes she has no towels. "HEY!"

Erik walks in. "What?"

Riley peeks out of the bathroom door. "I need a towel."

Erik goes into the laundry room and gets one for her. He opens the bathroom door and hands it to her.

"Thanks." She wraps herself up in the towel and walks out and reaches into her closet to get clothes when the rack falls hitting her in the head.

Erik runs over to her. "Are you okay?"

Riley holds her hand out.

"I'd be better if I was unburied." Erik laughs helping her get out of the closet from under her clothes. She fixes the towel.

"You said Sloan was coming over tonight. Do you want me to go get some hot wings or something?"

Riley shrugs liking the idea. "Sure, maybe we could spend a game night together." She grabs her scrubs and some cash out. As she is handing it to him, Tara walks in.

Tara huffs annoyed. "You are just a hoe, aren't you? Can't stand it that you lost him!" Erik shoves Riley behind him sticking up for her.

"She will always be my number one if you can't get over it, then leave."

Riley pokes her head out from behind him. "And just to add I was handing him money for food after almost being knocked out in my closet. So Erik is actually a hero. You should be proud."

Tara smirks. "Yeah, I'm sure Sloan would be okay with this."

Riley shrugs. "Yeah, he would be, considering he is a friend."

Riley grabs clothes from her dresser and gets dressed in gray sweatpants and a hot pink T-shirt. She scrunches her hair and does her makeup.

When she walks into the kitchen, Erik is standing around. "Sorry."

Riley looks at him confused. "What for?"

Erik shrugs looking around making sure she wasn't around. "For my girlfriend being rude to you. I wish she would just understand. You have a special place in my heart."

Riley giggles. "Erik, it's okay, I promise. She'll get used to it, just give her time. I mean it did look kind of crazy."

Erik nods as Sloan knocks on the door then walks in. Riley smiles cheerfully. Erik crosses his arms, looking at Sloan. Riley looks between both of them.

"Okay, both of you need to let the tension go. Yes, Erik lives with me, but we broke up and you need to be okay with that." She pauses and looks at Erik.

"And you feel bad for how your girlfriend treats me, you can't turn around and treat him the way she treats me and be mad. We had a mutual agreement of breaking up, now you need to accept that I have friends that are men."

Both guys look at her. Riley feels the tension lighten up. Erik looks straight to Sloan. "If you hurt her, I hurt you."

Riley sighs and climbs on top of the island and sits between both of them.

"Can we all just get along please? Sloan is a friend, and you are a friend. You are both the same to me, so let's move on."

Sloan shakes his head. "Riles, can I talk to you for a second?"

Riley nods looking at him. "Go for it."

Sloan pulls out his phone and shows her messages from his ex-wife. She looks up at him shocked.

"Dude, if she wants you back, go for it! You guys have kids together!"

Erik watches both of them and gains a whole new level of respect for Riley.

Riley helps him get ready to go meet her and hands him her rose he gave her. "I know you gave it to me, but give it to her. She likes purple too. Go!"

Sloan walks out.

Riley smiles cheerfully, shutting the door behind him. Erik stands behind her ready to be a shoulder for her.

"I'm sorry, Riles. I'm sure you're shattered."

Riley giggles amused. "Actually no, he really was just a friend."

She sits on the floor in the living room pulling out her laptop from under the coffee table. Erik sits on the couch watching a movie waiting on Tara to get back from the store.

Riley gets up and makes some hot chocolate. After all any season was perfect for hot chocolate, right? Tara walks into the kitchen setting bags down.

Tara is eyeing the hot chocolate. Riley turns to her and smiles. "You can have some."

Tara looks a little shocked, expecting Riley to be a jerk. "Where is your guy?"

Riley shrugs. "I sent him to be with ex-wife."

Without thinking, Riley helps Tara put up hers and Erik's groceries. Tara walks into the living room to Erik, and Riley hears them talking about her.

Riley gets a message from a dating site from one of Sloan's friends, Matt. The messages reads: What are you looking for?

Riley messages back saying just friends right now. She goes into the living room sitting on the floor and gets back on her laptop.

Tara stares at her. Riley feels her eyes and looks at her oddly. "What?"

Tara moves over beside Riley and sits on the floor next to her. "Why are you being nice to me?"

Riley sets down her laptop and looks at Tara. "Because there is no reason to be rude to you. If Erik wants to be with you, then that's what he wants to do, and everybody deserves to be with somebody who is great like him. I absolutely understand how everything looked earlier, and I'm sorry."

Tara smiles, accepting her answer. "Thank you."

Erik looks at the two of them tuning into their conversation. "Where did you guys become friends from? Thin air?"

Riley giggles. "No."

Riley shows Tara a picture of Matt. "GIRL! He is awesome you would love him!"

The more Tara and Riley talk, the better they become at being friends. Erik shuts off the TV and holds his hand out for Tara for bed. "Riles, you should get in bed too. It's pretty late."

Riley shrugs. "It's a night nurse thing. I'd like to keep my sleeping schedule but thanks."

Erik and Tara go to bed.

Riley keeps scrolling through and falls asleep on the floor.

Chapter 24

Tara leaves early for work, stepping over Riley, careful not to wake her. When she leaves, Erik wakes Riley up.

"Come on, Riles, go get in bed."

Riley rubs her eyes and realizes she fell asleep on the floor.

"Yeah." She gets up and takes her dead laptop with her to her room. She sits on her bed, messaging Matt.

Erik walks in and sits by her. "Can we talk?"

Riley nods shutting her laptop. "Sure, what's up?"

Erik feels his heart break. "Tara is pregnant."

Riley nods, hiding her broken heart.

Erik looks down. "I don't know if I want to really marry her."

Riley shrugs. "Then don't. I mean there's no way it's yours. You guys haven't even been together for a month."

Erik nods agreeing. "The thing is. It's Kasey's or so she says."

Riley's eyes almost pop out. "Well about time Karma gets Kasey."

Erik chuckles. "But I want to be a good friend, you know. Anyways, what are your plans for the day?"

Riley shrugs and checks her schedule. "Well, apparently I'm off tonight too, so I guess I can sit around bored."

Erik gets a smirk on his face. Riley meets his eyes.

"What?"

"You can hang out with me! Tara is going to her house tonight."

Riley giggles. "Sure, why not." Riley pushes him off her bed playfully. "But I'm going back to sleep. You should too."

Erik nods getting up and walks out. Riley covers up and goes to sleep.

Chapter 25

After a couple months, Riley had become best friends with Erik. Joking, laughing, cutting up together, and even able to be in the same room with each other's girlfriend/boyfriend.

Riley invites Matt over to the house for the first time to meet Erik and have a movie night. Riley puts on black leggings and a V-neck long-sleeve shirt that clings to her skin. She straightens her hair and pins her bangs bang, making a bump on top.

She then does her makeup. She walks out of her room shutting her door bumping into Erik, knocking the breath out of herself.

Erik laughs amused. "My bad."

Riley looks up at him giggling. "Yeah, your bad!"

She double takes him and looks him up and down. He's wearing a blue and white plaid button up shirt with the sleeves half rolled and nice jeans with nice tennis shoes.

"Well, somebody got fancy for date night."

Erik laughs at her. "You're one to talk."

Riley takes a selfie with Erik and posts it to her blog page. The two walks out into the living room together.

Riley takes a breath, kind of nervous about her first date since Erik.

Tara walks in smiling in a lacey short black dress and black heels.

"You look pretty!" Riley smiles warmly at her.

Tara smiles back. "Think so?"

"Absolutely!" Riley nods and walks into the kitchen where Erik is.

Erik looks up at the two and looks as if his eyes were going to pop out.

Riley walks out to the porch and sits there waiting. Matt shows a few minutes later. Riley walks over to him. "Hey!"

Matt looks up at her as he's shutting his car door. "Hey."

He takes her hand. "You look stunning."

Riley giggles. "Thanks."

Matt and Riley move to the porch. Riley sits on the swing with him.

"So, thank you for finally giving me a shot! Sloan has told me lots about you, you know."

Riley smiles interested. "Is that a good thing?"

Matt nods. "Absolutely. Lyss has too. She's my partner you know."

Riley nods. "I do!"

Tara opens the door and peeks out. "You guys coming in?"

Riley hops up and walks in with Matt behind her.

They find a horror movie. Riley sits on the floor with Matt. Her eyes glued to the TV.

When Erik and Tara go into Erik's room, Riley takes Matt into hers just to sit and talk.

"You know if you're tired I can stay with you if you want."

Riley nods, liking the idea. "That would be awesome."

Riley changes into pink plaid pajama shorts and a black T-shirt. She wipes the makeup off her face and lies down next to him.

She falls asleep.

In the middle of the night, Riley wakes up to Matt trying to get stuff. "Stop!"

Matt then positions himself on top of her, holding her on the bed.

"Matt this isn't funny please stop!"

He continues, covering her mouth. Riley fights to get out of his grip. "GET OFF OF ME!"

Riley sounds muffled, and she realizes nobody is going to come to rescue her in this is her battle. She bites Matt's hand and kicks him off her, flying into the wall as he flips off the bed.

He grabs her on the floor holding her arms down.

"GET OUT!"

Tara peeks in to see if everything is okay and sees Riley fighting him, she rushes out to get Erik.

Riley grabs the closest thing to her, hitting him on the face with her laptop. He lets go, jumping back, and Riley jumps up running for the door. Matt grabs her from behind as she is clinging on to it.

"NO!"

She loses her grip on the door. She kicks him in the face when he lets go and runs out of the room, running straight into Erik, bouncing off him.

"MOVE!"

She crawls around him and runs out, grabbing her car keys. Erik looks confused. Tara grabs Riley's arm before she can get out the door.

"What's wrong?"

She sees bruises on Riley's wrists and a busted lip. "What the crap happened?"

Riley looks like she just saw a ghost.

"I saw you fighting Riley what?"

Riley runs out the door and gets in her car locking herself inside, completely shutting down. Riley calms down as she sees the blue lights behind her car. Tara talks to the cops, and Matt is arrested.

When they leave, Riley gets out and walks back in, shutting her door. She hears Erik talking to Tara, sending her back to bed. Riley texts Mabel saying she can't be with somebody right now and tells her exactly what happened.

An hour goes by and Mabel knocks on her bedroom door. Riley lets her in, even though Erik had been trying since she locked herself in and sat by the door.

Mabel turns on the floor lamp and sees the room destroyed. "Are you okay, honey?"

Riley looks up at Mabel, feeling completely devastated. "I'm okay physically besides the fact I think Erik murdered my head."

Mabel laughs and looks confused. "What?"

Riley smirks finding it kind of funny. "I ran straight into him and bounced off."

Mabel laughs. "You know he's pacing around upset that you won't talk to him. I think he truly still loves you, Riley. Will you go out there and let him know you are okay?"

Riley shakes her head. "I don't want him to worry about me."

Mabel and Riley talk for a while until Mabel has her laughing. "I'm glad you are alright, Riles. But I am beyond exhausted, and Erik is your best friend. Talk to him, let him in, you know he loves you no matter what."

Riley nods, letting her go. She stands at her door with her arms crossed. Erik runs up to her and holds her in a tight hug before noticing the room.

"Riles, I can't do this."

Riley takes it the wrong way, thinking he meant living with her.

"Then you guys get your own place."

Erik shakes his head no. "No, I mean I can't be with her anymore. You are my best friend and—" He pauses looking around at the room. "What did he do to you?"

He notices her busted lip and lifts her chin up looking. "You can't date anymore."

Riley smirks. Erik takes her hands. "What did he do, Riles?"

Riley sighs letting his hands go and sits on her bed. "He tried to rape me, that's what he did. That turned into a fight."

Riley looks at the wall where she hit and sits an almost whole, "And destroyed my room." She looks around realizing how bad it looks.

Erik squats in front of her, meeting her eyes. She sees the loving look he had the first time he saved her. "I'm never letting you go again. Got it?"

Riley nods, kind of understanding what he's talking about. "Are you okay?"

Riley nods becoming tired. "Yes, I'm fine."

Erik stands up holding out his hand. "Come on."

Riley takes his hand. They go into the living room and he sits on the couch with her. Riley falls asleep with her head in his lap. He covers her and goes to talk to Tara since she is up getting ready for work.

Chapter 26

Riley wakes up to the door slamming shut. She sits up and looks at Erik.

"I broke up with her and gave her all of her stuff."

Riley starts processing everything. Erik is sitting beside her.

"I want my Riles back. I swear I will never hurt you again."

Riley walks into his room and sees all of Tara's stuff gone. She walks back into the living room.

"I'll give you this chance, but if you screw up again, don't ever ask me back again."

Erik hugs her, holding her against his body and kisses her forehead. She hugs him back. Finally, it wasn't a dream anymore. It was real. This was real.

"We still have a wedding to plan, you know."

Riley laughs and lets go. "Too soon, buddy."

She walks to the kitchen and makes a pot of coffee. She sits on the island counter, waiting. Erik pulls up the picture from last night. The selfie they took together and shows it to her, both look generally happy.

Riley smiles at it. "We're a cute couple you know that?"

Erik laughs at her comment. "Well, isn't somebody conceited?"

Riley hops down and makes herself a cup of coffee and looks at Erik. "Sure am!"

She plops on the couch and takes a big sip, forgetting that it's still hot and spits it everywhere. Erik looks a bit confused laughing.

"What was that about? Too hot?"

Riley nods. "Just a little."

Erik sits beside her. Riley leans against him with her head against his chest. She grabs her blanket, not wanting to go back into her room. "You know we can get in bed if you are tired."

Riley shakes her head. "I don't want to be in there."

Erik nods understanding. She closes her eyes remembering it all.

A deputy knocks on the door. Riley gets up and opens the door. "Ms. Carter, I'm here to collect a statement from you."

Riley sits down with the deputy telling him detail by detail what exactly happened. She takes him into her room letting him take pictures. The deputy turns to her. "You haven't showered or anything right?"

Riley shakes her head wondering what it had to do with anything.

"Great, we need you to come with us to the hospital for a rape kit."

Erik steps in, from behind her with his hand on her back. "Now wait a minute. I thought she told you, he tried but she fought?"

The deputy nods. "Sorry, but it's required."

Riley sighs and turns to Erik. "I'll just go."

Erik nods. "Do you want me to come with you?"

Riley shrugs. "Whatever you want to do, it's your choice."

Erik grabs his keys and goes with them. Riley goes into the emergency department with the deputy and gets everything done along with pictures of her bruises and busted lip.

When everything is over with, she walks out to Erik feeling every bit of embarrassment possible. A blonde female detective walks over to her. "So you guys are aware this is going to court. We will be in touch."

Riley nods wanting it over with. "I'll be around."

She walks with Erik getting into his car. Erik touches her hand. "I'll be by your side one hundred percent."

Riley smiles feeling loved. "Thank you." He drives home and takes her hand. They go inside. A smile forms on her lips and she goes into the kitchen grabbing ice cream out of the freezer.

Erik laughs. "Comfort food!"

Riley giggles and runs over to him. She sticks her finger in the carton and rubs it on his cheek. Erik laughs and grabs her from behind. Riley giggles flirting.

The two of them have an ice cream fight. After it's all said and done, she takes a selfie with them and posts it.

Tara comments on it saying, "adorable" and posts a picture of her and Sloan together under it.

Riley holds up her phone and shows Erik. "Awhh! Sloan and Tara are together!"

Erik smiles happy that she took his advice to move on.

Riley makes the discovery that she is still in her pajamas.

"Well, I guess I wasn't changing today."

Erik laughs at her comment. "Guess not."

Chapter 27

Riley goes into the laundry room and grabs clothes and a warm dry towel, then goes toward her room for a shower and stops right before walking in. She shrugs, letting it go and walks in taking a shower.

After her shower, she puts on a green capri work-out leggings and a light gray-colored T-shirt. She puts mousse in her hair to give it more volume, then dries it, does her makeup, and throws her hair up walking into the living room.

Erik looks up from his phone to her. "What are you fancy for?"

Riley laughs. "I'm not. I'm just going to hit the gym. What are you doing?"

Erik looks shocked at her. "I guess sit here bored. Might go hang out with Derek."

Riley nods. "Sounds good!"

She grabs her keys. Erik walks over to her and hugs her. She kisses his and walks out. She gets in her car and drives to the gym.

Riley walks in, goes to the elliptical machine and pushes ear phones in her ears. She blares music and does that for twenty minutes then moves to lifting weights with her legs.

She then does a ten-minute run on the treadmill. After her leg work out, she goes to the locker room and grabs her keys and walks out. She gets in her car and texts Erik asking if he's home or having man time.

Erik texts her saying she should come over too. He's at Derek's; Mabel wants to see her. Riley drives out there but stops on the way getting a big bottle of cold water.

She drinks half of it then goes to Derek's and Mabel's house. She walks in cheerfully. Mabel hugs her. "Hey! You look great! Especially after last night."

Riley shrugs. "Yeah, well, I wasn't going down without a fight." She notices Riley has water in her hand.

"I swear you are doing so much better for yourself."

Riley shrugs. "Actually, I've been talking to Ana about being overnight charge nurse in trauma."

Erik looks surprised. "You are?"

Riley nods. "I didn't say anything to you. You were busy." She smiles.

Erik is in deep thought, trying to figure out how to make this work if she doesn't talk about big changes.

"When did this happen?"

Riley looks a little confused. "Like two weeks ago."

Erik nods understanding now.

Riley sits on the floor, feeling bored. Erik grabs his keys. "I guess we need to get on home."

Riley hugs Mabel. "Thank you for helping last night."

She walks out and gets in her car driving home. She parks and walks in. Matt walks up behind her as she is unlocking the door.

"Can I talk to you?"

Riley jumps dropping her keys not expecting anybody. Erik had stopped to get gas in his car.

She turns and looks at him. "I'd rather not." She grabs her keys from the ground.

"I just wanted to apologize. I had been drinking and I guess just too much. I'm sorry."

Riley nods backing into the house, so she can close the door quickly, if needed. "Well, thanks for apologizing, but I'm tired, and I'm with Erik so please go home."

Matt nods and turns around leaving as Erik pulls up.

Riley's heart skips a beat, hoping he didn't start anything. Matt drives off as Erik gets out. He walks over to her, looking a little irritated.

"Why is he here?"

Riley hangs her keys. "He just came and apologized. Then left."

Erik doubts her and gets a text from Tara asking if she can come over. Erik tells her sure.

"Okay, well you look tired. Why don't you go on and get in bed."

Riley shakes her head. "I'm fine." She tilts her head noticing his distancing. "Erik, you know you don't have to be with me if you don't want to. If you want to remain friends then just tell me."

Erik looks away walking in. She goes inside and sits on the island pulling out her laptop. She tunes out everything until she hears somebody knocking at the door and Erik walking by catches her attention.

Tara walks in with a smile. "Sloan and I aren't going to work out. I really just can't stand being away from you."

Erik holds Tara close. "I don't think me and Riley are, either. There's just a distance there and we are better as friends than anything. I just don't know how to tell her. She had the heart to forgive me and give me another chance."

Riley texts him saying, "You know if you want to be with her then be with her. I'm not going to be mad. I kind of had the feeling anyway so just tell me what you want."

Erik reads the text and walks into the kitchen. "Can I talk to you for a sec?"

Riley looks up at him and nods. "Of course, go head!"

Erik sits beside her on the island. "I don't really know what to say, Riles. I love you I just don't want to hurt you, that's all."

Riley smiles. "You aren't. I heard you talking to Tara. It's okay really. I think of it as kind of a mutual thing."

Erik nods. "But I'd like to keep my room here, if that's okay?"

Riley smiles perky. "It's fine! And I like her. Just go for it."

Erik smiles thankful that she understands. He walks out to go to Tara.

Riley gets on her dating site, messaging people, and pops her headphones back in. She listens to music and looks through messages. Adam, a medic at the fire department with Alyssa, messages her asking if he could meet up with her.

Riley texts him saying, "Sure come on over. My doors are open."

An hour goes by and Adam knocks on the door. Riley hops down shutting her laptop and opens the door. Riley looks down realizing she's still in her gym clothes.

"Oh my gosh! I'm sorry I'm still in my gym clothes. I just didn't even think of it."

Adam chuckles handing her a rose. "It's fine. Alyssa has talked highly of you, and I wanted to take a chance and meet with you. Hang out, you know?"

Riley smiles cheerfully. "Awesome! Well, we can do whatever. My rooms is still destroyed from an attack last night, but we can hang out in here?"

Adam nods liking that idea. Riley sits on the floor talking with him.

"So you're the nurse moving to trauma?"

Riley nods with a smile. "Absolutely. I'm pretty excited it's a change. Besides the fact that I'm out of work for another week before I start."

Adam nods understanding. "Well as you know I'm a paramedic at the station. It's just nice to spend time with somebody who understands what my life is like, you know?"

Riley nods agreeing. "It is."

They talk about things they have in common. They share stories.

Erik and Tara walk out looking at them oddly, after hearing the laughing and another male voice in the house.

Riley looks up at him curious. "I thought you guys went to bed?"

Erik chuckles. "Nah, we watched a movie. Who is this?"

Adam stands up. "I'm Adam. I work at the fire department. I've ran into Riley a few times at the hospital."

Riley crosses her arms hoping Erik will approve. "Well, I'm Erik, Riley's my best friend. I work at the hospital. We live together that's not a problem, right?"

Adam chuckles. "No, of course not."

Erik and Adam talk while Riley and Tara wander into the kitchen talking. Riley sits on the island counter talking to her.

"You guys are so good together!"

Tara smiles. "Thank you for giving him the push he needed toward me. You're a good friend. I know it's got to be awkward."

Riley smirks. "Girl, I just had that feeling the second he asked. Besides, he's kind of like a brother to me now as weird as that sounds."

Tara smiles. "And you're a lot like a sister to me."

Adam and Erik walk into the kitchen, and Adam is paged to the station. "Hey, I got to go. Text me?"

Riley nods. "Sure! Be safe!"

Adam leaves, and Tara goes to bed.

Erik leans against the counter next to Riley, crossing his arms.

"I don't know what I want, Riles. Maybe I should just be single."

Riley shrugs. "What do you think I'm doing?"

Erik smirks. "Only you, Riles."

Riley hops down, texting Adam. She looks up at Erik.

"You know, I enjoy your company."

Erik chuckles being paged. "Well, I guess I got to get going. Going to miss you on the floor you know."

Riley smiles grabbing her laptop. "You'll be fine. Krista's got this."

Erik goes into his room to change. He walks out, and Riley hugs him. "Be safe."

Erik hugs her back. "You know I will." He walks out.

Riley goes into her room and shuts her door. She cleans it up the best she can and gets in her bed. She falls asleep.

Chapter 28

Riley wakes up screaming from a nightmare and a freaked-out Tara standing at the door on the phone. She sits up shaking, realizing it was just a dream.

"Are you okay?"

Riley doesn't say anything hugging her knees to her chest.

"Erik, she's like completely shut down. I don't know what to do! She really scared me can you just—"

Tara's water breaks. "Crap." Riley looks at her oddly.

"My water just broke! I'm only thirty-three weeks!"

Tara drops the phone freaking out. Riley hops up and jumps into action, calming her down. She calls an ambulance and acts as if she were in a hospital setting. "Okay, I'm really not trying to invade your personal space, but I just need to check dilation. Are you okay with that?"

Tara nods. Riley checks and looks at her, wide-eyed. "Just don't try pushing at all."

The ambulance gets there with Lindsey and Alyssa. Riley, still in her gym clothes, gets in the back with her. She keeps Tara calm and her mind occupied the whole ride.

They get to the hospital fast, and Riley runs up to the labor and delivery floor with her. She helps Krista get everything together for Mabel and gets pushed away.

"Walk away, Riles. This is our turf now."

Riley walks out worried for her friend. Erik grabs Riley's shoulders, who appears to be in a daze.

"Riles, you are covered in blood. What's going on? Is she okay?"

She snaps back to reality. "She's okay."

Erik holds her against him, needing his friend. She sits in the waiting room with him. Mabel walks out, pulling Erik in with her.

Riley sits alone in the waiting room, texting Adam. Adam walks up and sits by her.

"You know you did everything you could in your house. Let it go."

Riley looks at him. "I don't want him blaming me if anything happens to her and her baby."

Adam kneels in front of her. "Sweetheart, listen. You need a good night's rest, a shower, and some clean clothes. You can't do anything, you can come over to my apartment if you'd like? I'll take the couch and you can have my bed."

Riley nods agreeing. She takes his hand and walks out, texting Erik to keep her updated and that she is with Adam. She gets in his car with him and goes to his apartment.

Adam goes into his room and grabs a navy-blue T-shirt and some gray sweatpants. Riley takes it and gets in the shower. She gets done quickly and gets out and dressed.

She wipes the smeared makeup off her face and goes into his living room, throwing her hair up in a messy bun.

Adam gives her a comforting hug. "Get you some rest, okay? I'll be right here if you need me."

Riley feeling bad goes and gets in his bed and falls asleep quickly.

She wakes up at nine in the morning. She looks around seeing that he kept his word. She smiles thinking that maybe she found the right person this time.

Riley walks into the kitchen, smelling pancakes and the sweet smell of coffee.

Adam turns to her smiling. "Hey, sleepy, feel better?"

Riley nods. "Actually yes." She sits at his island counter.

Adam leans beside her. "You look well rested. I figured you might want breakfast, so I made it for you."

Riley smiles not ever having somebody like that. "Thank you. And thank you for letting me stay with you last night."

Adam smirks. "No problem."

Riley eats with Adam, and they both get cup of coffee and go over to the hospital to check on Erik and Tara.

Riley stands outside her room, nervous to know. Adam takes her hand and looks her in the eye. "You got this, no matter what. No feelings remember that."

Riley nods and goes in with him, still holding his hand. Tara looks at her half smiling. "I was farther than I thought. I was thirty-five weeks and she is doing really good!"

Riley smiles happy and hugs Tara. "I'm glad." She sees Erik asleep on the couch. "See, he cares about you."

Tara nods. "He loves that little girl too."

Tara tosses a pillow at him, waking him up. "Hey, your best friend is here."

Tara giggles looking at Riley's outfit. "We know what you guys did last night."

Erik jumps up hearing that.

Riley shakes her head. "No no! I just didn't go home. Adam was nice enough to let me take a shower at his house and gave me some clothes. Since I got your blood all over me."

Tara giggles. "Sorry."

Erik looks at Riley crossing his arms. "Nice."

Adam jumps in. "She slept in my bed, I slept on the couch. She needed sleep. And she was extremely worried about you, guys, so I kept her company."

Riley nods. "Yeah what he said."

Adam meets her eyes. "Speaking of that, I can take you home, so you can change if you'd like?"

Riley nods feeling uncomfortable. "Yes definitely!"

Erik breaks in. "I can take her home. I'm sure you have to be at work soon."

Adam shakes his head no. "Not unless they call. I'm off today. I just figured you like to spend time with your family."

Erik nods, appreciating him. "Thank you."

Riley hugs Tara and Erik. "I'll see you guys when you go home!"

She walks out with Adam and gets in his car. He drives her home. Riley gets out and goes inside changing into a rose-pink V-neck, and dark colored jeans that fit tightly.

She puts on navy-colored tennis shoes and walks out.

Adam smiles at her. Riley feels as if her heart were full.

"You look beautiful," he says. He then takes her hand. "I need to run by the station real fast, and then we can go do whatever you'd like."

Riley smiles, falling for him. "Sounds good!"

She gets in his car with him, and they go to the station. Adam gets out with her and goes inside, taking her hand.

The guys look at her. "Adam scored a girl!"

Riley's face turns blood-red.

Adam chuckles. "Yeah, make jokes."

He goes into the chief's office and talks for a second and then walks out taking her hand. They go back to his car and get in.

Riley tilts her head curious. "I'd like for you to meet my adopted parents."

Adam takes her to Mabel's house. She gets out pulling him inside. Derek looks curiously at her.

"Hi, I'm Derek and you are?" He stands up shaking Adam's hand.

"I'm her friend. Well, I guess you could say we're dating. It's our second date."

Riley smiles proudly. "And he is awesome!"

Derek talks to him for a while, and Riley listens to their conversation.

Riley gets anxious and takes his hand. They get in his car leaving.

Chapter 29

After about a month, Adam and Riley are officially a couple, and very close to each other.

Erik walks out of his room, tired from caring for their newborn. Riley is sitting at the island video chatting with Adam while he's at work. Her hair looks messy. Erik tilts his head trying to figure out why she looks different.

She had chopped her hair off that morning and dyed it blonde.

"What's different?"

Riley giggles looking at Erik and turns her phone where Adam can see.

"Say, hey! I'm talking to Adam. He's at work."

Erik waves, while making coffee.

"And I cut and dyed my hair."

The tone drops, and Riley looks at Adam.

"Alright, I got to go! Talk to you soon, sweetheart. Love you!"

Riley smiles. "Love you too, goose!" She ends the call. Erik leans against the counter.

"You guys are too cute. So I want to propose to Tara."

Riley jumps up excited. "You should!! You guys know you can stay here as long as you want. I love being Aunt Riley!"

Erik laughs, even though they had a history, they now had a sibling type of relationship. "We'll be here awhile."

Riley looks excited. "Well, I'll gladly keep Ms. Rose if you guys want to go out tonight. Adam gets off at seven, so he could come over and help."

Erik nods agreeing. "Sounds like a plan! Thanks, Riles."

Tara walks out after getting her daughter to sleep. "What's going on?" She looks like she saw a ghost looking at Riley. "Whoa, now that's different!"

Riley giggles. "You like?"

Tara nods tired. "Absolutely!"

Riley turns the conversation. "Oh, by the way, you and Erik are going out tonight. I got Rose."

Tara looks confused. "Are we?"

Erik nods smiling. "Yeah, I got plans for us."

The day goes by quickly, and Adam is off. Riley gets excited when he walks in. "We got Rose tonight!"

Adam laughs. "Alright, well you guys have fun!"

He looks to Erik. Tara and Erik leave.

Riley gets Rose and holds her; getting her, Riley and Rose snuggles.

She sits on the couch talking to Rose while Adam orders pizza for supper. He stands in the door way smiling at her.

"You'd make a great mother."

Riley looks up smiling. "Maybe one day. Not anytime soon though."

She feeds Rose and then gets her to sleep and in bed. Adam gets a plate ready for Riley and hands it to her as she sits on the couch.

"Thank you."

Adam smiles eating with her. She does the dishes and cleans up. Rose wakes up and Adam feeds her while Riley gets a shower.

When Riley gets out, Tara is holding her baby.

"He proposed!"

Riley smiles sitting beside Adam on the couch. "I know he told me!"

Adam puts his arm around Riley. "I told her she would make a great mother one day."

Erik laughs. "Good luck on that one."

Riley leans her head against Adam. He puts his arm around her. "Are you ready for bed already?"

Riley nods. "Yeah I have to go to work tomorrow. I'd like to sleep awhile."

Adam smirks. "Okay, well go to bed."

Erik and Tara go to bed with Rose.

Riley pulls him into her room and climbs in her bed with him. She snuggles up to him and goes to sleep with a big smile.

Chapter 30

Another couple months go by, Riley and Adam seem happy together; Erik, Tara, and Rose are living upstairs. Riley seems to be home a lot more than she was when she was with labor and delivery; she works twenty-four on and forty-eight hours off.

Riley clocks out from the hospital after a slow night. She gets in her car to drive home and realizes she left the headlights on. Her car won't start, and its thirty degrees outside. She's already catching a cold and is drained. She calls Adam almost crying.

"What's wrong, sweetheart?"

Riley chokes her tears back. "I can't get my car to start, and I don't feel good. I really just want to go to bed."

Adam chuckles on the other end. "I'm on my way, okay? I love you."

"I love you too." She hangs up and waits the fifteen minutes for him to get to her. When he pulls up, she runs to get in his car freezing. She turns the heat up and rubs her tired eyes.

"Thank you for coming to get me."

Adam hands her a biscuit. "I thought you might be hungry."

Riley shakes her head no turning it down. "No, I kind of feel sick, to be honest."

Adam nods and drives home. They get out, and Riley pukes her guts out the second she gets out. She sits on the cold ground not wanting to move. Adam picks her up and carries her inside.

Erik looks at them oddly. "What's wrong?"

"She isn't feeling good." Adam gets her into her room and sets her down on the bed. He kneels in front of her.

"Hey."

Riley opens her eyes, barely holding them open.

"You need to get changed. Maybe a shower?"

Riley shakes her head no.

"Yeah. Come on." He holds out his hand.

Riley gets up and goes into the bathroom getting sick again. Adam holds her hair out of her way.

She gets in the shower after and then grabs one of his T-shirts and gets in bed to sleep.

Adam walks out, shutting the door. Erik smirks biting his tongue. Adam shrugs and they sit together in the kitchen. Riley wakes up that afternoon feeling half dead and puts on a pair of Adam's sweatpants and goes into the kitchen.

Both Adam and Erik are leaning against the counter with their arms crossed.

"What?" Her hair looks crazy and is flapping around everywhere. She grabs some crackers and eats them.

"You look awful, Riles."

Riley shrugs. She lays her head on the island counter and sounds wheezy. Erik sits beside her, putting his hand on her back.

"Riles?"

Riley doesn't look his way, closing her eyes.

"Yeah?" she answers.

Erik gets up and comes back a few minutes later.

"I'm going to listen to your breathing. okay?"

Riley nods.

Adam gets toned and kisses her forehead. "I'll be back soon. I love you."

"I love you too."

"Hey, look at me for a second." Erik sets his stethoscope down. "You have a choice. Either you let me take you to the doctor or we can wait for Adam and then you go."

"I just want to go to bed."

Erik looks serious. "Riles, this isn't just some cold, you know. I worked the ER, you need antibiotics and steroids. You sound and look horrible."

Riley turns her head. "I'm okay."

Erik shakes his head no, disagreeing. "Riles, please."

Riley nods. "Okay, but you have to promise they'll make me feel better."

Erik gets up and holds his hand out. "I promise."

She takes his hand and gets up feeling weak.

Erik picks her up carrying her out to his car and drives her to the urgent care. She gets back quickly; the doctor checks her out and they take blood. She lies on the bed curled in a ball.

Erik stares at her. She looks pitiful. They come in an hour later.

"You have pneumonia. We're going to give you an antibiotic shot, steroid shot, and some pills as well."

Riley nods. The nurse walks in and gives her both shots in both hips. They get her prescriptions. Riley looks like a walking zombie. Erik takes her hand, trying to act as a caring brother.

They get in the car and drive home. Riley leans the seat back and curls in a ball. They get home, and Adam walks out to help Riley in. He carries her to their room and helps her in bed.

She lays her head on his lap when he sits down. He rubs her back. "Give it a couple days for those steroids to kick in."

She nods. Her body aches.

"Do you want me to go get you something to eat?" Adam asks.

Riley shakes her head no.

"Sweetheart, you have to eat something." Adam squats down in front of her and brushes her hair out of her face. "You look so miserable."

Riley opens her eyes. "I just feel horrible."

Adam nods in understanding. "Well, yeah. You have pneumonia. What about some ice cream?"

A big smile forms on her face.

"Yes?" Adam asks.

Riley nods. "Yes."

He stands and holds out his hand for her. She gets up and walks into the kitchen with him. She eats some ice cream and then takes her medicine. Adam sends her back to bed.

Chapter 31

After a couple days, Riley starts to feel better. Adam takes a couple days off to take care of her.

Riley wakes up feeling like crap but better than before. She rolls over to Adam, stealing his warmth. Adam wakes up, putting his arm around her. "How are you feeling, sweetheart?"

Riley smiles warmly. "I feel better than I did but not one hundred percent."

Adam smiles looking at her. "Good. I'm glad."

Riley nods agreeing. "You and me both."

She gets up and puts on fuzzy pajama pants and a long-sleeve shirt. Adam gets up with her, and they go into the living room. She finds a movie and lies on the couch, with her head on his lap.

Erik walks in from being on call, and fighting with Tara on the phone. Riley catches the end of his conversation.

"Well then leave, Tara. I'm done."

Riley looks confusedly at him. Erik hangs up and looks angry throwing crap together.

Riley sits up and looks at Adam. "What is it, sweetheart?"

Riley smiles feeling loved. "Do you want to go somewhere?"

Adam laughs sarcastically. "Unless you are going to lie down, you are not going anywhere."

Riley sighs and goes into the kitchen. She grabs an apple and starts cutting it. Her phone dings not paying attention and cuts into her finger. Blood rushes out.

"Yeah! Real good, Riley!" She goes over to the sink dripping blood and grabs the closest rag. She wraps it around her finger.

"Riles, you okay?" Adam walks into the kitchen. Riley turns to him.

"Yeah I just cut my finger."

Adam looks at the floor then to her. "Can I see?"

Riley nods, stepping to the side holding her hand over the sink. Adam looks at her finger and tries to look at tendons. Riley jumps. "Ow! I have feelings, you know!"

Erik walks in and looks at them oddly then at the floor. "What did you do? Murder the apple?"

Riley rolls her eyes. "Ha ha, very funny." Adam walks out to his car getting his medical bag.

Erik stands beside her. "So how exactly did you do this?"

Riley looks at her phone. "I was cutting an apple and looked at my phone, that's how."

Erik laughs looking at her finger. "You just need a couple stitches." He looks at the tendons and makes sure nothings cut. "Yup. You're good."

Adam walks in and digs out what he needs then stitches her finger up, then wraps it. "It'll be sore for a few days obviously."

Riley looks at both of them crossing her arms. "I'm a trauma nurse not stupid guy. Lord, now I got both of you teaming up on me. I need a female up in here!"

Both guys laugh amused. "You'll be okay."

Riley looks at her apple no longer wanting it.

"Well I was hungry, but not after trying to mangle my finger."

Adam frowns at her. "Eat something else."

Riley makes a salad and eats it. She then does the dishes and gets the house straightened up. After everything is done, she sits on the couch in between Adam and Erik.

Erik gets called for on call and jumps up leaving.

Riley snuggles up to Adam and watches a movie with him. After the movie, Riley makes a sandwich and eats. They both get a shower and in bed.

Riley has her head on his chest. "Thank you. You know you are such a wonderful guy."

Adam smiles kissing her, then holds up a ring. "Will you marry me?"

Riley sits up thinking he's joking and realizes he's not. "Are you serious?"

Adam nods, waiting for an answer. "Yes, I will!"

Adam kisses her and slides the ring on her finger. She looks at her pretty ring; it looks like it has a glow to it.

She smiles and goes back to sleep.

Chapter 32

In the morning, Riley gets up perky with Adam and takes him to the station for work. She drives home and puts a pork loin in the Crock-Pot for supper. She then gets laundry done and cleans the house spotless.

After wearing herself out, she gets in bed for the night. She wakes up to her alarm at five. She gets ready for work and eats something then leaves.

Riley rushes in through the emergency room, ready to jump in. She goes into a room and is already calling a code blue. She jumps in, not realizing her doctor in charge is Kasey.

She works by her brother until a surgeon gets there, and Kasey disappears. A wreck victim comes in—a child. Riley starts an IV and moves quickly. They push fluids and the kid codes as well. She starts CPR while waiting on Kasey.

After the kid comes a burn victim. She does what she can and moves them up to the Burn Unit. She goes into the emergency room to help with whatever is needed.

She walks in to a room and helps with stitches then moves to a room where somebody claims they hit their toe two weeks ago. Riley looks at the clock and sees that it's four in the morning. She sighs walking out of the room, letting Kasey know.

After everybody for the most part has been attended to, she gets things together for the next charge nurse. Even though it hadn't been much of a night, it was still kind of interesting. She missed her labor and delivery floor.

Riley gets off the clock and drives home. She walks in and gets a shower then collapses in bed. Erik wakes her up at two that afternoon. She looks at him groggily.

"Is everything okay?"

Erik nods. "I was just checking on you."

Riley rubs her eyes and looks at the time then jumps up. "I didn't realize it was that late! Sorry, I was exhausted."

Erik shrugs and sits beside her. "Me and Tara separated. Kasey and Alyssa separated too."

Riley looks confused. "Are you serious?"

Erik nods. "I'm actually about to date Alyssa."

Riley sits on her bed in her jammies.

"I'm sorry . . . you're what?"

Erik shrugs. "She's my girlfriend. She is coming over for a while today."

Riley nods, taking it in. "I liked Tara but okay whatever you say."

Erik chuckles. "She, Alyssa, is a good person, you know."

Riley shakes her head. "No, I don't know, but I do know she drives me insane, acting like a child that can't take care of herself."

Erik takes that into consideration. "True, but she'll grow."

Riley laughs. "Oh, wait, you're serious?"

Erik gives her a look. "Yes, I'm serious. So what's new with you and Adam?"

A big smile grows on her face. "Well, he proposed!" She holds up her hand showing her ring.

Erik smiles happy for her.

"And then you're totally going to be a Prego."

Riley shakes her head. "Oh no no, Riley is not having a baby, sorry."

Erik laughs. "Sure, you are! I bet you're already pregnant. You just don't know it yet."

Riley thinks for a second and bites her lip. Erik looks at her seriously.

"You have been taking your birth control, right?"

Riley looks away. "Riley!"

She looks at him. "No. I haven't taken it in like three months."

Erik looks at her going into doctor mode. "Get your butt up and go take a test!"

Riley looks at him like he's crazy. "I'm not pregnant Erik."

He stands up crossing his arms. "Now, Riley!"

She gets up not wanting to. "Can't I just do it later?"

Erik goes into his big brother mode, pointing at the bathroom door. "Go!"

Riley huffs and goes into the bathroom. She takes a test and watches it turn positive within seconds. She walks out biting her lip, not making eye contact with Erik.

He smiles already knowing. "You are, aren't you?"

Riley keeps her mouth shut.

"Hello?"

Riley looks at him for a quick second, then looks away. "Yes."

Erik hands her her phone. "Then get your appointment set!"

Riley grabs her phone calling and getting her appointment made. Unfortunately, Mabel was not available, and she got stuck with Erik being her doctor.

She walks in giving him a I-dislike-you look. "You know I really don't like you right now."

Erik looks at her curious. "Why is that?"

Riley crosses her arms. "Because I'm pregnant, and I got stuck with you as my doctor!"

Erik laughs amused. "On the bright side, we live together. Not like I haven't seen you anyways."

Riley looks irritated. "Mabel just *had* to go to your practice and I get stuck with you! Isn't that some crap?"

Erik laughs at her pouting. "Might want to tell Adam."

Riley nods agreeing. "Yup, I'm stuck with two guys that aren't going to let me even look at the sun."

Erik laughs walking out of her room. "You'll survive."

Riley texts Adam telling him she has something for him.

After about an hour, he stops by with Lindsey on the way back to their station.

"I got your text. Is everything alright?"

He hears Erik laughing from upstairs.

"What?"

Riley pulls him into the bathroom and picks up her test showing him.

"This. This is what and lucky me. I get stuck with my basically brother for my doctor!"

Adam laughs at her before looking at it. "Are you serious?"

Riley nods crossing her arms. "Because I'm stupid and forgot my birth control for like three months."

Erik chimes in. "Antibiotics cancel it out too."

Riley looks around Adam, shooting Erik a look that if looks could kill he would have been dead.

Adam hugs Riley excited. "This is awesome!"

The tone drops, and Adam kisses her rushing out the door.

Riley walks into the kitchen still pouting.

"Oh stop. You'll be fine. You have to see Mabel eventually anyways."

Riley shrugs agreeing. "True." She sits at the island staring at an apple.

"That apple isn't going to float over to you, you know. You have to get up and get it."

Riley ignores him and gets up getting it. She hands it to him with a sweet smile. "Will you cut it?"

Erik laughs. "You totally just pulled off the little sister look. I got it." He cuts her apple into little triangles. She looks at the plate and then back to him.

"Do I look like a child?"

Erik laughs again. "Nah, I just love messing with you."

He walks into the living room. Riley eats her apple and puts the plate away in the dishwasher. She pulls out her laptop and plays on it waiting for Adam to get off.

Eventually she gets bored and gets up making meat loaf for supper.

She eats before everybody does and then sticks the pan in the oven.

Adam walks in from work and has a big smile on his face. Alyssa walks in behind him and hugs Erik cheerfully.

Riley looks around Adam, staring Alyssa down. Adam blocks her.

"I know you don't like her much, but she isn't going to be a jerk to Erik."

Riley nods and hugs him excited. "So we're going to have a baby!"

Adam laughs at her. "Yes, we are." Riley starts feeling all kinds of excitement flow through her.

Adam eats supper and then gets a shower with Riley. They get in bed and watch a movie together. Riley falls asleep with her head on his chest and wearing a big smile.

Chapter 33

Riley gets up perky in the morning and scrunches her hair, pulls it half back with a clip, and then twists her bangs, pinning them to the side. She does her makeup and puts on jean-colored leggings and a black and gray half-sleeve shirt.

She walks out of the bathroom into Adam. He catches her, and their eyes meet. She giggles.

"You look beautiful," Adam murmurs.

Riley's face blushes. "You do too even with your bed head."

She walks into the living room, letting him take over the bathroom. She puts an egg and sausage croissant in the microwave and sits at the island waiting for it to cook.

Erik walks in ready for work with a cup of coffee in his hand. He looks at her, head tilted. "No breakfast?"

Riley looks up from her phone, at the microwave, seeing that the microwave already went off. She gets up and walks over to it pulling her plate out. "Yeah, I was just waiting."

She leans against the counter eating it, with a glass of grape juice. Erik smiles crossing his arms. "Somebody went on a healthier binge."

Riley shrugs putting her plate in the sink and then pulls down her prenatal vitamin from the cabinet while taking it with the juice. Adam walks in as Riley puts her cup in the sink.

Erik looks at her curious. "Are you doing this because you got stuck with me?"

Riley crosses her arms. "Doing what?"

Adam looks between the two. "Awh, are you guys fighting?"

Riley looks at Adam with a smirk. "I don't even know what about!"

Erik looks at the clock. "Hey, you have an appointment in three hours."

Riley looks annoyed. "Yeah, I know. I'm very aware. And you have a job to get to!"

Erik walks out the door. Riley rolls her eyes, shaking her head. "Little does he know I got Mabel to switch me over to her."

Adam laughs as he stands by the counter. "So what was he talking about?"

Riley bites her lip. "I guess because I took my prenatal and drank juice, ate breakfast too."

"No way!"

Riley giggles nodding. "Yup."

Alyssa walks by with Grace and the diaper bag and walks back into the kitchen. "Kasey is on his way to get Grace for the weekend."

Riley shrugs. "Well he can come in and be social." She looks at her niece shocked that she is walking around already.

Riley sits on the floor holding her arms open. "GRACIE!"

Grace runs over to her and hugs her. "WEEE!"

Riley giggles playing with her when Kasey walks in, irritated.

"I don't understand why you couldn't bring her out, Lyssa. I have to get to work!"

Riley picks up Grace and walks into the living room looking at her brother with Adam.

"Well, look who decided to actually come to my house."

Kasey looks at his sister crossing his arms. "And who is this guy? Aren't you with Erik?"

Riley laughs amused. "Where have you been? This is my fiancé, who also happens to be the father of my child. You know you work on the same floor as me and can't even say anything to me. So take your daughter and go on about your way."

Kasey looks shocked at his sister. "You know Mom is here. She's living with Dad. I'm sure she would love to see you."

Riley looks at him not breathing. Alyssa takes Grace out to Kasey's car. "What?"

Kasey nods. "Yup, she's at home go see her."

Riley nods. "Only if you promise to try to be a better brother."

Kasey thinks for a second. "We'll work on it together." He walks out the door.

Riley turns to Adam. "My mom. My real mom. She went missing and they never found her."

Adam shakes his head, meeting her eyes. "Riley, I need you to push it to the back of your mind and come back to me."

Riley nods and puts on a smile. They leave for the doctor. On the way there, they pass her dad's house. Riley puts her hand on the window.

"She's really there?"

Adam shrugs not answering. They get to the hospital and walk up together while holding hands.

She walks in and signs in. She sits close to the door and texts Mabel.

Not long after arriving, they get her back and into an ultrasound. The tech looks at her with a big smile. "Fourteen weeks and three days."

Riley shoots up. "Wait, fourteen weeks?"

The tech nods printing the pictures and hands it to her. They take her into a room and a new nurse practitioner walks in. She smiles warmly. "Hey, I'm Claire. Dr. Sheeran is busy on a delivery, but I understand you used to work with her."

Riley nods. "Yes, ma'am. I did."

Claire smiles and writes something on her sheet. "Okay, we'll just go to lab F and get some blood work, and we will see you in two weeks since you have miscarried before."

Riley nods and hops up with Adam. They walk into the lab and the nurse takes blood. Riley then sets up her next appointment with Mabel then and they go out to where the car is parked.

"So I'll tell Jasper that I need that day off."

Riley takes his hand cheerfully. "Okay. Can we stop by my parents' house?"

Adam nods getting in the car with her. "If that's what you want to do."

Riley smiles. "I do."

They drive to Jase's house.

Chapter 34

Riley takes a breath as they park and gets out of the car with Adam. She knocks on the door. A teenage girl opens the door and looks at her, tilting her head.

"Riley?"

Riley looks shocked. "Yeah."

The girl lets her in with Adam. "Dad has been talking a lot about you to Mom. I'm your half sister by the way. I'm Chelsea."

Riley nods, taking in that kind of news. Chelsea walks up to the stairs.

"MOM! DAD!"

Riley takes Adam's hand nervously. Melanie and Jase walk down the stairs.

Melanie looks up at her daughter and smiles. "Riley?"

Riley sighs. "Yes."

Jase stands back watching with his arms crossed. Melanie runs over to her and hugs her tightly. Riley pushes her back a little.

"I'm not trying to be mean, but I don't really know you. I just wanted to see if Kasey was lying."

Jase huffs and walks over to his daughter. "You look a little fat, Riles."

Riley looks at her start of a baby bump and at her dad.

"I'm pregnant, Dad. Not that you have much to do with me."

Melanie looks at her daughter teary-eyed. "I've missed so much of your life. I'm so sorry that I walked away from you and your brother!"

She then looks at Jase. "How could you just walk away from her? She needs you and Kasey too!"

Grace runs out from the kitchen. "WII YEE!"

Riley smiles and kneels to catch Grace and hugs her. "GRACIEEE!!!"

Adam chuckles. "That's their thing."

Kasey walks out of the kitchen with Taylor and looks at his sister with his daughter.

He watches the smiles on both faces and listens to the laughter between them. He catches himself smiling. "So, Mom, you know Riley is getting married?"

Melanie smiles at her daughter, her eyes full of happiness. "I didn't! Is this him?"

Riley smiles turning to Adam. "He is. He's a wonderful man."

Adam smiles at his fiancé.

"Well, your daughter is very beautiful and has been through a lot. Erik is very much a brother to her."

Melanie looks at her son, taking Grace from Riley. "You two go talk now."

Kasey and Riley both huff and go out on the porch talking. Riley stares blankly at the ground.

Kasey stares at his sister. "You've grown up a lot."

Riley refuses to even look at Kasey. "I have."

"Can I ask what happened between you and Erik?"

Riley looks at her brother. "He cheated on me. We separated. A lot of crap has happened. We got back together for a day and then decided it wasn't right and have been broken up ever since."

Kasey thinks back and remembers seeing his sister in a room but was too busy to go check on her. "It's not that I didn't want to see you and make things right with you. It's just I've been busy."

Riley nods. "Yeah, well, I hope you aren't like that with Gracie. She's very intelligent, you know."

Kasey nods. "So Adam is a good guy, right?"

Riley smiles happy. "Absolutely. Erik approved."

Kasey looks confused. "I thought you guys broke up?"

Riley nods. "Yup and he lives in your room and acts as my big brother."

Kasey looks a little hurt. "Well, I want to make things right okay? We need to."

Riley nods agreeing. "We do. I'm also fourteen weeks pregnant."

Kasey looks at her shocked. "Really?"

Riley smiles. "I am."

Jase walks out and looks at his kids. "I got shoved out to mend things with Riley too." He rolls his eyes. "So what are we talking about?"

Kasey looks up at his dad. "Dad, you don't have to be so cold to her. You know she grew up."

Jase looks annoyed. "Family time over yet?"

Kasey stands up. "Dad just sit down and talk to her!"

Riley shakes her head. "No, don't because why would I want a father all of a sudden when I already have one?"

Jase and Kasey look at her confused. "What?"

Jase steps toward his daughter. "What was that?"

Riley stands up. "Yeah, while you were off living in your own dreams, I made my own family. I thought maybe I could meet my mom, but you know things are still broken in this family. Derek is my dad. Anybody can make a baby, but it takes a real man to take care of that child."

Jase backs down hearing her stand up to him. Riley walks in and grabs Adam's hand. "I want to go home."

Adam looks at her curiously and walks out with her. Kasey meets his sisters' eyes with an apologetic look. "Text me, Riles."

Riley looks at her brother with a cold-hearted look. "You don't call me Riles."

She walks to the car and gets in with Adam.

He drives toward the station. "So what happened?"

Riley shakes her head. "Kasey wants to be that brother. My dad is still my dad . . . and my mom? Well I don't even know her."

Adam nods agreeing and pulls in. "Everybody wanted to see you."

Riley smiles and gets out with him pushing everything to the back of her mind. They go inside. Jasper and Chase walk over to them. "Hey, how is everything?"

Adam smiles. "Fourteen weeks."

Lindsey runs up to them. "Did you find out the gender yet?"

Riley giggles. "No, I'm only fourteen weeks. Six weeks and I'll know."

Lindsey sighs, the bright expression in her face fades. "Well—"

She is interrupted by a big crash sound. Everybody walks outside and sees a car crashed into a tree. Adam looks at Riley. "I want you to go sit inside, okay?"

Riley gives him a yeah-right look. "I'm a trauma nurse. I got this."

They get the ambulance and fire truck over to the scene and call it in.

Lindsey pulls Riley into the ambulance, up front. "Adam would be livid if he sees you out here."

Riley sits in the truck bored. Then they pulled a man out in a backboard. Riley sees what they don't see. A child in the back seat.

She gets out and runs toward the car. Chase grabs her from behind. "You can't."

Riley kicks and screams. "NO! You have to get the kid out! I'm a nurse. I have to get the kid!"

Lindsey walks over to her, blocking her view. "Can you come with me for a sec? I need your help."

Riley goes to the back of the ambulance with her. "The kid that you thought you saw was an empty car seat."

Lindsey waits on Ashley, a medic working with her today. Riley walks over to the station and sits in the lounge waiting. Adam walks in and holds out his hand to her.

"Ready?"

Riley nods and gets in the car with him. "And that is why I cannot be a fire fighter or medic. I can't just walk away."

Adam nods understanding. "I know."

They drive home and get out. Riley walks in with him and sits on the couch.

Chapter 35

Riley wakes up on the couch not realizing she fell asleep. She gets up and sees a car pulling up in the driveway.

"Hey, hubby!"

Adam walks out of the kitchen. "Yes, sweetheart?"

Riley looks out the window. "Who is here?"

Adam shrugs. "Looks like your brother by the looks."

Riley gets excited, ready to tell Erik all about her day but sees Kasey instead. The excitement fades away. She huffs opening the door.

Kasey hugs his little sister. "I'm sorry for ever being the worst brother possible." He hands her a baggy of candy.

Riley laughs. "No. I don't do a lot of sweets."

Adam walks up behind her. "But . . ."

Riley bites her lip. "But thank you for the thought."

Adam nods walking back into the kitchen. Kasey chuckles.

"Adam told me I could come by. I just want to work my way back around, if you are okay with that."

Riley nods. "Okay, we'll try"

Erik pulls in with Alyssa. They come in. Erik looks at Alyssa and Kasey oddly. "Did somebody die?"

Alyssa looks at Kasey. "Is Gracie okay?"

Riley pulls Erik into the kitchen with Adam. "Kasey told me my mom was here. My real mom. I went over, and my mom is trying to make everybody mend everything. I give it a week, and he'll disappear."

Erik nods agreeing. "Me too. Want to know a secret?"

Riley shrugs taking a sip of water.

"Lyss is pregnant."

Riley spits her sip out. "Nah uh!"

Erik nods. "With my baby."

Riley laughs. "No way!"

Erik looks between Adam and Riley. "You guys act too much alike."

Riley giggles. "I know." She walks over to Adam putting his arm around her. He hands her a plate of lasagna.

"Eat."

Riley shakes her head. Adam nods. "Now."

Riley shakes her head again.

"Riley Elisse, sit your butt down and eat. You haven't had anything but breakfast this morning."

Riley's face goes blood red. Erik crosses his arms, narrowing his eyes. "What did I just hear?"

She sighs sitting at the island and eats half her lasagna. "I'm not that hungry."

Adam stands beside her, with his elbow on the counter and his head tilted. "You got five minutes to eat."

Riley smirks. "Or?"

Erik and Adam both stare at her, both have eyebrows raised. She sighs eating.

"You guys, I swear!"

She finishes and puts the plate in the dishwasher.

"See? Was that too hard?"

Riley shakes her head. "No."

Kasey walks into the kitchen with Alyssa looking irritated.

"What's going on?"

Riley shrugs. "Nothing."

She gets a text asking for her to come up to the labor and delivery floor they are out of a charge nurse and need one desperately.

She looks at Adam. "I just got called in."

Kasey looks at his phone waiting. "I didn't."

Erik gets a text as well. "Me too! Let's roll, Riles."

Riley giggles and kisses Adam. "I'll see you in the morning?"

Adam kisses her back and hugs her. She runs her fingers through his thick red hair. "I love yooouu!"

Adam smirks. "Take it easy, sweetheart."

Riley gets in the car with Erik and off to the hospital they go.

Chapter 36

Riley blares music in the car on the way there.

They get to the parking garage and park close to the doors, then walk inside. "You should come back. We miss you."

Riley smiles. "I want to."

They both take a breath and open the doors, then they walk into together. Taylor looks at both of them relieved.

"Thank the good lord! Riley, grab rooms and go. Erik, come with me. We have four that need C-sections. I called Derek and Mabel as well."

Riley takes off, handing files to the three other nurses. She starts at Room 1.

"Hey, I'm—" She looks down realizing she looks nothing like a nurse. "I'm Riley. I'm your charge nurse. How are you feeling?"

The patient looks like she is in a lot of pain. She checks monitors and watches contraction after contraction. "How long has it been since somebody was in here?"

"Three hours."

Riley looks irritated. "Alright, I'm going to check you."

She checks dilation and gets a full ten; she's ready to push. Riley pages for Room 1 delivery. NICU comes in, and Riley gets everything thrown together.

Sarah runs in. "There is no doctor available."

Riley nods ready. "Alright, then I'm taking you, you are with me."

Riley and Sarah deliver the baby and hand the baby off to the NICU.

Ana walks in smiling. "I'm a nurse practitioner. I'm covering for OB tonight."

Riley looks at her thankful to see her best friend she hadn't seen in so long except for work.

After Ana took over, Riley goes to Room 4. She walks in to a screaming patient. Riley looks like she just lost hearing.

"Alright that answers my question. Let me check you."

She checks the patient. "Eight. Let me go ahead and page." She walks out paging on call and moves to Room 7.

Destiny, a newer nurse, walks out of Room 6 and toward Riley. "I need on call OB now. This is an emergency."

Riley turns before opening the door. "What's wrong?"

Destiny looks panicked. "I felt cord."

Riley looks like she saw a ghost. "I'll page and we'll go."

Ana walks toward Riley. "What?"

"I need you to take Room 7. I have to get this patient to OR"

She runs in and unlocks the wheels and grabs the IV bags and runs down the hall with Sarah to the OR. They meet Erik, and Riley goes in with him.

She keeps the patient calm, and baby is delivered quickly and safely.

After delivery, Riley shows the patient the baby and then Sarah takes the baby to NICU, then comes back for the patient. "Room 4? What do you want me to do. Is she full and complete?"

Riley looks at Mabel as she is walking out. "Room 4, meet me there!"

She runs to the floor and to the room, walking in with Ana and Sarah delivering. Mabel walks over to them and takes over.

Riley walks out and sits on the floor by the door. Erik sits beside her. "Crazy night isn't it?"

Riley nods. "I really need to change."

Erik laughs looking her up and down. "You and Sarah are close in size. see if she has a set."

Sarah walks out and looks at them oddly. Riley looks up at her. "Hey, do you have scrubs I could borrow for the night?"

Sarah giggles and goes with her to the locker room. Riley changes and uses her brush brushing out the curls and throws her hair up. She walks out, shoving her shoe back on.

Erik pulls Riley to the side. "Slow down, okay?"

Riley nods sitting at the desk. "I will."

Sarah walks up to her and Erik. "So you're pregnant?"

Riley smiles. "I am. Fourteen weeks and four days now."

Sarah looks at the two. "Are you guys even still together?"

Both of them laugh amused. "Oh no!"

Riley looks at Erik with a smirk. "He's my best friend, but we went our separate ways. His girlfriend is actually pregnant!"

Sarah looks at them strangely. "Well, that's different."

Erik laughs. "Crazy thing is they actually get along."

Sarah nods walking off. Krista walks in. Riley looks at the time. "Already seven?"

Krista laughs. "It is, and it is so strange to see you up here and with Erik."

Riley giggles. "I'm sure it is."

Taylor and Mabel walk over to Riley with pleading eyes. "I'll give you the same pay as trauma if you come back. It's like three days off before you come back, but please!"

Riley smiles happy. "Absolutely."

Mabel looks out of breath. "So how are you feeling. Are you feeling okay?"

Riley nods cheerfully. "I am."

She gets up and grabs her clothes from the locker room. She walks out with Erik and gets in his car.

They drive home.

Riley walks in as Adam is getting up. She walks over to him. Adam kisses her.

"You look pretty happy."

Riley smiles. "I am! I'm going back to labor and delivery. I'm off for three days and then I'll be back."

Adam smiles. "Good! You look tired, sweetheart. Go get some rest, and I'll see you in the morning?"

Riley hugs him tightly. "I love you."

"I love you too."

Riley goes into their room, gets a shower, and goes to bed.

Chapter 37

Riley gets up at two. She texts Adam just to tell him she loves him and then gets up to change to black yoga pants and an aqua T-shirt. She sits on her bed with her laptop on and shops online for their wedding, planning it. She picks a date in about a month and orders her dress and decorations, then books a church.

Riley orders the bride's cake and books the caterer. She sets her laptop down and goes into the kitchen not expecting to find Erik. She makes a bowl of cereal and looks at a barely awake Erik.

"Did you not go to sleep?"

Erik laughs. "Nope."

Riley shrugs and pulls out her phone.

"Look!" She shows him her wedding dress. "It's going to be here in like two days!"

Erik tilts his head. "You want to look like a sparkle princess?"

Riley giggles. "Duh!"

She eats her bowl of cereal, takes her prenatal, and then eats some Greek yogurt. She stands up and leans against the counter.

"Alyssa is in pain."

Riley looks at him curious. "How so?"

Erik holds up his phone. "She won't take a leave. She is mad that I wanted her to go to our group of doctors so on and so forth."

Riley walks over looking at his phone reading the texts.

"She acts like a child. Tell her to get over it."

Erik smirks. "Her mom is her doctor."

Riley shrugs. "And mine is my brother and my father. So what's the difference?"

Erik crosses his arms. "Somebody got mad and went to Mabel"

Riley smirks. "Yeah, I did." She finishes her yogurt and throws her trash away.

"You are so getting a bump."

Riley looks down noticing her bigger belly. "Yeah. It grew."

She giggles realizing her shirt fits tight. "Yeah. Maybe it's time I go clothes shopping."

Erik nods. "Yeah this is a you-and-Alyssa conversation not mine."

Riley giggles. "Yeah, or Mabel."

She texts Mabel, asking her to go shopping with her.

Mabel shows up a couple hours later. Riley goes out and gets in her car and they drive to the Grand Central Mall.

Riley goes in with Mabel excited. She picks a maternity clothing store and walks around looking. Mabel holds up a cute black lacey dress. Riley grabs it and a red one like it then she finds maternity leggings, yoga pants, and lots of striped shirts and shirts with hearts and different designs.

Riley pays and goes out to the car with four bags full of clothes. She gets in and Mabel looks at her. "Now, what have you eaten? Are you hungry?"

Riley shrugs. "Yeah. I had a bowl of cereal."

They go to a burger joint, and Riley gets the biggest cheeseburger with everything on it. She gobbles it up then later, Mabel drops her off at home.

"You know your dad would like to see you."

Riley texts Derek. "Why don't you guys come over for dinner? I'll make pork chops or something?"

Mabel smiles and agrees, then drives off.

Riley goes inside and throws her clothes in the wash along with her scrubs she borrowed from Sarah. She starts dinner and makes mashed potatoes and corn to go with it.

She has everything ready when Mabel and Derek walk in.

Riley smiles, wearing her black lace-styled dress that goes to her knees and has her black ankle boots on with it. She walks over to Derek and hugs him.

"Hey, sweetheart, how are you feeling today?"

Riley smiles. "I'm doing good today."

Derek smiles, and Riley goes into the kitchen with everybody and sits at the island eating with everybody. Riley does dishes after and puts away everything.

Derek, Alyssa, Mabel, and Erik are sitting in the living room talking.

Riley walks in and sits on the couch texting Adam missing him like crazy. He video calls.

Riley answers it. "Hey! Slow night?"

Adam smiles. "Don't you look fancy. Who's there?"

Riley moves the phone around, so he can see everybody.

Erik takes the phone. "Your fiancé thinks she needs to have girl conversations with me."

Adam chuckles. "Welcome to my world."

Derek looks at Alyssa and Riley. "Lyss, you could learn a lot from her, you know."

Alyssa rolls her eyes. "Well, I'm not her. Anyways, I'm pregnant."

Mabel looks at her daughter irritated. "Excuse me?"

Alyssa stands up. "Come on. You guys don't get mad at Riley for getting pregnant!"

Mabel looks at Riley. "Don't worry, Riley got in trouble."

Derek nods. "She did."

Riley bites her lip watching Erik talk to Adam. "Right, Riles?"

"Yeah."

Mabel laughs.

"Wait, what?"

She looks at both Mabel and Derek.

Derek leans forward and looks at both girls. "If I hear that either one of you are pregnant again there will be consequences. Got it?"

Riley looks at him confused. "Hey, I didn't do anything! What'd you do?" She looks at Alyssa.

Alyssa stomps her feet. "You! You got me in trouble!"

Riley looks lost. "I have no idea what you're talking about."

Mabel laughs. "It's a joke. Lyss. Chill."

Alyssa screams irritated and walks into her room, slamming the door.

Riley rolls her eyes. "Drama queen."

Erik looks at everybody. "Great she's in that kind of mood?"

Riley smirks. "Sure is."

Riley takes her phone back.

The tone goes off. Riley sighs. "I know you got to go. I love you!"

Adam frowns. "Hey, cheer up. I'll be home before you know it. I love you too."

Riley hangs up and looks up at them. Mabel stands up. "Well I think we better get going, honey. You look beautiful tonight. Get some rest, alright?"

Riley nods and hugs Mabel and then goes over to Derek and hugs him. "I love you, guys."

Derek hugs her extra long. "We're just a phone call away if you need us."

Riley nods and watches them leave. She goes into her room and changes into shorts and a tank top. She walks out, turning off lights.

Erik meets her in the living room. "Hey, what's wrong?"

Riley looks at him, with a tear in her eye. "Nothing I'm just having Adam withdrawals."

Erik hugs her. "He'll be home in the morning. It'll be okay."

Riley smiles hugging him back. "I know it's a medic thing. He has to suffer without me too."

Erik laughs agreeing. "Go to bed, Riles, you look exhausted."

Riley nods and goes to her room, shutting the door behind her.

She gets in bed and stacks up her pillows. Before falling asleep she texts Adam telling him she loves him.

Riley snuggles up to the pillows and closes her eyes, falling fast asleep.

Chapter 38

Adam wakes up Riley when he comes in. Riley sits up rubbing her eyes.

"It's just me go back to sleep."

Riley scoots over to him and lays her head on his chest. "I missed you last night."

Adam chuckles. "And I'm wide awake."

Riley nods and looks up at him. "We can get up."

Adam shakes his head. "No, you need sleep."

Riley sits up. "Let's get up."

Adam gets up giving in, with Riley. She puts on a pair of blue shorts and a white T-shirt and walks out of the bedroom with him. She goes into the kitchen and makes some toast and a fried egg.

As she's about to take a bite of it, Adam grabs her hand. "You can't eat that."

Riley looks confused. "Why, what's wrong with it?"

Adam looks at her seriously. "You can't have raw egg when you're pregnant."

Riley looks down at her egg and pushes it to him. She then makes herself a scrambled egg and puts ketchup on it, then sits down and eats it. Erik walks into the kitchen and looks at her oddly.

"Didn't you just eat? I swear I just saw you eating."

Adam looks at Erik. "No, she was going to eat a raw egg."

Erik looks at her like she's stupid. "Riley!"

Riley shrugs, putting her plate in the sink. "It wasn't completely raw, it was fried."

Erik shakes his head and grabs a cup of coffee. Riley stares at it wanting a cup but resists it. She grabs a soda. Both Adam and Erik stare at her.

"Well I need caffeine."

She goes into the living room and sits on the couch crisscrossing her legs. All of a sudden she gets hot. "Oh, my lord, you guys are going to sweat me out of here!"

Adam looks a little confused. "It's not hot in here. It's a good temperature."

Riley feels her face burning. "It's hot."

She gets up and turns the air conditioning on setting it at sixty-five. Erik watches her.

"Riles, are you sure it's not your blood pressure?"

Riley shakes her head no. "No, if it was up, I'd have a pounding headache."

Riley sits back on the couch and pulls Adam down beside her. She lays her head on his lap and falls asleep.

"I knew she was still tired. She wouldn't stay in bed."

Erik smirks. "She missed you last night."

Riley hops up not long after falling asleep, running into their bathroom. Adam and Erik stay in the living room.

Riley pukes her guts out and then blacks out hitting the floor.

Erik looks at Adam. "You know she's been in there for about ten minutes. Might go check on her."

Adam walks in. "Riles?"

He doesn't get a response and knocks on the door. "Riles, are you okay?"

When she doesn't reply he walks in finding her passed out on the floor.

Adam checks her pulse and figures she's got to be just dehydrated or something. He picks her up carrying her into the kitchen elevating her legs higher than her head.

Erik walks into the living room and drops his glass mug. "Is she okay?"

Riley starts to come to.

"She passed out."

Riley looks at them groggily, real out of it. Her head is pounding and her body aches. She feels extremely exhausted.

"Hey, how are you feeling?"

Riley sits up. "I feel like crap."

Adam looks at her sympathetically. "Well, yeah. You passed out."

Riley looks at him wide eyed. "What?" She hops up and goes into their room stumbling and grabs her shoes.

Adam and Erik follow her curious.

"Where are you going, love?" asks Erik.

Riley looks at Erik; he knows she hates it when he does that. "Well I'm pregnant. Are you sure you two didn't pass out? I have to go to the hospital! The baby?"

Erik holds up a finger calling Mabel. Adam grabs Riley's arm to keep her stable. "Let's sit down for a second." He pulls a penlight out of his pocket and makes sure she doesn't have a concussion.

Erik texts Adam saying Mabel and Derek are both in the living room.

Adam kneels in front of Riley after making her sit for a while. "Feel ready to get up?"

Riley nods. "Yes, I'm fine."

She gets up. Adam takes her hand, taking her into the living room. Riley looks around with a migraine, and still feeling dizzy.

She sees Mabel sitting on the couch with Derek talking to Erik. She goes to sit on the couch missing it completely. They turn to the sound of the thud.

Riley lies there, not wanting to move. Adam stands over her. "Well, are you going to get up or just lay there?"

Riley looks at him. "Just give me a second."

Mabel walks over to her and sits beside her. "How are you feeling?"

Riley stares at the ceiling. "Well, I have the worst headache, my body hurts, and I just want to go to sleep."

Mabel nods. "Well do you want to go to the hospital? I mean I can check you out here."

Riley sits up. "We can do it here."

Mabel goes out to Derek's car grabbing her medical bag. She comes back in. Riley goes into her room with Mabel not wanting to be on the spot.

Mabel checks her vitals, then listens to the baby's heartbeat with a Doppler. "You got low blood pressure, but other than that, you're okay and baby is okay."

Riley smiles. "Good. It was probably just my blood pressure then."

Mabel nods agreeing. "Probably a mild concussion too, if you hit the floor."

She goes into the living room with Riley. Everybody stares at them.

"She's fine, baby's fine."

Adam nods. "Good. She has a concussion."

Riley rolls her eyes thinking fantastic. She gets up and goes to the kitchen, grabbing a cold bottle of water and goes back into the living room. Adam gets a text from Lindsey asking if she could come over.

Riley gets a text reminder about meeting with the pastor for their wedding. She looks at Adam. "I forgot about the wedding date! It's set for next week! We have to go meet the pastor!"

Adam looks at his phone, with the date set. "Well, let's go."

Riley goes into her room and gets changed into leggings and a white lace dress shirt. She pulls on boots, scrunches her hair, and does her makeup and then walks out.

Mabel looks at her shocked. "You got ready that fast?"

Riley smiles. "Well, yeah!"

She grabs her keys. "You guys can come with us if you want."

Derek grabs Mabel's hand standing up. "Let's go."

Riley gets in the car with Adam and they drive to the church.

She gets out with Adam and goes in with everybody behind her. The pastor sits down with Riley and Adam alone and they talk about the wedding, the meaning of love, and if this is what they really want.

After their meeting, the pastor shakes Derek's hand. "Beautiful daughter you guys have there."

Derek smiles. "Thank you."

The pastor talks with Mabel and Derek while Riley decides where she wants everything and how to decorate. She walks out with Adam excited, despite the pounding headache.

"I can't wait!"

Adam smiles and takes both her hands looking in her eyes. "You'll be fifteen weeks too."

Riley nods smiling. "I know I got a baby bean in there!"

They stop in front of Derek and Mabel.

"You guys want to go out to eat or something?"

Mabel and Derek's phone buzz. Mabel looks at Riley apologetically. "I think we have to get to work. Thank you for letting us come with you guys though."

Riley nods understanding. She gets in the car with Adam and smiles excitedly. "We're finally getting married! It's getting real!"

Adam chuckles at her.

Chapter 39

The week goes by quickly and then it's their wedding day! Riley is in the bridal room getting ready with Ana, Alyssa, and Mabel. Riley has on a dress that is white, long, and flowing. It sparkles and is sleeveless with silver glitter lines around the top like a princess dress.

She styles her hair with a curling iron and then pins it half down half up.

She then does her makeup. She has on maroon lipstick, rose pink eyeshadow, and thick eyeliner. She puts on concealer and face powder along with reddish pink blush. Her long red hair shines under her veil. Mabel places a tiara on top.

Riley puts on dangle diamond earrings and a purple teardrop-shaped necklace.

Derek knocks on the door. Mabel smiles and turns to Riley. "You okay with Derek coming in?"

Riley turns to face her. "Of course!"

Derek walks up behind her and smiles. "You look beautiful. Not the Riley we are used to."

Riley smiles and hugs him. "Thank you for walking me down the aisle."

Derek hugs her. "You know I love you as my own."

Riley smiles. "Yes, I do, and I am thankful to have a father like you."

Erik knocks on the door next. Mabel opens it. "Yes?"

Erik smiles hopeful. "I want to see the bride!"

Mabel turns to Riley. "What about Erik?"

Riley tilts her head and looks at her. "What about him?"

Mabel laughs. "He wants to talk to you."

Riley sighs. "Sure."

Derek walks away. "I'll give you two a second."

Mabel nods agreeing. "I think we all should."

They all walk out, letting Erik in. He shuts the door behind her and smiles. "You look so beautiful."

Riley smiles. "Thank you."

Erik looks down. "I'm sorry I missed out on this."

Riley giggles. "You're my brother Erik, let it go."

Erik nods. "One last selfie?"

Riley looks confused. "Sure?"

She walks over to him and takes a silly selfie with him.

Erik walks to the door with a sad expression. "Congrats, Riley. Take care of yourself." He walks out.

Riley looks a little confused and everybody walks in. "Don't know what he's talking about. But okay."

Mabel nods. Ana comes in. "Alright bride, it's time!"

Riley gets nervous and walks out with them. The music starts. Ana walks first, then Alyssa, and then Mabel. Finally, Derek steps up to Riley, and she wraps her arm around his.

They walk down the aisle together. When they get to the end, they stop.

The pastor looks at them. "Who gives this bride away?"

Derek smiles proudly. "I do."

Riley walks up to Adam and hands Mabel her flowers.

The pastor goes on about love, and then there is the candle-lighting service. They say their vows. They give each other a ring.

"I know pronounce you husband and wife. Ladies and gentlemen, I present to you, Mr. and Mrs. Clements."

Riley and Adam walk down the aisle together and go to the reception. They cut the cakes and have their first dance then eat. After the reception, they go to get their stuff out of their rooms, and Riley changes into black leggings and a short hot pink dress that shows well her baby bump.

She gets her stuff in Adam's car and they drive away.

Chapter 40

After their wedding, they fly to Paris for two weeks and come back. Riley and Adam are on their way home when Adam looks at Riley.

"There's something you need to know that I was asked not to say anything until now."

Riley looks confused. "Like?"

Adam sighs, not wanting to break her heart.

"Riley, Erik moved out and away. He has no plans of coming back."

Riley's heart shatters. She stares out the window. "Okay."

They get home. Riley goes inside the house, thinking it's just a joke. She looks in the room and sees it completely empty. She sighs and decides to let it go.

Mabel texts her saying, "Your appointment is in two hours, see you soon, honey!"

Riley looks at Adam. "Apparently I have an appointment in two hours."

Adam nods. "Well, let's go."

Riley has her hair curly, half up half down and her bangs twisted and pinned to the side. She has on white leggings and a navy-colored longer shirt with one shoulder showing and the other not. Her bump shows big time now.

She was seventeen weeks after all. She goes out to the car and gets in with Adam and off to the hospital they go. They park and go inside. Riley signs in thinking she is seeing Mabel.

They get called back and Riley has her gender ultrasound, and vitals taken, they get into a room.

Doctor Vickery walks in smiling. "Hey, how are we doing?"

Riley smiles half way. "Great!"

Doctor Vickery measures her belly and gets the heart rate of the baby. "Everything looks great. Baby is measuring a week ahead but that's alright."

Riley nods getting up. They get checked out and the next appointment set with Mabel. She walks out taking Adam's hand. "So I go to work tonight."

Adam nods. "Me too."

Riley smiles and kisses him. "I'm excited."

Adam chuckles. "Yeah you're first night at work as Mrs. Clements."

Riley nods smiling proudly. They go home, and both get in bed before work. Riley gets up and dressed at five. She puts on her pink tennis shoes and has on navy-colored scrubs.

She wakes up Adam. "Hey, I'm heading out for work."

Adam gets up. "Alright, let me know when you get there, love."

Riley kisses him. "You too!"

She walks out and drives to work. She gets there fast and goes in, clocking in.

Her hair is still styled as it was earlier, and she has on makeup. Taylor walks by and looks at her. "You have a surprise tonight."

Riley looks confused. "Okay?"

Taylor smiles. "Just wait."

Ana walks over to Riley. "I already saw your surprise."

Riley walks over to the monitors and watches. She then assigns rooms to nurses there tonight and goes to Room 1.

"Hey, I'm Riley. I'll be your nurse tonight. How are you doing?"

The patient smiles cheerfully. "Great for now!"

Riley asks questions and then looks at the monitor in the room and records contractions.

"What is your pain level?"

The patient seems calm. "A four."

Riley nods keying it in and then checks dilation.

"You are about a five. I'll get the doctor to come in in a second to break your water."

Riley walks out and sees everybody staring at the double doors. She looks at them odd. "What are all we looking at?"

Taylor smiles. "Go open the doors."

Riley, feeling like this is a set-up walks over and kicks the door open, hitting Erik in the face.

"Ow!"

Riley runs around the door and looks at him with her hand over her mouth. "I am so sorry!"

Erik looks up at her and chuckles. "Miss me?"

Riley screams excited and jumps on him, hugging him.

Erik catches her, hugging her back.

"I absolutely one hundred percent miss you!"

Erik laughs putting her down. "You got a big baby bump going on! I miss you too. I'm living with Kasey now. And Lyss is back with him."

Riley looks shocked. "No way!"

Erik nods. "I'm with Sarah."

Riley smiles happy for him.

"That's awesome! I'm happy for you. Hey, are you on call tonight?"

Erik nods almost afraid to ask. "Why?"

Riley smiles handing him a file. "Good, Room 1 needs her water broken."

Erik sighs taking the papers and walks away. Riley walks into Room 4.

"Hey, I'm Riley. How are you feeling?"

The patient looks like she's very much in pain. Riley checks dilation and finds a baby's head out. She sets up everything not having time and delivers the baby paging on call.

She hands the baby to NICU, and turns to get a doctor, tripping. Erik catches her. "Careful, love." He lets her go and walks over to the patient.

She bites back, missing him, and goes to the desk watching monitors, having a boring night. Seven rolls around, and she clocks out and mopes over to the door.

She looks back seeing Erik smiling. She walks through the door and goes to her car. She texts Adam telling him she is on her way home and apologizes for not telling him she was at work.

When she gets home, she sees the fire truck there. Riley gets out confused. A deputy walks over to her.

"Mrs. Clements?"

Riley nods. "Yes?"

"I think we need to go inside and talk."

Riley walks inside not seeing Adam's keys. She sits down and looks at the deputy.

"I regret to inform you that your husband was in a fatal accident this morning. He did not make it."

Riley's eyes fill with tears. "NO! This is just some sick joke!"

The deputy shakes his head. "I'm afraid not."

Riley walks around the house. "Adam this isn't funny! Come out!"

Lindsey walks in and takes Riley's arms.

"Riley, I'm sorry! He really is gone."

Riley falls on the floor balling.

Lindsey picks up her phone when Erik calls.

"Hey, Riley just lost her husband now might not be a great time to talk."

Within seconds, Erik is there walking in the door. "Riles?"

Riley looks up at him with tears still pouring down her face.

He hugs her tightly. "Hey, you have to calm down. The baby."

Riley is shaky. "No, he just . . . he can't!"

Erik nods rubbing her back. "It's alright, Riles. It's going to be okay."

Riley becomes hysterical.

Erik wipes her tears and looks into her eyes. "Riley, you have to listen to me, okay?"

Riley nods.

"You are going to send yourself into preterm labor you have to calm down," Erik warns.

Riley slows down her breathing, feeling her heart shatter to pieces.

Erik holds her close to him. "You just worked a long shift. Let's get you in bed."

Riley shakes her head no. "No!"

Erik picks her up carrying her to her room and sits her on her bed. "I'll stay with you. It'll be okay."

Riley falls asleep after crying until she couldn't.

She dreams of Adam smiling at her but as an angel. "Sweetheart, I'll be by your side no matter what. I will always be with you. Please don't cry. Move on. Be happy. I love you."

Chapter 41

Riley wakes up with more tears falling. Erik rubs her back calming her down. "Hey."

Riley stares at the wall not wanting to talk. She was pregnant and alone. Erik walks around to her kneeling down meeting her eyes. "Riles, you are going to be just fine. I'm right here, I'm not going anywhere. Do you understand me?"

Kasey walks into the bed room with a sad look in his eyes. "She okay?"

Erik shakes his head no.

Kasey sits by his sister rubbing her back. "You have us both, Riles. Mabel and Derek are on the way over."

Riley stares at Erik not saying a word. Her heart is broken.

Erik takes her hand. "Have you eaten anything yet?"

Riley doesn't answer him. Kasey gets up. "I'll make her something."

Mabel walks in. "How is she doing?"

Erik looks at Riley. "I'll be right back, okay?"

He walks away. Riley grabs Adam's pillow and hugs it close to her. Mabel lies down beside Riley and hugs her like a mother would. "Hey, you know Adam would be livid if you weren't eating."

Riley nods.

"I know you don't want to, but you have that baby to think about. We are all here with you. We got you breakfast."

Riley nods again. "I just can't believe he's gone."

Mabel nods. "Me either, but you have to eat something. Come on." She gets up holding her hand out.

Riley sits up but refuses to move. "This was his pillow."

Mabel sighs. "Would you talk to Erik?"

Riley looks at her. "I want Erik. I want to hug him and never let go."

Mabel nods going to get him. Erik walks back in and sits behind Riley with his arms around her. Riley leans back on him. Erik looks down at her.

She looks up meeting his eyes.

"What about a shower?" asks Erik.

Riley shakes her head. "I don't want to move."

Erik nods. "Okay we can stay here like this for as long as you want."

Riley nods. "Good, because I'm having some awful contractions."

Erik bites his lip, wanting to make sure the baby is okay. "Well, why don't we get you to the hospital, get it stopped, and me and you will come back here and sit in this bed until you are ready to get up."

Riley nods. "That sounds okay."

Erik gets up and holds out his hand.

Chapter 42

After checking on the baby everything seems okay, but Riley has been put on light duty. She is now about thirty-four weeks pregnant. Erik left Sarah and is staying with Riley, falling for her all over again.

Riley and Erik are sitting on the bed, Erik behind her with his arms around her as they are watching a movie. Riley starts having contractions again.

Riley keeps it to herself until they get intense. She squeezes Erik's leg tightly. "Riley, you're pulling hair!"

Riley holds her breath until the contraction ends. "Okay that one was awful."

Erik looks at her confused. "What was?" Another one hits her.

She squeezes his leg again holding her breath.

"Riles!" He takes her hand making her let go of his leg.

"Are you okay?"

Riley shakes her head and then all the sudden feels like she peed on herself. "Okay, I think we should really go to the hospital now. Like right now."

Erik feels the wetness on his legs. "Did you just . . . ?"

Riley shakes her head no slaps him playfully. "No, you goober! My water just broke! And these are some awful contractions!"

Erik jumps up. "Your what just broke?"

Riley moves slowly getting up out of the bed. "My bag is in the closet for the hospital. We have to move now!"

Erik stands there in shock.

"HELLO! Riley to Erik." Erik snaps back and grabs everything.

"So help me if you don't get me to the hospital right now. I promise you I will scream in your ear."

Erik puts everything in the car and then comes back and picks her up carrying her out to the car. He grabs her seatbelt buckling her in.

"I can buckle myself, you know."

Erik chuckles a nervous chuckle and flies to the hospital.

"Lord, I'm going to die in labor."

He gets her there, and let's Lindsey know so the fire department can come up. They get her in a room and ready for delivery.

Erik walks into the room and sits beside her, taking her hand. "Strange how I'm here with you, isn't it?"

Riley shoots him a hush-it look. "Well, I can tell you one thing if these people don't get in here when you're delivering this child."

Sarah walks in taking vitals and asking the questions. "And your pain level?"

Riley gives her a look. Erik looks at Sarah.

"I'd go with a ten because that's how my hand feels right now."

"Get this kid out of me!"

Sarah smirks. "Let me go get the doctor."

Riley looks irritated. "HEY! You didn't check dilation."

Erik laughs. "Riles, you are the patient, you are not here to work."

Sarah walks out getting Ana. Ana walks in and checks. "Girl! How long have you been having contractions?"

Riley thinks for a second. "About ten hours off and on."

Ana nods. "I'd say so! You're a nine."

Erik looks at Riley unhappy. "And you waited until your water broke to tell me?"

Riley smirks. "Sure did. Now get it out!"

Ana smiles looking at Erik. "At least, you're already in here."

She walks out. About thirty minutes go by, Riley looks at Erik. "You are about to deliver this child because I really feel like I need to push."

Erik's eyes widen, and he freezes. Riley waves her hand in front of his face.

Erik moves to the end of the bed and checks. "You better not even think about pushing." He rushes out. A few minutes Later Erik, Ana and NICU nurses walk in. Erik delivers Riley's baby.

When her son is born, he seems a hundred percent healthy. No problems for a preemie baby. He weighs seven pounds eight ounces. Erik walks out for about an hour and then comes back in with a smile.

"Hey. You did good!"

Riley laughs and smiles. "Not many people can say their best friend delivered their baby."

Chapter 43

A couple months after Damian is born, Erik acts as the father. He and Riley are testing the waters of dating again. But this time they still act as if they were best friends.

Riley is holding Damian and looks at Erik as he walks into the living room with Mabel.

Mabel holds out her arms, "You two are going out tonight, Riles. We got little man, don't worry, okay?"

Riley nods and hands him to her feeling bare. "But I love him."

Mabel giggles. "I know, sweetie, but you need a break. Go out, have fun. We got him tonight, go on!"

Erik takes her hand. "Come on, love."

Riley sighs and kisses her son's forehead. She walks out to the car with Erik and gets in. They go over to Kasey's house.

Riley walks in with Erik to Alyssa's party. The music is loud and there is a lot of people. Alyssa hands Riley a drink. "It's wine coolers, you'll be fine for a night!"

Riley takes a sip and dances around with Alyssa.

Riley ends up dancing with Erik after a while. All of a sudden it gets quiet, and Erik is nowhere to be found. Riley looks around for him. Slow music starts.

Erik walks over to her taking her hand and gets on a knee. "Riley Elisse Clements, would you do me the honor of being my wife?"

Riley smiles and tears fall. "I would."

Everybody screams excited.

Erik holds up a finger. "But?" He stands up.

"But are you sure you really want that?"

Erik nods. "Absolutely."

Riley smiles. "Then yes, I will."

Erik picks her up spinning her and kisses her.

After the party they go home late and see that Mabel had already left with her son.

Riley gets in bed with Erik and lays her head on his chest. "I still have my dress and the decorations. All we need is to set a date."

Erik smiles. "Tomorrow."

Riley looks at him shocked. "What?"

He nods with a big smile. "I had a feeling you would, so I already had everything taken care of."

Chapter 44

Wedding day number two. Riley gets up and gets her stuff together then gets in the car with Erik. They drive over to Kasey's house. Alyssa takes Riley into her room and helps her get ready.

Riley curls her hair and pins her bangs back, thus making a poof. She puts on the tiara and does her makeup. Dark colored lipstick, dark blush, face powder, and white eye shadow.

She puts on her necklace and earrings and finally her dress. Kasey walks in. "Ready?"

Riley nods. "Absolutely."

Kasey takes her out to his backyard where Alyssa had everything set up. The music starts, and Riley walks with her brother down the aisle. They stop in front of the pastor.

"Who gives this woman away today?"

"I do."

Erik takes her hand and smiles. "You look beautiful."

The pastor goes right to the vows. Riley says hers, and Erik says his. They put the rings on and the pastor smiles. "I pronounce you husband and wife, Mr. and Mrs. Valentine, ladies and gentlemen."

Riley turns seeing all the people she works with and her friends. Erik walks with Riley, and they have the cutting of the cake and the first dance.

Mabel hands Damian to Riley and the newly wedded couple get in the car and leave.

They go to their house where Riley changes into shorts and a gray T-shirt.

Erik walks into his wife. "Man, it feels good to call you my wife."

Riley giggles and kisses him.

"It does, doesn't it?"

Erik looks at Damian in his swing. "He is so sweet."

Riley nods agreeing. "He sure is!"

Erik picks him up lovingly while Riley puts away the wedding gifts.

Mabel and Kasey walk in smiling. "How was that for a quick wedding?"

Riley hugs her brother. "Thank you. You have earned your brother rights back."

Kasey laughs. "I love you too, Riles. So when are you and Erik having a baby?"

Riley laughs amused. "I am not having another baby yet."

Erik looks up at Kasey and Riley. "You can have another after a year if you really wanted to."

Riley shakes her head. "Nope. I got the five-year IUD. I'm good. Damian can be in school when we have a baby."

Erik laughs and feeds Damian. "I want a girl."

Riley nods. "Yeah well, you're going to be waiting a while for that girl."

Chapter 45

Some time has passed. Damian is now two. Riley and Erik are still married, but they seem to have a lot of issues. Riley isn't sure she even still wants to be with Erik who seems to be a cheater still.

Riley is sitting in the living room with her son, waiting on Mabel to get him for the night. Damian walks up to his mom. "Mama!" He holds his hands out to her.

Riley picks him up when Erik walks in late. He looks irritated and reeks of a sweet-scented perfume. Riley rolls her eyes, not wanting to say anything until Damian had left.

Mabel walks in with a smile; it instantly fades when she feels the tension. "Come talk with me for a second."

Riley looks at Erik who hadn't said one word to her. "Keep an eye on Damian, please?"

Erik huffs and walks into the living room, sitting on the floor with him. She walks outside with Mabel. "You guys still not talking?"

Riley shrugs. "I don't know. I just wish Adam was still here. Things were just so much better with Erik being my friend." Riley breaks down crying. "I just want him back. Not a day goes by that I don't wish things were different."

Mabel hugs Riley. "Honey, you are so unhappy, and it is obvious. I'm going to take Damian for a couple nights. You guys need to sit down and talk."

Riley nods facing the obvious—they weren't supposed to be together. "Okay."

Mabel walks in with Riley, who looked like she had been crying. Mabel picks up Damian and his overnight bag. "Tell, Mama, bye! Say we'll see you in a couple days!"

Riley hugs Damian and kisses his forehead. "I love you, sweetheart!"

Damian smiles and bats his eyes at her. "Love you, Mama. Bye!" He waves and Riley smiles waving to him as they walk out together.

Erik looks up at her from his phone on the couch. "What's wrong with you?"

Riley sighs sitting down, feeling like her best friend was gone.

"We have to talk Erik."

Erik puts his phone down. "Okay what?"

Riley bites her lip. "I'm tired."

Erik shrugs. "So go to bed."

Riley shakes her head. "No that is not what I mean. I mean I am tired of constantly fighting with you. I'm tired of doing this by myself while you go screw everything that walks. I'm tired of us. I just want Adam back!"

Riley's heart shatters after hearing herself.

Erik sits up, staring directly into her eyes. "I think you need help."

Riley stands up irritated. "I do not need help, Erik. I need a divorce! I need my best friend, but I guess that's gone too. Just sign the friggin papers and we will be just fine!"

Erik looks at her hurt. "Wow, Riley."

Riley sighs sitting down. "I can't do this anymore. I just I can't. You know you always have a room here, but I shouldn't have married you. I just can't do this! I can't do *us*."

She pulls her ring off, putting it on the coffee table. "I'm done."

She gets up going into the kitchen and grabs the divorce papers and sets them in front of him. She whispers. "I'm done."

Erik signs the papers and gets up. "I'm going to a friend's house. Have a good night."

Riley stands there alone, watching him go. She crawls into her bed and cries until she can't. She stares at the ceiling. "Why did you have to go?"

She lies there staring at the wall until the sun comes up. The front door opens and closes. She assumes it's Erik and ignores it. Erik walks into their room and starts throwing stuff in a box.

Riley looks toward him not saying a word.

Erik looks at her and sits beside her. "I'm moving out."

Riley ignores him.

"Did you hear me?"

Riley nods. "Then go."

Erik continues grabbing his stuff. "I don't understand you Riley."

Riley sits up. "Just go Erik get your stuff and go. I can take care of my son and myself just fine without you I've done it this entire marriage so just go."

Erik gives her a hurt look. "I'll see you around then."

He walks out with two boxes of his stuff. Riley texts Lindsey, who had become a good friend of hers since Adam passed away.

Lindsey comes over and crawls in bed with her, being a good friend.

"You need to get up out of bed and get a shower."

Riley shakes her head. "I miss him. I want him back."

Lindsey forces her best friend to sit up. "Riley you have got to pull it together because you are getting divorced you are going on the market I have the perfect guy in mind for you!"

Riley looks at her serious. "Who?"

Lindsey smiles. "He's a firefighter and a medic too. His name is Micah."

Riley bites her lip. "Well, okay. I got to get my papers to my lawyer."

Lindsey pulls Riley out of bed. "Get a shower."

Riley gets up and goes to get a shower. She puts on sweatpants, a black shirt, and a light gray jacket. She walks out with Lindsey and goes to her lawyer's office.

She gives her papers to him and had copies made. "Alright Mrs. Carter, you will have a notice whether it is approved or not in a few days."

Riley nods and walks out taking back her last name. She walks out with Lindsey.

Lindsey drives toward the fire department. Riley looks at her confused. "Where are we going? My house is the other way."

Lindsey smirks. "I told you to get dressed."

They pull in. Riley crosses her arms. "Lind's, I look crazy!"

Lindsey giggles. "Just come on!"

Riley sighs getting out and walks in behind Lindsey.

Lindsey takes Riley into the lounge room and smiles perky at Micah. "You know the girl I was telling you about earlier?"

Micah turns to her. Riley's heart skips a beat. He has short sandy hair, is tall and in between pale and tan. He has pretty green eyes.

"Yeah?"

Lindsey smiles excited. "This is her! Riley, this is Micah."

Micah smiles at her. "Hey, nice to meet you finally!"

Riley smiles. "You too." She glares at Lindsey for making her meet somebody when she looked crazy.

Riley and Micah exchange numbers. Lindsey walks off going to talk to Jasper, leaving Riley and Micah alone.

Riley sits on a chair nervously waiting for Lindsey. Micah sits beside her.

"So Lindsey says you were married to Adam."

Riley nods. "Yeah for like a week. Then he was taken away from me. I married my best friend at the time after, who I am currently getting divorced from."

Micah nods in understanding. "So are you sure you really want to get back out there?"

Riley shrugs. "I've been done for about six months. He's cheated for about a year."

Micah nods. "Well, I don't know what she told you about me, but I have a five-year-old daughter, Maliah. Her mother and I are separated. Never married though. I work a lot."

Riley smiles. "I know. I work nights at the hospital in labor and delivery."

The two continue talking. Riley invites him over for the night just to hang out and get to know each other. Lindsey grabs Riley by the arm and they leave.

Riley goes home with Lindsey, and she drags Lindsey in.

"Help! He's coming over tonight."

Lindsey squeals excitedly. She picks a black lace-designed dress for Riley with her boots. Riley styles her hair half up half down, does her makeup and then gets dressed.

Lindsey snaps a pic and sends it to Micah. "I totally just did that."

Micah texts Riley telling her she looks beautiful. Riley smiles. "I hope this works."

Lindsey smiles at her. "Now that is a smile I haven't seen since Adam."

Chapter 46

Riley and Micah have been dating for a couple weeks, but not officially a couple. Micah comes over with his daughter for the first time.

Riley opens the door letting him in, not expecting to meet her. Riley smiles.

"Hey! I'm Riley!"

Maliah smiles. "Hey, I'm Maliah." She looks up at Micah, feeling kind of shy.

Damian runs into the living room so excited and full of energy.

"Daddy, who is that?" Maliah looks at her dad curious.

Riley smiles warmly. "This is my son, Damian."

Maliah walks over to him and sits down with his blocks with him, playing. Micah sits on the couch with Riley, with his arm around her. "So what are the plans for the day?"

Riley shrugs. "At least they get along. She is so pretty!"

Micah smiles. "She is beautiful. I know it's only been two weeks, but I kind of feel like this is right."

Riley nods agreeing. "Me too."

Damian knocks over Maliah's block tower and giggles. Maliah screams. "DADDY!"

Micah looks at his daughter. "What is it, honey?"

Maliah runs over to him. "He knocked down my blocks!"

Riley jumps in. "Sweetheart, he's just a baby. He doesn't know right from wrong just yet."

Riley gets up and walks over to Damian. "Go apologize and give her a hug."

Damian crosses his arms. "Hmph!"

Riley sighs. "Go tell her you are sorry, Damian."

Damian walks over to her and hits Maliah. Riley looks at him shocked. "No, sir! Sit in the corner!"

She picks him up and sits him in the corner facing the wall. Damian screams pitching a fit.

Maliah cries climbing in Micah's lap. Riley squats in front of her. "Hey, want to see something cool?"

Maliah nods sniffing. Riley kisses her arm where Damian hit her. "See, all better now right?"

Maliah nods giggling. "Daddy, she does the same thing you and Mommy do!"

Micah smirks. "She's pretty cool, isn't she?"

Maliah nods. "I like her. Are you going to marry her, Daddy?"

Riley giggles and pokes her nose. "You are silly! Do you want a snack?"

Maliah nods and looks at her dad. "Can I, Daddy?"

Micah nods. "Of course, honey."

Riley takes her hand and goes into the kitchen pulling down some gummies. Maliah runs to her daddy with a packet.

Riley lets Damian get up. "Now go tell her you are sorry and give her a hug."

Damian listens to her. "I'm sorry." He hugs her and then hands her a block.

Maliah gets off the couch and plays with him.

Riley sits beside Micah. He looks at her impressed. "Brownie points for the girl that treats my daughter as her own."

Riley giggles. "She is adorable!"

Maliah runs up to Micah. "Daddy, can we stay the night?"

Micah looks unsure at her. "Let me think about it okay?" Maliah nods and goes back to playing.

Riley looks at him. "You know you are welcome to stay if you want to. I can make her a bed."

Micah shrugs. "Yeah, but I want to do things the right way. I'm not sure her mother would be okay with her being here overnight."

Riley nods understanding. "Yeah, I have to share Damian with Erik even though he isn't really his father. Erik is getting him in the morning for the weekend."

Micah nods thinking. "Maybe I should be here just in case. Okay?"

Riley nods liking the idea, starting to really fall for him. "I think that might be okay."

Maliah runs over to her daddy. "Daddy, I want to spend the night!"

Micah thinks about it. "Let me talk to your mom and we'll see okay?" Maliah nods excited.

"Okay, Daddy!"

Riley smiles. "I think she likes me."

Micah nods agreeing. "Again, a first."

Micah calls Maliah's mother. "Hey, April, quick question."

He walks into the kitchen on the phone with her. Maliah runs over to Riley with Damian. "I hope Mommy says it's okay! I like you."

Riley giggles. "You do?"

Maliah nods. "And we can stay up late and play princesses!"

Riley shows excitement. "No way! That sounds like so much fun!"

Micah points at Maliah. "Mom wants to talk to you." Maliah runs over grabbing the phone. "Mommy! I want to spend the night, please please, Mommy! Ms. Riley is so cool!"

Micah looks at Riley apologetically. "She wants to meet you first. Are you okay with me giving her your address?"

Riley nods. "Of course! She is welcome to come in."

Maliah hands the phone to Micah. Micah talks to her for another few minutes and hangs up. "She is on her way."

Maliah looks sadly at her dad. "I don't want to go to Mommy's house, Daddy!"

Damian chunks a block at Riley hitting her collarbone. Riley bites her lip trying not to be mad or scream. Micah steps in on this one.

"Damian, you can't be throwing things at your mommy. Go hug her."

Damian runs over and hugs her then tries to kiss her where he hit her. "I'm sorry, Mommy!"

Riley smiles; she can't stay mad at her son. "It's okay, sweetheart!" She hugs him and then tickles him. He laughs.

"Mommy, stop!"

Riley giggles. Micah walks out to meet April. Damian pokes her and runs Riley runs slowly toward him. "Oh no, I'm going to get you! What are you going to do?"

Damian runs around giggling. Riley grabs him up and swings him around giggling with him. Maliah runs up to her.

"My turn!"

April walks in hesitantly. Riley smiles warmly, holding Maliah. "Hey, I'm Riley. Nice to meet you!"

Maliah smiles and reaches for her. "MOMMY!"

Riley hands her to April. Micah waits for the tension to start in.

April smiles. "I'm April. My daughter sure seems to love you."

"Well, I'm glad."

"So does her father, so I guess I can make a sacrifice to let her get to know you."

Riley nods. "Girl, she is your daughter. If you don't feel comfortable with her being here, I understand."

April smiles looking at Micah. "Boy, did you catch a good one. I already like her!"

Riley giggles. Maliah hops down. "Mommy, Damian hit Ms. Riley." She points at the mark on Riley's collar bone.

Riley shakes her head. "Sweetheart, I'm okay. He doesn't know better, he's just a baby."

Maliah looks at Micah. "Daddy! Damian hurt her."

April giggles. "If she truly likes you, this is how she acts. Could I have your number?"

Riley nods. "Absolutely!" She gives April her number, and April gets ready to go.

"Well I won't pry anymore. I guess I better get going. You guys have a good night."

Riley nods. "You too! Let us know you got home safely!"

April looks at Micah. "You better not ever leave her. I don't like her. I already love her."

She giggles and hugs Maliah and leaves.

Riley cooks supper and gets the kids fed, bathed, and in bed.

After cleaning up, Micah picks up Riley sitting her on the island counter.

"Now let's take care of you."

Riley giggles a little confused. "With what?"

Micah checks out her collarbone, just in case.

"I'm fine, it's just a block they can't do much."

Micah chuckles. "Love, you have a nasty-looking bruise. I just wanted to be on the safe side."

Riley giggles. "Well, don't you think we should get in bed? Erik will be here early, and Maliah has school, and you have to go to work."

Micah nods. "Yes, we should. You sleep on your bed, and I'll be out here on the couch."

Riley hops down and hugs him. "If you are sure you really want to do that."

Micah nods. "Absolutely."

Riley kisses him goodnight and goes into her room, leaving the door open. She gets into pajama shorts and a tank top then climbs on her bed already falling asleep.

Riley wakes up in the morning to Erik calling her. She answers in a sleepy voice. "Yes?"

She gets up and gets things together for him for Damian.

Micah hears her opening and closing drawers and walks in.

"You okay, love?"

Riley looks up while shoving clothes into Damian's bag.

"Erik's on his way over."

Micah grabs her hands stopping her as she tries rushing.

"What's making you rush?"

Riley looks up with tears in her eyes. "I still have to get him up, dressed, fed, and have him ready to go in about twenty minutes."

Micah puts his hand behind her hear. "I'll get him up and dressed and some breakfast. You get him some clothes and his stuff ready. You aren't doing this alone anymore, Riles."

Riley nods hugging him feeling thankful. "Thank you."

Micah kisses her forehead and gets Damian up.

Riley gets his bag packed and looking organized and walks out putting his bag by the door and looks into the kitchen. She sees Micah with Maliah and Damian playing with them as they eat breakfast.

Riley walks into the kitchen as the kids finish eating. Micah looks up at her smiling. "He's all ready!"

Erik walks in minutes after. He looks at Riley annoyed. "Where is his stuff?"

Riley points at the door. "It's ready to go." Erik glances and then double takes seeing Maliah and Micah.

"Who is this? Why is he around Damian?"

Riley crosses her arms. "He is my boyfriend, and that is his daughter."

Erik sees the bruise on her collarbone. "Did he do that?"

Riley looks irritated. "Actually, no. Damian chunked a block at me."

Erik looks at Damian. "Did you hurt Mommy?"

Damian giggles and nods. "Yah!"

Erik shakes his head. "No, we don't hurt Mommy. Did you give her kisses and hugs and tell her you are sorry?"

Damian nods. "Yah!"

Micah walks over to Riley putting his hand on her back. "Well, I'm Micah."

Erik shakes his hand. "We'll get along as long as you don't hurt her."

Riley rolls her eyes. "Yup." She hugs Damian. "I love you, sweetheart. Have fun with Daddy."

Damian hugs her and kisses her cheek. "Love you too, bye!" He waves.

Erik picks up Damian. "We'll be back Sunday night." He walks out with Damian.

Micah looks at Riley. "I didn't realize that was him."

Riley nods. "Unfortunately."

April comes by picking up Maliah for school. She hugs Riley.

"Thank you for treating her no different than your own."

Riley hugs her back, shocked. "Girl, I adore her. She is awesome."

Maliah hugs Riley. "Bye, Ms. Riley!" They leave.

Micah looks at her apologetically; he is already in his work clothes.

"I don't want to leave you alone," he says.

Riley smiles and hugs him, feeling the most loving touch she had ever felt. "I know you have to work . . . it's okay."

He kisses her. "I'll be back tonight. I love you."

Riley nods and kisses him back. "I love you too. Let me know when you get there."

Riley walks around the house, cleaning it up. Mabel texts her asking her to come in for the day shift and take tomorrow night off. Riley agrees and changes into navy-colored scrubs and leaves for work.

When she gets there, she texts Micah letting him know. He replies with "Good. Have a good day love, see you tonight."

Riley sees there are only three patients; she checks the monitors. She walks to Room 3 where the patient delivered an hour ago. She checks her uterus.

"Is there anything you need?"

Mrs. Jones shakes her head. "No, thank you though!"

Riley nods and walks out to the next room. "Hey, I'm Riley. How are you feeling?"

She gets all the questions out of the way and checks dilation. "What is your pain level?"

Mrs. Clearwater smiles cheerful. "Great! I just got the epidural."

Riley smiles warmly. "Good! And you are a seven!"

She walks out and goes to the last patient who had already delivered the day before. She gets vitals and looks at the new mom breastfeeding her infant. She smiles.

"Do you need anything? Are you hurting?" asks Riley.

Mrs. Davenport shakes her head. "No, ma'am, thank you!"

Riley smiles. "Okay if you need anything, just let me know."

She walks out and goes to the desk and watches her one room. Mabel walks over to her.

"Could you possibly switch to days to work with me?"

Riley nods. "Absolutely!"

She sees a drop in the baby's heart rate and jumps up. "Come with me. The baby's rate is dropping." She goes into the room.

"Mrs. Jones, how are you feeling?"

Mrs. Jones looks a little pale. "I don't really feel too good."

Riley checks her vitals and gets a low heart rate. "Alright, let's move!"

She unlocks the wheels and takes the patient to C-section.

Riley keeps the patient calm while Mabel delivers and stitches the patient back up. Riley holds the patient's hand as she is scared.

"Everything will be just fine," says Riley.

Riley talks about the beach with her. Mabel finishes.

"Mrs. Jones, you did really good. Let's get you to recovery." Riley takes the patient to recovery.

Riley gets a text from Micah asking how her day is going, now that it is almost over. Riley smiles texting him back with good pretty slow.

Mabel leans over the desk. "I haven't seen that smile in a long time. What's going on?"

Riley smiles realizing she hadn't told them. "My divorce is finalized, and I've been dating a guy from the station. He and his daughter stayed over last night. I met her mom. It's been going really good!"

Mabel looks at the bruise on her collarbone. "What is that from?"

Riley sighs. "My son and his attitude."

Mabel shakes her head. "No, no. Damian and I are going to have a little talk when he comes home from Erik's."

Riley nods. "Micah got onto him."

Mabel smiles. "I want to meet him. I'm sure your father would like to as well. You guys come over for supper?"

Riley hugs her. "Of course!" She clocks out and walks out to her car with Mabel. She gets in and drives home.

Riley gets out and goes up the stairs, as she steps on the middle stair, it collapses and she hears a crunch. Before the pain shoots up her leg. She screams falling.

She texts Micah asking if he was on his way home.

Micah calls her. "Hey, I'm leaving the station. Do you need anything before I come home?"

Riley can't hold back the tears. "I'm stuck!"

"What do you mean are you okay?"

He hears Riley crying on the other end. "No, I fell through the stairs, and I'm stuck."

Micah hangs up and flies there. He gets out running over to her.

"Hey are you okay?"

Riley has tears rolling down her face. "Just fix it!"

Micah looks down seeing bone poke out of her ankle. He makes an *ouch* face.

"Just don't try to kill me because you are about to hate me."

Riley nods. "Call my brother!" She hands him her phone.

Micah calls Kasey telling him what's going on. Kasey flies up in the driveway.

"I know it's not a good thing, just get it out."

Kasey looks in the hole and sees the bone. "Oh, Riles."

Micah and Kasey work together to get her out as quickly and easily as possible and set her ankle.

Riley holds her breath, trying not to scream.

"We got to go to the hospital, Riles." Riley puts her arm around Micah's shoulder. He picks her up putting her in his truck.

Chapter 47

Riley has surgery right there at the hospital and has her ankle basically reconstructed. They put her in a cast and on crutches.

Riley is discharged to go home. Micah helps her inside and to their bed. "You know you can't be alone. Why don't I just stay with you until you're better?"

Riley nods liking that idea. "And I'm now out of work for eight weeks."

Micah nods agreeing. "You are going to lose your mind."

Riley giggles amused. "I sure am."

Riley picks up her phone. "I want to tell Damian goodnight. Erik never puts him in bed early."

Micah takes the phone calling Erik.

"Hey, Riles wants to talk to Damian."

"Well, sorry she isn't the one on the phone."

Micah looks at her. "Look, I don't know what your issue is. Riley just got home from the hospital and just wants to talk to her son. She just got out of surgery."

"A C-section?"

Micah sighs. "No, she broke her ankle."

Erik is walking in a few minutes later. "Did he hurt you?"

Riley jumps. "No! I fell through the stairs, I guess it was just rotten. He saved me because I was more freaked out about bugs than I was about falling. But you know, at least it was me and not Damian."

Erik nods agreeing. "So I have a girlfriend staying the night. Damian loves her."

Riley nods. "And I live with my boyfriend. What's your point?"

Micah hands Riley a plate with a pork chop, green beans, and mashed potatoes. Riley shakes her head. "I'm not hungry."

Micah pulls up a fold-out table beside her. "Hungry or not you have to eat so you can get meds in your system."

Erik smiles at Micah. "Hey, I like him."

Riley shakes her head no. "I don't want anything."

Micah crosses his arms. Riley sighs and eats half the plate. Micah takes her plate and walks away with Erik behind him.

"I like you. You are good to her."

Micah nods. "Yeah, well I do have a daughter that doesn't like eating either. You find ways."

Riley hears the two of them laughing and talking in the kitchen. Riley gets up to go join them and slips in the hallway. She falls and sits in the hallway irritated.

Micah looks around the corner and sees her.

"Are you okay, love?"

Riley shakes her head no. "No, I'm not okay!"

Micah gets her in bed and gives her some meds.

Erik leaves shortly after, and Micah gets in bed with her and goes to sleep.

Chapter 48

Riley is having her cast taken off and being put in a boot. No more crutches. She walks toward Micah, feeling like a new person. Micah smiles at her. "Feel different?"

Riley smiles. "Absolutely!"

She gets in the car with him and they drive home. Riley gets out with him excited and goes inside. Erik is sitting on the couch with April and the kids. Riley looks between both of them confused.

"What are you guys doing in my house?"

Erik shrugs. "I had to bring Damian by to get some stuff. April called me, so I told her to come by. Nice to know somebody who was with Micah before."

Riley crosses her arms. "Okay, well go on."

Erik stands up taking her hand. "Actually, could you keep Damian tonight?"

Riley rolls her eyes. "Sure. Bye!"

Erik walks out with April.

Maliah walks out of Damian's bedroom with a toy, and Damian follows behind her carrying blocks.

Riley takes the back of blocks from him. "Daddy had to go do somethings tonight, so your stuck with me tonight."

Damian nods. "Okay, Mommy."

He slings the bag over his shoulder and walks out into the living room and plays with Maliah in the living room. Riley smiles watching them. Micah sits on the floor, building towers with them.

Riley snaps pictures of them. After a couple hours, she sends both kids to bed and gets in bed with Micah, feeling tired.

"We both have to work tomorrow night."

Micah nods. "Yeah. Is Erik taking Damian?"

Riley shrugs. "If not, I'll ask Derek."

Chapter 49

After some years have passed, Maliah is now thirteen and Damian, ten. Micah and Riley are still together, married and happy. Riley is still a labor and delivery nurse.

Riley walks into the living room, where Damian is doing his homework, and Maliah is playing on her phone.

"Maliah is your homework done?"

Maliah rolls her eyes ignoring her.

"Maliah!"

Micah walks in from the kitchen. "Maliah, do we have a problem?"

Maliah looks at her dad and then to her phone. "No."

Micah walks over to her, taking the phone. "Thank you. Riley is talking to you."

Maliah huffs, crossing her arms. "What?"

Riley sighs, irritated. "Is your homework done?"

Maliah shrugs. "Mom and Erik aren't like this."

She stomps up the stairs to her room. Riley looks at Damian as he finishes his math homework and sticks it in his backpack.

"Done."

He walks into his room. Riley rolls her eyes and looks at Micah. "Attitudes! Ugh!"

Micah nods. "Of course. I'm going to go talk to Maliah."

Riley nods. She sits down on the floor and pulls out her laptop, studying up for a test she has to take for work. Erik walks in the door, shutting it lightly.

Riley jumps when he touches her shoulder. "Lord, dude! Don't scare me like that!"

Erik chuckles. "Sorry, is everything okay? Maliah texted and said she wanted to come home tonight."

Riley rolls her eyes shutting her laptop. "MALIAH!"

Micah and Maliah walk over to the rail. "What?"

Riley looks up and gets up, crossing her arms. "Why do you want to go home tonight?"

Maliah's face turns red, scared of being in trouble. "I don't know."

Erik sits on the couch. "Let's talk."

Maliah sighs and stomps down the stairs with Micah behind her. "What?"

Damian walks out of his room and turns back around, then goes back in seeing the meeting they are having.

Riley focuses on Maliah. "What is your problem tonight?"

Maliah sighs. "Mom said I could go hang out with my friends tonight."

Riley bites her lip. "Really? So if I call her, she's going to say that?"

Maliah looks between her parents and slumps. "No."

Micah and Erik walk outside with her, talking. Damian walks into the living room. "She wants to go see her boyfriend, Mom."

Riley shakes her head. "No. Have you eaten?"

Damian nods. "Yes, ma'am. Mom, I have a question."

Riley sits down with him. "What's that?"

Damian gets a big smile. "Can I go see Grandma Mabel and Grandpa Derek tonight?"

Riley thinks for a second. "Let me ask Dad and we'll see, okay?"

Damian nods. "Thank you, Mama."

Micah and Erik walk back in with Maliah. "Go up to your room. Until I'm ready to talk to you."

Maliah stomps up the stairs. "I'm telling Mom."

Riley turns to both Erik and Micah. "Damian wants to go spend the night with Mabel. I told him we would talk and see."

Erik shrugs. "Have you talked to them yet?"

Riley shakes her head no. Micah shrugs. "I guess, it's okay."

Riley texts Mabel asking. Mabel calls. "Let me talk to him."

"Damian, Grandma Mabel wants to talk to you."

Damian runs out of his room taking the phone. Riley sits on the couch bored.

Maliah walks down the stairs quietly, trying to sneak into the kitchen.

Riley catches her out of the corner of her eye. "Maliah, were you told to come out?"

Micah and Erik look at Riley.

"What?"

Micah crosses his arms. "How did you know she came down?"

Riley looks behind her. "I saw her."

Maliah's jaw drops. "You can see from the back of your head!"

Riley smirks and points at the stairs. Maliah sighs, going back up them.

Erik smiles. "How times have changed."

Riley giggles and sits crisscrossed on the couch. "Sure have."

She looks at Micah. "I have a question to ask you."

Micah looks to her waiting for her to ask. "Yes?"

Riley smiles a big smile. "So I've been thinking—"

Erik cuts her off laughing. "Riley thinking? Did your brain smoke?"

Riley glares. "Oh, come on! I didn't even ask yet!"

Micah chuckles. "Well, get it out."

Riley smiles. "I want to go for my EMT."

Micah and Erik laugh together. "Now that is a good one."

Riley looks at them serious. "I'm not joking, I want to get my EMT and go to the fire department."

She looks at both of them staring at her.

Chapter 50

Micah shakes his head. "No, that's too dangerous for you."

Riley sighs. "No, it's not."

Micah laughs. "Sweetheart, if that's what you want to do, then I say go for it. You know I'll support you one hundred percent."

Riley smiles feeling excited. "Really?"

Micah nods. "Absolutely."

She jumps up hugging him. "Thank you!"

Erik looks at her. "You're going to stay at the hospital until you leave, right?"

Riley nods. "Sure am!"

She texts Lindsey telling her that Micah is going to let her go to school to get her certifications to become an EMT. Lindsey texts her back saying she needed to volunteer first, see how she liked it before doing that.

Riley replies with, "then let me."

She looks up at Micah with a smirk, waiting for him to get a text. Micah looks at her a little worried. "What?"

Riley smiles. "Oh nothing." Damian walks out with her phone.

"Aunt Natalie is coming to get me. And Grandma Mabel said if it was okay with you and Daddy and Daddy Micah that Maliah could come over too."

Riley looks at Erik. "That's your call."

Erik looks at Micah. "Technically she is here, so it is your call."

"Maliah?"

Maliah walks over to the rail of the stairs. "Yes?"

"Would you like to go over to Grandma Mabel's house tonight?"

Maliah gets excited. "Yes!"

Riley looks up at her. "Well go get your bag ready. Aunt Natalie is on the way to pick up you and Damian."

Maliah and Damian take off to their rooms.

Micah looks up at his wife. "So a medic, huh?"

Riley smirks and runs off into their room.

Erik and Micah talk about Riley and the fire department.

Natalie knocks on the door before walking in. "The best aunt in the world is here to get the kiddos!"

Damian and Maliah run down to her. "Bye, Mom! Love you!"

"Love you too, son! You too, Maliah."

"Yup, bye!"

They leave with Natalie. Lindsey shows up not too long after the kids leave.

"Riley boo!"

Riley runs into the living room and tackles her best friend. "Lindsey!"

They both giggle. "I miss your face!"

Lindsey nods agreeing. "Right? Jas said you can go on a ride along with me tonight? If the hubby approves."

Riley looks at Micah pleading. "Pleeaaseee?"

Micah laughs. "I guess. Just be careful."

Riley jumps up and changes into jeans and a gray T-shirt. She walks out with Lindsey and gets in the car with her. They drive to the station.

Chapter 51

Riley gets out and goes inside the fire department with Lindsey. Alyssa looks up at Riley and double takes. "What are you doing here?"

Lindsey rolls her eyes at Alyssa. "Lyss, she'll ride along with me tonight. Jas said it was fine."

Alyssa calls Kasey. "I'm telling your brother."

Riley shrugs. "So?"

Alyssa hands the phone to Riley after telling him. "Hey, buhbah."

"You're doing what?"

Riley giggles. "Yeah."

"Watch Lyss for me, make sure she stays safe and you stay safe. I love you, Riles."

"Love you too." She hands the phone to Alyssa smiling. "I was put in charge of your safety."

Alyssa's jaw drops taking the phone back. "Fine, I'm calling Dad."

Riley's eyes widen. "No."

Alyssa nods walking away.

Lindsey looks at Riley. "So are you ready for this? Nights can get crazy. He said if you do well tonight, you can do a ride along on the trucks tomorrow."

Riley nods excited. "Of course!"

The first tone drops for a CPR in progress. Lindsey grabs Riley, shoving her in the front seat. "How are you with loses?"

Riley shrugs. "I guess I'm okay."

Lindsey nods. "Well, get ready just in case."

Alyssa hops in then looking at Riley; she feels smashed. "This is going to be an enjoyable night. And Dad is mad at you, and Mom said you are in trouble."

Riley sighs. "Oh well." They take off to the call.

Lindsey hands Riley the board to fill out before grabbing the medical bag. They walk into a house, with a teenage-looking girl who appears to be on drugs, unconscious, and a young man freaking out.

"She just dropped. I don't know what happened," cried the young man.

Lindsey nods hooking her up to an AED. "Alright, Riles, start CPR."

Riley starts CPR. "Clear."

Riley steps back. Lindsey shocks the girl getting a heartbeat. They get her on a gurney and into the ambulance. "Get in the back with Lyss. She can teach you some things."

Riley gets in the back as Lindsey drives. Riley starts an IV on Alyssa's count. They get the girl hooked up to oxygen, and they hit her with Narcan. "Get ready for the violence."

The girl regains consciousness almost instantly and starts screaming trying to yank out the IV.

Riley stares like she had never seen anything like it before.

They get to the hospital rather quickly, and Alyssa has Riley help unload the girl and take her in. Kasey walks over to Alyssa. "Riles doing okay?"

Alyssa giggles. "She looked terrified."

Kasey chuckles, taking over. Riley gets in the front seat with Lindsey. The tone drops for a roll over wreck. They fly to the scene. Lindsey hops out with Riley and has Alyssa stand back on this one. She guides Riley through things.

Riley climbs in through the window, checking for a pulse as Lindsey had instructed her to. When she gets the patient out, she crawls back through the glass, cutting her arm.

"Ow!"

She takes a breath and looks, seeing a gash with blood.

Lindsey grabs her arm. "Lord, Micah is going to kill me, you have to get checked out."

Riley shakes her head. "I'm good."

Chapter 52

Riley has her certifications and is now working on the fire department with Lindsey as her new partner overnight. Riley walks in cheerfully for the start of their shift.

Lindsey hugs her, excited. "Girl, I cannot wait for our shift!"

Riley giggles. "Me either!"

They go into the lounge room. Micah looks up at his wife. "You get to work with us both tonight!"

Riley smirks. "I know."

They are toned for a house fire. Lindsey grabs Riley, and they hop on the ambulance. They fly there behind the fire trucks. They arrive to a large house on fire. Lindsey gets out with Riley, and they get ready for the first patient.

Chase walks over to Riley. "You are going in. I need you as a firefighter at this exact moment."

Riley nods and suits up. Lindsey hugs her. "Go show up Micah, girl."

Riley giggles going in with Chase. They search the top floor and Riley steps wrong, and almost goes through the floor. Chase catches her. "Micah would be livid if anything happened to you."

Riley nods agreeing. They continue to the next room. "Fire department call out."

Nobody answers. All of a sudden the door slams shut behind them, and Chase can't get it open. The start of a back draft begins. Chase looks at Riley. Riley has fear in her eyes and begins to freak.

"We have to go. How do you feel about going through a window?"

Riley looks out the window and down. About a good ten-foot drop. She looks at Chase shaking her head. "You've lost your mind."

"Hey, guys, were trapped."

Riley looks at Chase nervous. "The floor. What about the floor?"

Chase looks down, finding a weak spot. They both stomp it through, and Chase grabs Riley jumping down. Riley hits the second floor hard, knocking the breath out of her.

"Sorry. We have to move."

Jasper comes over the radio. "Chase, I need you guys out now—that roof is coming in."

Chase grabs Riley's hand. "We have to get to the basement."

They find the hole in the floor and, again Chase grabs Riley jumping down to the basement.

Chase shoves Riley out the door and goes out behind her.

Riley walks over with Chase to the ambulance. "She might need medical attention. She took a good hit."

Riley pulls off her turnouts. Lindsey watches Riley close.

"How did you guys get trapped?"

Riley shrugs. "The door shut behind us, back draft, went through the floor twice."

Lindsey looks at her shocked. "You did what?"

Riley nods. "Yeah."

Lindsey bites her lip. "Micah was called in he is going to be livid."

Riley giggles. "He'll be fine."

Lindsey shakes her head, watching an angry Micah walk toward them. "You got a choice. Pretend we have a call or face him."

Riley jumps in the back of the ambulance and shuts the doors. Lindsey shrugs and gets in the driver's seat and turns around leaving with lights on.

She takes off to the station and figures they'll just take the heat for leaving later. Riley pops up in the window. "So he saw that?"

Lindsey nods. "We all did."

Riley nods waiting on the call from Micah. Instead she gets a text from him asking if she's okay. She calls him.

"Hey, sweetheart are you okay?"

Riley bites her lip. "Yes why?"

"You guys took off pretty fast we didn't hear a tone."

Riley looks at Lindsey thinking.

"Yeah, we're good. We're just on standby."

"Okay. I love you."

"I love you too." She hangs up as they pull into the station.

Riley hops out when they park and sits on the step on the back. Lindsey walks around to her. "Everything okay?"

Riley nods. "Yeah, I just told him we were on standby."

Lindsey sits by her. "So no heat?"

Riley shakes her head with a smile. "No, no heat."

Chapter 53

Riley is asleep sitting in the ambulance at the fire. Micah comes over opening the door. Riley jumps as she falls out.

"Shit!"

Micah looks at her oddly and laughs. "Wake up. We're being toned for a wreck. Lindsey wants to stay here in case she is needed. Do you want me to go with you?"

Riley nods, half asleep. "I didn't realize she even got out. Yah, let's go."

Micah gets in the driver's seat and drives to the scene. When they get there, there is a car flipped and a truck that appears to be the one that hit them. Riley gets out, grabs the medical bag, and walks over with Micah. Nobody seems to be in sight.

The driver of the truck walks up. "They got out and ran. I don't know where they went."

Micah nods. "Well are you okay, sir?"

The man nods. They hear gun shots coming toward them. Micah grabs Riley shoving her to the other side of the ambulance and calls it in. Riley sits by the tire a little freaked.

"Well this is a first."

Micah holds a finger in front of his lips as if he were saying *shh*. The man that hit them sits on the other side of Riley. "Are you okay?"

Riley nods. "Yeah, why would I not be?"

A man walks out of the woods, before Riley notices the man is in her face grabbing her up.

"Micah!"

The man points the gun at her. Micah jumps up ready to fight for her. "Let her go!"

Riley feels a big ball of emotions hit her all at once. The guy with the gun smiles. "Give me the keys."

Riley freezes up. Micah shakes his head no. "I can't do that."

The guy moves the gun to her head. "Give me the keys."

Micah hands them to the guy. He shoves Riley in the ambulance and drives off with her still holding her at gunpoint. Riley thinks of Damian and Maliah.

"You are going to help me."

Riley nods. "Okay, well what's wrong?"

The man pulls off into the woods. Inside she feels like she's in a horror movie, and on the outside, she is as calm as can be. "My friend was shot. I was trying to get him to the hospital."

Riley nods. The man yanks her out of the ambulance and then realization hits her. The voice was familiar, but the face wasn't. It was Liam.

He pulls her a mile into the woods to a house. He walks behind her and shoves her in. She sees a man that looked pale on the couch. She feels for a pulse.

The man was shot in the arm. But has a good pulse. She finds the bullet. She pulls it out and cleans him then stitches him up and wraps it up.

Liam looks at her shocked. "I know you are still afraid of me. Why is that?"

Riley shrugs. "Maybe because of the fact that you are still holding a gun at me?"

Her phone rings. She hands it to him. "It's probably for you."

Liam yanks it from her and answers it.

"Let her go, Liam. She didn't do anything."

"I can't do that. Not until she tells me why she is scared of me."

"Just put the gun down and let her walk out."

Liam gets irritated and throws her phone on the floor shattering the screen. Riley jumps. Liam grabs her by her hair and drags her outside.

"IF YOU WANT HER COME AND GET HER!"

He drags her back in. "You aren't going anywhere."

Liam sits on the couch talking to the other guy. While he's not paying attention, she tries to make a run for the door. Before she can open it, he's grabbing her.

"Where do you think you are going?"

The other guy gets up. "Liam, you are taking this too far. Let her go."

Riley recognizes the voice as well.

"Shut up, Sloan."

Riley looks through the darkness at a guy she thought was her friend so long ago.

"Sloan?"

The guy turns to her. Liam duck-tapes her hands and feet together. "Try to run now."

Riley huffs. "I'll get out of here without you."

Liam turns to her and hits her, knocking her out. "Now maybe you won't talk back."

Chapter 54

Riley wakes up, taped to a chair and with tape over her mouth. Sloan is sitting beside her and whispers, "He is on drugs, he shot me. I wouldn't test him."

Riley nods. Sloan looks at her, feeling bad. "They are going to save you, Riley."

Liam walks back into the kitchen where she is duck-taped. "Looks like you aren't going to be going anywhere soon, Riley. I disconnected the GPS on your ambulance."

All of a sudden, the cops come busting in the door with guns. Liam runs through the house hiding. When the first officer walks around the corner, he finds her.

Riley looks at them. The deputy calls for an ambulance and clears detectives as his partner continues past Riley. The deputy pulls the tape off her mouth and whispers to her.

"Are you okay?"

Riley nods. "He ran behind me."

A couple other deputies walk past her, covering each other. They find him arresting him and clear for the paramedics to come in. They take the tape off her wrists and ankles and walk out with her.

When she gets to the ambulance, Micah and Erik are standing there with Lindsey. Micah hugs her tight.

"I'm sorry! I didn't even see him!"

Riley nods. "Me either. Until he was right on me." She hugs him back.

"I'm okay, Micah. I mean my head is pounding, but I'm okay." She sits on the steps of the ambulance. "I am just ready to go home."

Micah shakes his head. "Oh no, you are going to the hospital." He checks her pupils. She has a pretty good concussion.

"Yeah, you are going to the hospital."

Lindsey holds a mirror up to her. Riley sees a nice-sized bruise on the side of her head.

"Well that's a honker."

Lindsey giggles. "A honker?"

Riley nods amused. "Yup, a honker."

Chapter 55

They get her to the hospital and checked out then home.

Riley is asleep on her bed. Micah walks in to check on her, with Damian.

"Dad, Mom looks like she doesn't feel good."

Micah sits on the side of her. "She probably doesn't, son. She took quite a hit."

Riley opens her eyes, with her head pounding; she squeezes them shut. "Ohhh . . . make it go away! I feel hung over!"

Micah laughs. "Damian wanted to come check on you, love."

Riley opens an eye and looks at her son. "I'm okay, sweetheart, just tired."

Damian nods and hugs her. "I love you, Mama."

Riley smiles. "I love you too." She hugs him back.

Damian walks out of the room to go tell everybody that she is okay.

Micah meets her eyes. "How are you feeling?" Riley shrugs.

"Feel like coming out into the living room? Mabel, Derek, Kasey, and Lindsey are out there wanting to see you."

Riley nods and sits up, feeling dizzy. She grabs his hand. "Okay, let's do this."

Micah chuckles and walks with her into the living room. Her whole world is spinning, and she feels like she's drunk. She looks at everybody, sitting down.

"Oh, how are you guys awake?"

Mabel giggles and hugs her. "We just wanted to check on you. I mean it is like ten in the morning."

Riley rubs her eyes. "In the morning? I went home at ten in the morning."

Micah shrugs. "Love, you've been asleep for a couple days."

Riley looks at him shocked. "Alright then."

Kasey hugs his sister. "Don't ever scare me like that!"

Riley giggles. "Me, scare you? Yeah, okay!"

He chuckles. "Get some rest, you look exhausted."

Riley nods. "Just a little."

Micah holds out his hand. "If you want to lie down, go on." Riley takes it and goes into their room lying back in bed. She then falls asleep.

Chapter 56

Riley wakes up a couple hours later and goes into the living room to find Micah. Derek and Kasey look up at her from their phones.

"Hey, sweetheart, how are you feeling?"

Riley sits beside her brother and looks at Derek. "Okay, I guess. Where is Micah and Damian?"

"Micah got called in, and Damian is with Erik and April, everything okay?"

Riley nods. "Yeah, just curious."

She crisscrosses her legs, then picks up her phone from the coffee table. Kasey stares at his sister, watching her.

"You sure?"

Riley nods. "Yeah, why wouldn't I be?"

"You just look a little pale."

Riley shrugs. "I'm sure."

Kasey and Derek text each other about Riley, and how she looks. Riley decides to get up to get something to eat, feeling dizzy and blacking out a little. She gets in the kitchen and makes a turkey and cheese sandwich.

Before she can even take a bite of it, she blacks out hitting the floor. Kasey jumps up hearing the plate shatter and the thud. "Riles, are you okay?"

When she doesn't answer, he looks at Derek and they both run into the kitchen finding her on the floor with a shattered plate next to her and the sandwich everywhere.

Derek looks at Kasey, growing concerned. "Last time she did this, she was pregnant with complications."

They move her to the couch, getting her legs higher than her head.

Derek sits beside her, while Kasey calls Micah. "Hey listen is there any chance Riles could be pregnant?"

"I don't think so, but I guess there could be she's on pills now," says Micah.

Kasey hangs up.

Riley wakes up, feeling her head pounding. She looks at Derek, with a concerned expression. "What?"

Derek sits on the coffee table in front of her and meets her eyes. "Is there any way you could be pregnant again?"

Riley sits up. "No, absolutely not, why?"

Kasey walks into the living room. "Micah said there is a slight chance."

Riley looks at both of them confused. "Would somebody tell me what is going on?"

Kasey sits beside his sister. "You passed out."

Riley shrugs. "And I also haven't had food in two days?"

Kasey nods taking that into consideration. "Yeah, but Derek said last time you passed out you were pregnant."

Riley nods. "And? That was like way before Damian. Like a year before Damian."

"Do you think you could be again?"

Riley gets up. "No, I'm not. I'm just starving."

She walks into the kitchen realizing how bad that sounds and makes a bowl of cereal instead eating it. Kasey and Derek walk in and sit in front of her.

She looks up at them. "Just to clarify, I am not pregnant. I have an IUD. I'm good."

Kasey crosses his arms. "Really because Micah said you had pills."

Riley hops up. "I'm calling Mom!"

She looks at Derek annoyed, and walks into the living room calling Mabel.

She answers. "Honey, I'm in the middle of something right now can you talk to your father about whatever it is?"

Riley huffs. "He is the whatever it is."

Mabel sighs on the other end. "Here, I have Erik beside me. I'll tell him what to tell you."

Erik takes over the call. "What's up, Riles?"

Riley rolls her eyes. "This is not a me and you conversation."

Erik chuckles. "Sure, it is. What's up?"

Riley sighs. "Derek and Kasey are harassing me trying to tell me I'm pregnant which I most definitely am not."

She hears Erik laughing harder. "Are you sure?"

She looks a little annoyed. "Yes, I am sure! What kind of question is that?"

"Well when was the last—"

Riley cuts him off. "Don't even finish that because I am not talking about this with you. I want to talk to my mom."

"I'll have her call you back. Okay?"

Riley sighs. "You guys had to leave me with the two worriers? Okay."

She hangs up and looks up to Kasey and Derek staring at her.

"What?"

Chapter 57

Riley is waiting for three hours for Mabel to call her back, so she texts Erik asking.

Erik calls her. "I'm on my way. There she is in a C-section right now."

Riley sighs. "And I get stuck with all three of you. Peachy." She hangs up sitting on the couch texting Micah saying she absolutely dislikes him for leaving her with Derek and Kasey.

Erik walks in with a smirk on his face. Riley looks up at him. "What?"

"Mabel wants you to come to the hospital."

Riley rolls her eyes not moving. "Can we not today? I look homeless, I feel gross, and I do not want to move."

Erik laughs. "Come on, it won't take long, I promise."

Riley gets up rolling her eyes and goes into her room changing into sea-green shorts and a white T-shirt that clings to her skin. She slips on her blue tennis shoes. She throws her hair up and walks out of her room.

"Okay, fine."

She walks out to Erik's car huffy.

Erik and Kasey laugh. "She is so pregnant."

Erik gets in the car with her with the same smirk on her face. She looks at him oddly, and they drive to the hospital.

Riley walks with Erik to the labor and delivery floor, finding Mabel at the desk. Mabel smiles. "Oh good, you're both here. Erik, take Room 3. Riley, come with me."

Riley giggles. "Totally rhymes."

Erik smiles and mumbles. "Totally pregnant." He walks off.

Riley goes with Mabel to her office. "So you're one hundred percent sure you aren't pregnant?"

Riley looks away. "Well no, but I have the IUD."

Mabel nods. "Yup."

Mabel opens her door to her office and walks over to her desk typing in something. Riley watches her sitting in a chair.

"Mom, I'm not pregnant."

A nurse walks into her office. "You needed me?"

Mabel nods. "I need an ultrasound and blood work with a urine sample on her."

Riley feels like a child again, rolling her eyes to go with the nurse for a blood work and the urine sample first as well as vitals. They take her to the ultrasound and don't find the IUD.

Riley is taken back into Mabel's office.

Mabel looks up at Riley. "Riley, are you sure you didn't have it removed last year?"

Riley thinks for a second and gets an *oh-shit* look.

"Yup, I think I did."

Mabel nods. "Taking your pills?"

Riley shakes her head no.

"Well, when was your last cycle, Riles?"

Riley thinks for a second. "Like six years ago, Mom."

Mabel looks up from her computer at her adopted daughter. "And you didn't think to mention this?"

Riley shrugs. "No? I was on the IUD."

Mabel shrugs. "So you decided 'oh well I'm just going to get pregnant again'? 'Oh well, Mom doesn't have to know everything'?"

Riley bites her lip looking at her. "No, ma'am."

Mabel looks irritated at her. "Well guess what, you're negative. But I think with everything going on, you need a couple weeks off and a week of rest."

Riley stares at her like she's looking through a wall. "No way!"

Mabel texts Derek telling him. "You better be glad you aren't under my roof, young lady. When you get home, I want you on bed rest for a week. Understand?"

Riley nods. "Yes, ma'am."

Mabel walks to the door. "In the car. Now."

Riley walks out going to Mabel's car getting in. Mabel drives her home and gets out walking in with her.

"You know you don't have to walk in with me."

They walk into the living room arguing.

Mabel stops and looks at Riley. "Just stop, Riley! Lose your attitude!"

Riley turns to face her. "I'm capable of taking care of myself." She then goes into her room, slamming the door.

Kasey and Derek look at the door then to Mabel.

"No, she is not pregnant, but I told her she needed rest."

Riley yells back. "I DO WHAT I WANT!"

Micah walks in, feeling the tension. His smile fades. "Okay, what did my wife do, and I thought you were at work?"

Mabel tells him everything. Micah goes into their room, closing the door behind him.

"Love?"

Riley looks at him from the bed. "I don't need babysitters you know."

Micah hugs her. "I'm sorry I just wanted to make sure somebody was here if you needed help."

Riley nods. "I just, I'm tired . . . tired of having issues."

Micah laughs. "Things happen. Life happens. We'll get through them together. Remember through the whispers in the wind I'll be there till the end."

Riley smiles thinking of Adam, but things don't hurt as bad. She had a wonderful husband and father to her son.

"I love you."

Chapter 58

Riley sits outside on the porch swing, staring into the woods. Micah walks outside and sits by her. "Love, why don't you come in? It's two in the morning. Everybody is getting ready to leave."

Riley shrugs. "Just thinking."

"About what?"

Riley shrugs again.

Micah meets her hazel eyes. "You can talk to me, you know. Nobody blames you for isolating yourself. We all understand that what you went through was traumatic."

Riley nods. "You know he was my abusive ex? He was before Erik. Like way before Erik. Like when I didn't exist to Kasey before."

Micah nods. "I know, sweetheart, but everybody is inside wanting to see how you are doing and wanting to spend time with you to keep you from shutting down."

Riley nods. "I know, but I just need time alone to process everything."

Micah takes her hand. "I won't let you be alone. Maybe we could talk to a therapist. Maybe that would help."

Riley looks at him taking it the wrong way. "I can't believe you would ever say that."

She gets up walking in with Micah grabbing her hand in the living room. "Riley, that isn't what I meant, and you know that!"

Riley yanks her hand away. "Yeah." She goes into her room locking herself in. Everybody stares at him.

Erik sighs. "What did you say to her?" He walks to the door knocking. "Riles?"

Riley sits by the door wanting to be alone. "What?"

The doorknob twists from Erik trying to get in. "Can I come talk to you?"

Riley shakes her head. "No, just let me be."

Micah uses a butter knife to get into her bedroom. Then he sits beside her. "I'm sorry. I just thought that maybe talking would make you feel better."

Riley hugs him. "I just want to go to bed."

Micah nods. "Well let's go." She takes his hand getting up and gets in bed. She lays her head on his chest and closes her eyes.

"I love you."

Micah smiles putting his arm around her. "I love you too."

Chapter 59

Riley wakes up from a call from Lindsey. She rubs her eyes seeing it's still dark out.

"Hello?"

"I'm on my way to you. I need help. I'm in the ambulance."

Riley jumps up getting her work clothes on. She stubs her toe on the dress and hops.

"Ow!"

Micah jumps up out of bed seeing Riley's figure in the dark hopping around shoving her shoes on. He starts laughing.

"Where are you off to?"

Riley jumps hitting the dresser again. "Oh, this is so not going to be a good shift. Lindsey is by herself. I'm going in."

Micah nods okaying it. "Good luck getting past your brother on the couch. He wanted to make sure you listened to your mom. But text me every chance, okay?"

Riley nods and kisses him. "I love you."

"Love you too, sweetheart."

Riley smiles and opens the door hitting her face on it. She bites her lip and walks out quietly. Kasey is already at the end of the hallway with his arms crossed shaking his head.

"Bed."

Riley huffs at her brother. "I love you, but I really have to go. I got called in."

She sees the flashing lights in the window. Kasey blocks her. "Micah can go, you cannot."

Riley crawls between her brother's arm and the wall and runs out the door.

"Love you!"

She giggles and runs out to the ambulance. She gets in quickly and looks at Lindsey who looks half asleep.

"I got called in too. We got a domestic, it's like two houses away from you. I'm on standby."

Riley nods. "Alrighty then. I guess get ready?"

Riley looks at the clock seeing she only slept for an hour. "Oh, peachy. One hour of sleep."

Lindsey laughs. "Yeah. I got like four. Sorry."

Riley smirks. "I rammed my foot into the dresser, and then Micah gave me a heart attack. I also hit my hip on the corner—that felt wonderful."

Lindsey giggles and they are given the all clear. They go to the scene. The deputies have a female who looks half beaten and another woman who looks livid with a few bruises.

Riley takes the easy one, being half asleep, and Lindsey takes the one that is pretty beaten.

Riley checks her out and doesn't find any cuts or anything. The deputies take her off. Riley walks over to Lindsey and helps get the victim on the gurney.

Deputies walk over to them. "We will be sending somebody soon to the hospital. The story is this one was sleeping with that one's husband."

Riley nods. "Alright then." They get the girl into the back of the ambulance, and Riley drives while Lindsey works. She flies to the hospital trying to stay awake and pulls in.

They unload the girl, and Lindsey fills in the doctors and nurses.

They get the gurney loaded back up, and Riley gets in the driver's seat. They head back to the station.

Riley starts to doze off. "RILEY!"

Riley jumps and gets back in her lane. Riley slows down a little and blows cool air to stay awake. All of the sudden a tire blows, and Riley goes to pull off, getting t-boned by a larger pick-up truck.

Glass shatters all over both of them. Lindsey blinks looking at Riley.

Riley meets her eyes. "Riles, you got a cut on your cheek."

Riley shrugs. "I'll be okay." She opens the door to get out and sees a drop. She scoots over toward Lindsey. "No, I won't at all."

Lindsey opens hers, and there is barely any ground under her door. They both realize the only thing that keeps the ambulance from going down is the tree.

"Call it in. We have to move like now."

Riley picks up the radio. "Uh, dispatch medic twenty-one?"

"Dispatch, go head."

Riley looks at Lindsey. "We're in a bit of a situation the only thing holding us is a tree."

"10-4, sending help your way."

Lindsey slides out clinging on to the ambulance until she is completely safe and holds out her hand for Riley. The ambulance tilts as Riley leans to get out.

She clings to the door. "Lord, I knew I shouldn't have gotten out of bed."

Lindsey giggles nervously. "Riley, you aren't helping me anything. Let's go! Take my hand!"

Riley grabs her hand as the ambulance leans more. Lindsey pulls her out as the ambulance goes down with the tree. The edge of the door hits Riley's side.

She bites her lip not to scream. They both hit the ground and walk over to the side, looking down seeing the ambulance on its side in a thirty-foot drop.

They both look at the smashed front of the truck and sees a man getting out a little beat-up but not much.

"Are you guys, okay? I looked down for just a second to grab my drink."

Lindsey crosses her arms. "We are now!"

Riley holds her side, feeling a sharp pain. "I'm iffy on that one."

Police cars and their fire truck is pulling up. Chase runs over to his sister after parking and hugs her.

"You better not have been driving. You always wreck that thing!"

Lindsey hugs him back. "It was Riley this time. The door hit her. Might want to check her out and call Micah."

The guys check out the guy that hit them.

Chase looks at Riley. "Are you okay? How are you feeling?"

Riley sits on the road. "Peachy."

Chase walks over to the deputies to send somebody to inform Micah.

Lindsey looks at Riley seeing a red stain on her. "Riley, let me check you." Riley lifts her shirt not realizing it was a gash.

"Oh well. That's fantastic."

Lindsey's jaw drops. "Riley, we have to get you to the hospital!"

Riley shrugs. "It can wait."

Lindsey shakes her head. "No, it can't!"

Another ambulance pulls up. Jasmine walks over to them with her medical bag. "Hey, guys, how are you feeling?"

Lindsey shrugs. "I'm fine, but she needs to get to the hospital," pointing at Riley.

Riley sees Alyssa walking over with a gurney. She turns so maybe her sister-in-law won't realize it's her.

Jasmine points at Riley. "She's the one going." Riley turns and sees Alyssa right next to her. She jumps and feels the stabbing pain, grabbing her side she bites her lip.

Alyssa's jaw drops. "Does Micah know?"

Lindsey nods. "Yes, they sent a deputy."

Alyssa whips out her phone. "Get on."

She walks away calling her dad.

Riley looks at Lindsey. "I don't want to go. My mom is going to be so mad."

Lindsey shrugs. "So is Micah."

Chapter 60

Riley is in the ambulance somewhat sitting up. "This is so uncomfortable."

Alyssa shrugs. "Mom and Dad are super livid with you."

Riley stares out the window. "Yeah, I'm sure my brother and Micah are too."

Alyssa nods. "Micah and Kasey are at the hospital already. Mom and Dad are on their way."

They pull into the bay. Alyssa opens the doors to pull the gurney. Riley stops her. "Just let me walk."

Alyssa shakes her head. "You have lost your mind!"

She pulls the gurney out and goes in. They get her into a trauma room, and people are all around working on her.

She feels the pain in her side get worse. A nurse looks at her and taking her hand. "I'm sorry, you have some glass in there."

The pain gets worse.

"Please stop!"

Riley starts wiggling. They start to stitch her up.

One nurse holds her hands and the other holds her legs making her be still. They finish and get her wrapped.

"We have to get some X-rays but if everything is okay then in a week you come back for the stitches to be taken out."

Riley nods.

"I'll go get your husband. He's anxious to see you."

A few minutes later Micah and Kasey walk in. Micah hugs her tight. "I'm so glad you are okay!"

Riley smiles hugging him back. "Me too, that was definitely an adventure."

Kasey takes her free hand. "Micah freaked."

Riley smiles. "I'm okay, really. I mean I can't really go to work for a week now."

Kasey agrees. "No, really? Don't worry, Micah, I'll hang out around the house with her."

Micah nods. "Sounds good to me. Miss accident-prone here lately."

Riley giggles and feels real sore. A tech comes in taking her for X-rays.

Kasey and Micah walk out to the waiting room.

Mabel and Derek look up at them.

Micah smiles. "She's good. Staying strong. She's all smiles right now. You can see it in her eyes though she's never been good at hiding that."

Mabel hugs him. "I'm so glad she's okay!"

Riley goes back into the room and waits for discharging. A nurse walks out with a doctor into the waiting room. "Family of Riley?"

Micah and Kasey walk over to them. "Hey, so she has no fractures or anything just a good-sized gash, no damage to organs. I'd say two weeks with no work, light duty at home, then come back in a week for stitches to be removed."

Micah nods. "Okay. Thanks."

"And family may go home. She is waiting for discharge papers."

Riley sits on the bed ready to go. Not ready to be chewed out for working. Micah walks in with everybody. Mabel hugs her.

"Don't you ever scare me like that!"

Riley flinches when she hugs. "Okay, but letting go would be great."

Mabel steps back. "Sorry."

Derek hugs her but more with his arms closer to her shoulders. "You can see the pain in your eyes. It's okay to be human, Riles."

Riley shakes her head. "I'm good."

A nurse comes in with discharge papers. Riley signs and gets up to walk out. Micah takes her hand and picks her up carrying her to the car.

He helps Riley in and gets in the driver's seat. "I love you."

Riley smiles. "I love you too."

They go home, and Micah helps her inside and into bed. Riley snuggles up to him and closes her eyes with a smile.

She falls asleep quickly.

Chapter 61

Micah makes breakfast for her in the morning. Riley wakes up; she gets up feeling as if she got hit by a bus, then makes a joke to herself. She has been hit but it felt much worse today than last night.

She walks slowly into the kitchen, holding on to the wall as she goes. Kasey looks at his sister from the couch. "Need help?"

Riley shakes her head and makes herself suck it up. She stops taking a couple breaths. Kasey walks over to her, taking her hand.

"I got you. Be easy on yourself."

Riley accepts his help and walks with him to the couch. She leans back on the couch not wanting to even be up.

Micah brings her some eggs, a pancake with a chocolate chip and whipped cream smiley face on it, and maple sausage. Riley giggles and looks at him with a smile.

"Thank you."

Micah smiles later sitting beside her. "I told you through the whispers in the wind I'll be there until the end. I'll never leave you alone."

Riley giggles and eats her breakfast he made for her.

He hands her some medication for pain. She takes it with a bottle of water and then lays her head on his lap. Damian and Maliah walk in with Erik.

He looks at them missing everything. "Riles, its wake-up time. Get up!"

Riley flinches as Damian runs toward her. Micah stops him. "Sorry buddy, Mommy had an accident last night and isn't feeling too well."

Erik tilts his head while setting down the kid's bags. "What?"

Micah and Kasey look at him dead serious. "You didn't hear about it?"

Erik sits down. "No."

Micah shows Erik pictures of the truck that hit them and the ambulance in the drop off. Erik looks at her shocked.

"Riles! You didn't tell me?"

Micah shrugs. "She's been asleep, just got up and ate. She's out of work for two weeks."

Riley looks at him. "Nah uh, they told me one."

Micah looks down at her, meeting her eyes. "Two. One for stitches to be removed, two until you can work."

Riley sighs. "Okay."

Erik looks at her confused. "Stitches?"

Micah pulls up her shirt on the side to show the dressings on her side wrapped around her tiny frame. "She's a one hundred-pound miracle, right?"

Erik nods. "Wow! Do you guys want me to keep Damian and Maliah a couple more nights? Just to give her time to heal."

Riley shakes her head no. "It's okay. I got him."

Micah shakes his head disagreeing. "Love, you have to rest. It won't hurt him to spend a couple more nights with April and Erik."

Riley nods. "Okay."

Damian hugs her lightly. "I love you, Mommy."

Riley smiles with tears in her eyes. "I love you too, sweetheart!"

Chapter 62

Riley's one week is up. She has her stitches removed and is given another week to let her body just rest and heal. Riley walks out of the hospital still a little sore. She stops and gets Micah a couple of burgers for his lunch and drives to the station.

She walks in and Micah spots her. He walks over to her. Riley hugs him, smiling. "Did you get released?"

Riley shakes her head no. "No, I still have a week before I can come back."

Micah takes the baggy of food. "Well, thank you for bringing me lunch, love."

Riley smiles cheerfully. "You're welcome."

He kisses her. "Alright, get back home and rest!"

Riley hugs him again, just wanting his attention. "I will."

She turns and walks back to her car. She drives home and goes inside. Riley sits on the couch bored. Erik texts her asking how she is.

She replies with "okay I guess."

Erik calls. "What's up, buttercup?"

Riley smiles. "Just bored, I guess. I hate being alone. Damian and Maliah are at school and Micah is at work. I got another week before I can go to work. So just bored and alone."

"Well, Kasey and I are off. Why don't you come over?"

Riley smirks. "Okay, give me like ten."

She hangs up and puts on gray sweatpants and a hot pink T-shirt. She grabs her keys and drives over to her brother's house.

She gets out and goes inside. Mason runs up to her. "Aunt Riley!"

Riley giggles while hugging him. "Hey! Tell your mom to stop hogging you!"

Kasey walks out of the kitchen with Erik. "Hey, Riles."

Riley looks at her brother and Erik since her accident. "Hey!"

Kasey smiles and hugs her. "You look livelier."

Riley nods. "Oh yes. Still pretty sore, but you know . . ."

Kasey points to the couch. "Well, why don't you sit down for a while."

Riley shrugs. "I've been sleeping for a week except when Damian and Maliah are home."

She walks over to the couch, sitting down anyways. Micah calls her. She answers. "Yeah?"

"Where are you?"

Riley bites her lip. "At my brother's house, why?"

"Riley! I said to rest not go run the roads. What is your problem?"

Riley looks up at her brother and Erik.

"Okay, well give me a few minutes and I'll be home."

Kasey looks confused at his sister. "What's going on, Riles?"

She hears Micah huff on the other end. "You know I'm getting tired of acting like your dad, Riles. Just friggin' get home."

Riley rolls her eyes. "Whatever. I'll be home in a minute so chill out."

"Don't even start with me."

Click.

Riley sighs and looks at her brother standing up. "I guess I'm not hanging out. I'll see you guys whenever I'm allowed to leave the house, I guess."

Kasey grabs his sisters' arm. "Do you want me to go with you?"

Riley shakes her head no. "No, I'm good. Micah is probably just in a bad mood." She hugs him and Erik, walks out then drives home. When she pulls up in the driveway, she sees a car she doesn't recognize.

She gets out walking in. "Micah?"

Micah walks out of the kitchen with a woman. "Yeah?"

Riley sighs, feeling a sting in her heart. "Who's this?"

The girl holds out her hand. "I'm Grace. I'm transferring to the station. You are?"

Riley looks between the two. "I'm Riley, Micah's wife?"

Grace looks at both of them. "Sorry. I didn't mean to step on toes. If you aren't comfortable with me being here, I can leave."

Riley shrugs. "You're fine." She walks into their room putting her bag and keys down. Micah goes into the bedroom.

"You don't have to be rude, Riles."

Riley turns to him. "Since when am I Riley to you?"

Micah shrugs. "Are you jealous?"

Riley crosses her arms. "You know the more we grow apart the more I miss Adam every single day! If only he wasn't killed."

Micah looks away. "Grace is his sister."

Riley's jaw drops. "What?"

She walks into the living room and stares at Grace. "Adam was your brother?"

She looks at Riley, shocked. "Yes, why?"

Riley stares at her and then hugs her. "I'm the one he married. Right before his death. I had his son."

Grace stares at her. "You know how they never actually found him?"

Riley nods. "Yeah."

Grace smiles. "Well, he didn't ever actually pass away either, he just couldn't remember anything. He lived with me up until recently. He just got his own house around here."

Riley's jaw drops. "You mean I went through hell without him, thinking he was gone all this time? I had dreams of him telling me to move on!"

Grace holds up her phone with a picture of her and Adam. "Is it okay if I got him to come over to meet his son?"

Riley nods. "Absolutely!"

Grace calls Adam. "Hey, you know you never told me you got married."

"Yeah, well, I'm at her house, and you have a son! Did you know that? They told her you died in that accident. Adam, you need to come over here!"

Riley walks into Micah, sitting on the bed looking sad. "What's wrong?"

Micah looks up at her. "Riley, I want you to sign this."

He hands her divorce papers. Riley looks up at him with a heartbroken look. "Why?"

Micah stands up. "Because, Riley, the universe is bringing you two back together. You need to be with your son's father."

Riley shakes her head no; she sits beside him. "I have been with you for eight years, Micah. Eight years. Why in the world would I leave you?"

Micah looks away from her. "Because I don't love you anymore, Riley. I don't want to be with you anymore. I cheated on you with Grace."

Riley feels her heart shatter and does what he asks—she signs the papers. "So I guess you're moving out."

Micah nods. "I have my stuff in the truck."

Chapter 63

Riley watches Micah leave with her heart shattered to pieces. She pulls the ring off from him and sits on the island. Grace walks over to her. "Adam will be here at four. Good luck, girl. He's starting to remember you."

Riley sits on the couch when Grace leaves. She texts Kasey saying, "Lord, what a rollercoaster."

Riley walks out to the driveway to get Damian off the bus. She walks with her son inside and sits down with him. "Son, we have to talk."

Damian looks at her, wondering what's going on. "Okay, Mom, what's wrong?"

Riley bites her lip. "Son, Micah only is a part of us for a little while, you may not understand today or next week or month, but he left us. And you know how your father passed away before you were born?"

He nods. "Yes, why?"

Riley sighs. "Well, I met his sister today. Damian, your father never died. This is new to me as well."

Chapter 64

A few years pass in time, Adam is around but hasn't completely remembered everything about Riley and him. Damian is now sixteen. Riley desperately wants Adam back as a part of her life, as well as another child.

Damian wakes up Riley on the couch. "Mom?"

Riley looks at him with an eye open. "Yes?"

Damian sits beside her. "You look like crap."

Riley sighs, sitting up, hugging her knees to her chest.

"Uncle Erik is on his way here, with Uncle Kasey," says Damian.

Riley looks confused. "Why?"

Damian smiles. "Because I was worried about you. You've only been asleep for ten hours."

Riley jumps up. "What!"

She runs into her room, grabbing clothes to get ready for her shift at the fire department. Damian walks in standing in the doorway. Riley looks up at her son while shoving her shirt over her head.

"Mom, I told Micah to let you have the night off. You look pale."

Riley shakes her head and starts coughing, with the start of a cold. "No no, I'm fine."

Damian raises his eyebrows at his mom. "Mom, you are sick. I also called Dad. He's going to come over when he gets off."

Riley's eyes widen. "Damian!"

Damian smirks. "I love you too, Mom."

Riley runs into the bathroom, tripping over the fan she had sitting in front of the door.

Damian laughs and helps her up. "Mom, slow down. Dad doesn't care how you look. You know that."

Riley sits on the floor. "I'm sorry."

Damian hugs his mom. "Mom, I think if you truly love Dad. You should try again."

She hugs him back. She hears the door open and close. Damian goes into the living room. "Mom is being emotional and she's sick."

Erik walks in. "Riles, what's up?"

Riley looks up at Erik while putting on the fakest smile possible. "Nothing is up. I'm just . . . Adam is coming over."

Erik laughs at her. "Riley, obviously you still love him. After sixteen years you can always start over."

Riley sighs, holding the ring on her necklace. "I just wish I could. It's not him anymore."

Erik shrugs. "And you sound like crap."

Adam walks into the room. "Hey, Riles, how are you feeling? Damian said you weren't feeling good."

Erik smirks. "She sounds like crap." He gets up and walks out leaving Riley with Adam.

Riley looks up at him nervous. "I'm fine. Damian is just over reacting."

Adam squats down, meeting her eyes. "You don't look fine. Come on let's get in bed."

He holds out his hand.

Riley shakes her head no. "Adam, I'm fine, really." She gets up. "I'm sorry he called you."

Adam stares at the rings on the necklace, taking them in his hand. "I remember."

Riley looks at him confused. "Remember what?"

Adam meets her eyes. "Riley, I remember our wedding. I remember telling you Erik had moved out. I remember leaving you heartbroken when I went to work that night. I can't remember the wreck, but I remember."

Riley looks at him hopeful.

Adam takes her necklace off her and places her ring on her finger. "And I remember being your husband."

Riley has tears roll down her cheeks. Adam wipes them away. "Don't you dare cry, sweetheart. You are too pretty to cry."

Damian peeks in listening.

Riley hugs Adam. "Sixteen years. I waited. Sixteen years."

Adam smiles. "Please forgive me, I took too long to come back home."

More tears fall.

"I love you, Riley Carter."

A big smile forms on her lips. "I love you too, Adam."

Chapter 65

Riley and Adam get remarried; Damian walks Riley down the aisle, giving her away to his dad.

The ceremony brings back many memories for the couple. A couple months after the wedding, Riley gets out of bed in the middle of the night, feeling horrible.

Adam wakes up to her pacing around. "Love, is everything okay? What's wrong?"

Riley meets his eyes.

"I feel like I'm going to be sick, and I don't want to be. So I'm trying to make it go away."

She runs into the bathroom puking up her guts. Adam hold her hair up. "I remember you doing this sixteen years ago."

Riley glares at him. He gets a wet cloth and wipes her face off.

"Well, it's the truth."

Riley gets back in bed with him, laying her head on his chest.

She wakes up in the morning, feeling horrible again, and she goes into the bathroom to grab a digital pregnancy test and takes it. The word "pregnant" appears on the little screen.

Adam meets her at the door as she opens the door. She holds up the digital pregnancy test. Adam looks at it seeing the word pregnant.

CPSIA information can be obtained
at www.ICGtesting.com
Printed in the USA
BVHW070942110319
542311BV00008B/205/P

9 781796 019841